IN THE TEETH OF THE EVIDENCE

In the Teeth
of the Evidence

DOROTHY L. SAYERS

NEW ENGLISH LIBRARY
TIMES MIRROR

First published by Victor Gollancz Ltd. in 1939

∗

First published as a Four Square edition 1960
Reprinted 1962
Reprinted June 1965
Reissued in an NEL edition January 1969
New edition November 1970
New edition April 1973

∗

NEL Books are published by New English Library Limited from Barnard's Inn, Holborn, London, EC1. Made and printed in Great Britain by Love & Malcomson Ltd., Redhill, Surrey.

45001554 8

IN THE TEETH OF THE EVIDENCE

A Lord Peter Wimsey Story

"WELL, old son," said Mr. Lamplough, "and what can we do for you today?"

"Oh, some of your whizz-bang business, I suppose," said Lord Peter Wimsey, seating himself resentfully in the green velvet torture-chair and making a face in the direction of the drill. "Jolly old left-hand upper grinder come to bits on me. I was only eating an omelette, too. Can't understand why they always pick these moments. If I'd been cracking nuts or chewing peppermint jumbles I could understand it."

"Yes?" said Mr. Lamplough, soothingly. He drew an electric bulb, complete with mirror, as though by magic out of a kind of Maskelyne-and-Devant contraption on Lord Peter's left; a trail of flex followed it, issuing apparently from the bowels of the earth. "Any pain?"

"No *pain*," said Wimsey irritably, "unless you count a sharp edge fit to saw your tongue off. Point is, why should it go pop like that? I wasn't doing anything to it."

"No?" said Mr. Lamplough, his manner hovering between the professional and the friendly, for he was an old Winchester man and a member of one of Wimsey's clubs, and had frequently met him on the cricket-field in the days of their youth. "Well, if you'll stop talking half a moment, we'll have a look at it. Ah!"

"Don't say 'Ah!' like that, as if you'd found pyorrhoea and necrosis of the jaw and were gloating over it, you damned old ghoul. Just carve it out and stop it up and be hanged to you. And, by the way, what have you been up to? Why should I meet an inspector of police on your doorstep? You needn't pretend he came to have his bridge-work attended to, because I saw his sergeant waiting for him outside."

"Well, it was rather curious," said Mr. Lamplough, dexterously gagging his friend with one hand and dabbing cotton-wool into the offending cavity with the other. "I suppose I oughtn't to tell you, but if I don't, you'll get it all out of your friends at Scotland Yard. They wanted to see my predecessor's books. Possibly you noticed that bit in the papers about a dental man being found dead in a blazing garage on Wimbledon Common?"

"Yonk—ugh?" said Lord Peter Wimsey.

"Last night," said Mr. Lamplough. "Pooped off about nine pipemma, and it took them three hours to put it out. One of those wooden garages—and the big job was to keep the blaze away from the house. Fortunately it's at the end of the row, with nobody at home. Apparently this man Prendergast was all alone there—just going off for a holiday or something—and he contrived to set himself and his car and his garage alight last night and was burnt to death. In fact, when they found him, he was so badly charred that they couldn't be sure it was he. So, being sticklers for routine, they had a look at his teeth."

"Oh, yes?" said Wimsey, watching Mr. Lamplough fitting a new drill into its socket. "Didn't anybody have a go at putting the fire out?"

"Oh, yes—but as it was a wooden shed, full of petrol, it simply went up like a bonfire. Just a little bit over this way, please. That's splendid." Gr-r-r, whizz, gr-r-r. "As a matter of fact, they seem to think it might just possibly be suicide. The man's married, with three children, and immured and all that sort of thing." Whizz, gr-r-r, buzz, gr-r-r, whizz. "His family's down at Worthing, staying with his mother-in-law or something. Tell me if I hurt you." Gr-r-r. "And I don't suppose he was doing any too well. Still, of course, he may easily have had an accident when filling up. I gather he was starting off that night to join them."

"A—ow—oo—oo—uh—ihi—ih?" inquired Wimsey naturally enough.

"How do I come into it?" said Mr. Lamplough, who, from long experience was expert in the interpretation of mumblings. "Well, only because the chap whose practice I took over here did this fellow Prendergast's dental work for him." Whizz. "He died, but left his books behind him for my guidance, in case any of his old patients should feel inclined to trust me." Gr-r-r,

6

whizz. "I m sorry. Did you feel that? As a matter of fact, some of them actually do. I suppose it's an instinct to trundle round to the same old place when you're in pain, like the dying elephants. Will you rinse, please?"

"I see," said Wimsey, when he had finished washing out chips of himself and exploring his ravaged molar with his tongue. "How odd it is that these cavities always seem so large. I feel as if I could put my head into this one. Still, I suppose you know what you're about. And are Prendergast's teeth all right?"

"Haven't had time to hunt through the ledger, yet, but I've said I'll go down to have a look at them as soon as I've finished with you. It's my lunch-time anyway, and my two o'clock patient isn't coming, thank goodness. She usually brings five spoilt children, and they all want to sit round and watch, and play with the apparatus. One of them got loose last time and tried to electrocute itself on the X-ray plant next door. And she thinks that children should be done at half-price. A little wider if you can manage it." Gr-r-r. "Yes, that's very nice. Now we can dress that and put in a temporary. Rinse please."

"Yes," said Wimsey, "and for goodness' sake make it firm and not too much of your foul oil of cloves. I don't want bits to come out in the middle of dinner. You can't imagine the nastiness of caviar flavoured with cloves."

"No?" said Mr. Lamplough. "You may find this a little cold." Squirt, swish. "Rinse, please. You may notice it when the dressing goes in. Oh, you did notice it? Good. That shows that the nerve's all right. Only a little longer now. There! Yes, you may get down now. Another rinse? Certainly. When would you like to come in again?"

"Don't be silly, old horse," said Wimsey. "I am coming out to Wimbledon with you straight away. You'll get there twice as fast if I drive you. I've never had a corpse-in-blazing-garage before, and I want to learn."

There is nothing really attractive about corpses in blazing garages. Even Wimsey's war experience did not quite reconcile him to the object that lay on the mortuary slab in the police station. Charred out of all resemblance to humanity, it turned even the police surgeon pale, while Mr. Lamplough was so overcome that he had to lay down the books he had brought with him and retire into the open to recover himself. Meanwhile Wimsey, having put himself on terms of mutual confidence and esteem with the police officials, thoughtfully turned over the little pile of blackened odds and ends that represented the contents of Mr. Prendergast's pockets. There was nothing remarkable about them. The leather note-case still held the remains of a thickish wad of notes—doubtless cash in hand for the holiday at Worthing. The handsome gold watch (obviously a presentation) had stopped at seven minutes past nine. Wimsey remarked on its good state of preservation. Sheltered between the left arm and the body—that seemed to be the explanation.

"Looks as though the first sudden blaze had regularly overcome him," said the police inspector. "He evidently made no attempt to get out. He'd simply fallen forward over the wheel, with his head on the dashboard. That's why the face is so disfigured. I'll show you the remains of the car presently if you're interested, my lord. If the other gentleman's feeling better we may as well take the body first."

Taking the body was a long and unpleasant job. Mr. Lamplough, nerving himself with an effort and producing a pair of forceps and a probe, went gingerly over the jaws—reduced almost to their bony structure by the furnace heat to which they had been exposed—while the police surgeon checked entries in the ledger. Mr. Prendergast had a dental history extending back over ten years in the ledger and had already had two or three fillings done before that time. These had been noted at the time when he first came to Mr. Lamplough's predecessor.

At the end of a long examination, the surgeon looked up from the notes he had been making.

"Well, now," he said, "let's check that again. Allowing for renewal of old work, I think we've got a pretty accurate picture of the present state of his mouth. There ought to be nine fillings in all. Small amalgam filling in right lower back wisdom tooth; big amalgam ditto in right lower back molar; amalgam fillings in right upper first and second bicuspids at point of contact; right upper incisor crowned—that all right?"

"I expect so," said Mr. Lamplough, "except that the right upper incisor seems to be missing altogether, but possibly the crown came loose and fell out." He probed delicately. "The jaw is very brittle—I can't make anything of the canal—but there's nothing against it."

"We may find the crown in the garage," suggested the Inspector.

"Fused porcelain filling in left upper canine," went on the

8

surgeon; "amalgam fillings in left upper first bicuspid and lower second bicuspid and left lower thirteen-year-old molar. That seems to be all. No teeth missing and no artificials. How old was this man, Inspector?"

"About forty-five, Doc."

"My age. I only wish I had as good a set of teeth," said the surgeon. Mr. Lamplough agreed with him.

"Then I take it, this is Mr. Prendergast all right," said the inspector.

"Not a doubt of it, I should say," replied Mr. Lamplough; "though I should like to find that missing crown."

"We'd better go round to the house, then," said the Inspector. "Well, yes, thank you, my lord, I shouldn't mind a lift in that. Some car. Well, the only point now is, whether it was accident or suicide. Round to the right my lord, and then second on the left—I'll tell you as we go."

"A bit out of the way for a dental man," observed Mr. Lamplough, as they emerged upon some scattered houses near the Common.

The Inspector made a grimace.

"I thought the same, sir, but it appears Mrs. Prendergast persuaded him to come here. So good for the children. Not so good for the practice, though. If you ask me, I should say Mrs. P. was the biggest argument we have for suicide. Here we are."

The last sentence was scarcely necessary. There was a little crowd about the gate of a small detached villa at the end of a row of similar houses. From a pile of dismal debris in the garden a smell of burning still rose, disgustingly. The Inspector pushed through the gate with his companions, pursued by the comments of the bystanders.

"That's the Inspector . . . that's Dr. Maggs . . . that'll be another doctor, him with the little bag . . . who's the bloke in the eye-glass? . . . Looks a proper nobleman, don't he, Florrie? . . . Why he'll be the insurance bloke. . . . Coo! look at his grand car . . . that's where the money goes. . . That's a Rolls, that is . . . no, silly, it's a Daimler. . . . Ow, well, it's all advertisement these days."

Wimsey giggled indecorously all the way up the garden path. The sight of the skeleton car amid the sodden and fire-blackened remains of the garage sobered him. Two police constables, crouched over the ruin with a sieve, stood up and saluted.

"How are you getting on, Jenkins?"

"Haven't got anything very much yet, sir, bar an ivory cigarette-holder. This gentleman"—indicating a stout, bald man in spectacles, who was squatting among the damaged coach-work, "is Mr. Tolley, from the motor-works, come with a note from the Superintendent, sir."

"Ah, yes. Can you give any opinion about this, Mr. Tolley? Dr. Maggs you know. Mr. Lamplough, Lord Peter Wimsey. By the way, Jenkins, Mr. Lamplough has been going into the corpse's dentistry, and he's looking for a lost tooth. You might see if you can find it. Now, Mr. Tolley?"

"Can't see much doubt about how it happened," said Mr. Tolley, picking his teeth thoughtfully. "Regular death-traps, these little saloons, when anything goes wrong unexpectedly. There's a front tank, you see, and it looks as though there might have been a bit of a leak behind the dash, somewhere. Possibly the seam of the tank had got strained a bit, or the union had come loose. It's loose now, as a matter of fact, but that's not unusual after a fire, Rouse case or no Rouse case. You can get quite a lot of slow dripping from a damaged tank or pipe, and there seems to have been a coconut mat round the controls, which would prevent you from noticing. There'd be a smell, of course, but these little garages do often get to smell of petrol, and he kept several cans of the stuff here. More than the legal amount—but *that's* not unusual either. Looks to me as though he'd filled up his tank—there are two empty tins near the bonnet, with the caps loose—got in, shut the door, started up the car, perhaps, and then lit a cigarette. Then, if there were any petrol fumes about from a leak, the whole show would go up in his face—whoosh!"

"How was the ignition?"

"Off. He may never have switched it on, but it's quite likely he switched it off again when the flames went up. Silly thing to do, but lots of people *do* do it. The proper thing, of course, is to switch off the petrol and leave the engine running so as to empty the carburettor, but you don't always think straight when you're being burnt alive. Or he may have meant to turn off the petrol and been overcome before he could manage it. The tank's over here to the left, you see."

"On the other hand," said Wimsey, "he may have committed suicide and faked the accident."

"Nasty way of committing suicide."

10

"Suppose he'd taken poison first."

"He'd have had to stay alive long enough to fire the car."

"That's true. Suppose he'd shot himself—would the flash from the—no, that's silly—you'd have found the weapon in the case. Or a hypodermic? Same objection. Prussic acid might have done it—I mean, he might just have had time to take a tablet and then fire the car. Prussic acid's pretty quick, but it isn't absolutely instantaneous."

"I'll have a look for it anyway," said Dr. Maggs.

They were interrupted by the constable.

"Excuse me, sir, but I think we've found the tooth. Mr. Lamplough says this is it."

Between his pudgy finger and thumb he held up a small, bony object, from which a small stalk of metal still protruded.

"That's a right upper incisor crown all right by the look of it," said Mr. Lamplough. "I suppose the cement gave way with the heat. Some cements are sensitive to heat, some, on the other hand, to damp. Well, that settles it, doesn't it?"

"Yes—well, we shall have to break it to the widow. Not that she can be in very much doubt, I imagine."

Mrs. Prendergast—a very much made-up lady with a face set in lines of habitual peevishness—received the news with a burst of loud sobs. She informed them, when she was sufficiently recovered, that Arthur had always been careless about petrol, that he smoked too much, that she had often warned him about the danger of small saloons, that she had told him he ought to get a bigger car, that the one he had was not really large enough for her and the whole family, that he *would* drive at night, though she had always said it was dangerous, and that if he'd listened to her, it would never have happened.

"Poor Arthur was not a good driver. Only last week, when he was taking us down to Worthing, he drove the car right up on a bank in trying to pass a lorry, and frightened us all dreadfully."

"Ah!" said the Inspector. "No doubt that's how the tank got strained." Very cautiously he inquired whether Mr. Prendergast could have had any reason for taking his own life. The widow was indignant. It was true that the practice had been declining of late, but Arthur would never have been so wicked as to do such a thing. Why, only three months ago, he had taken out a life-insurance for £500 and he'd never have invalidated it by committing suicide within the term stipulated by the policy.

Inconsiderate of her as Arthur was, and whatever injuries he had done her as a wife, he wouldn't rob his innocent children.

The Inspector pricked up his ears at the word "injuries." What injuries?

Oh, well, of course, she'd known all the time that Arthur was carrying on with that Mrs. Fielding. You couldn't deceive her with all this stuff about teeth needing continual attention. And it was all very well to say that Mrs. Fielding's house was better run than her own. *That* wasn't surprising—a rich widow with no children and no responsibilities, of course she could afford to have everything nice. You couldn't expect a busy wife to do miracles on such a small housekeeping allowance. If Arthur had wanted things different, he should have been more generous, and it was easy enough for Mrs. Fielding to attract men, dressed up like a fashion plate and no better than she should be. She'd told Arthur that if it didn't stop she'd divorce him. And since then he'd taken to spending all his evenings in Town, and what was he doing there—

The Inspector stemmed the torrent by asking for Mrs. Fielding's address.

"I'm sure I don't know," said Mrs. Prendergast. "She did live at Number 57, but she went abroad after I made it clear I wasn't going to stand any more of it. It's very nice to be some people, with plenty of money to spend. I've never been abroad since our honeymoon, and that was only to Boulogne."

At the end of this conversation, the Inspector sought Dr. Maggs and begged him to be thorough in his search for prussic acid.

The remaining testimony was that of Gladys, the general servant. She had left Mr. Prendergast's house the day before at 6 o'clock. She was to have taken a week's holiday while the Prendergasts were at Worthing. She had thought that Mr. Prendergast had seemed worried and nervous the last few days, but that had not surprised her, because she knew he disliked staying with his wife's people. She (Gladys) had finished her work and put out a cold supper and then gone home with her employer's permission. He had a patient—a gentleman from Australia, or some such a place, who wanted his teeth attended to in a hurry before going off on his travels again. Mr. Prendergast had explained that he would be working late, and would shut up the house himself, and she need not wait. Further inquiry showed that Mr. Prendergast had "scarcely touched"

12

his supper, being, presumably, in a hurry to get off. Apparently, then, the patient had been the last person to see Mr. Prendergast alive.

The dentist's appointment-book was next examined. The patient figured there as "Mr. Williams 5.30," and the address-book placed Mr. Williams at a small hotel in Bloomsbury. The manager of the hotel said that Mr. Williams had stayed there for a week. He had given no address except "Adelaide," and had mentioned that he was revisiting the old country for the first time after twenty years and had no friends in London. Unfortunately, he could not be interviewed. At about half-past ten the previous night, a messenger had called, bringing his card, to pay his bill and remove his luggage. No address had been left for forwarding letters. It was not a district messenger, but a man in a slouch hat and heavy dark overcoat. The night-porter had not seen his face very clearly, as only one light was on in the hall. He had told them to hurry up, as Mr. Williams wanted to catch the boat-train from Waterloo. Inquiry at the booking-office showed that a Mr. Williams had actually travelled on that train, being booked to Paris. The ticket had been taken that same night. So Mr. Williams had disappeared into the blue, and even if they could trace him, it seemed unlikely that he could throw much light on Mr. Prendergast's state of mind immediately previous to the disaster. It seemed a little odd, at first, that Mr. Williams, from Adelaide, staying in Bloomsbury, should have travelled to Wimbledon to get his teeth attended to, but the simple explanation was the likeliest: namely, that the friendless Williams had struck up an acquaintance with Prendergast in a café or some such place, and that a casual mention of his dental necessities had led to a project of mutual profit and assistance.

After which, nothing seemed to be left but for the coroner to bring in a verdict of Death by Misadventure and for the widow to send in her claim to the Insurance Company, when Dr. Maggs upset the whole scheme of things by announcing that he had discovered traces of a large injection of hyoscine in the body, and what about it? The Inspector, on hearing this, observed callously that he was not surprised. If ever a man had an excuse for suicide, he thought it was Mrs. Prendergast's husband. He thought that it would be desirable to make a careful search among the scorched laurels surrounding what had been Mr. Prendergast's garage. Lord Peter Wimsey agreed, but committed himself to the prophecy that the syringe would not be found.

Lord Peter Wimsey was entirely wrong. The syringe was found next day, in a position suggesting that it had been thrown out of the window of the garage after use. Traces of the poison were discovered to be present in it. "It's a slow-working drug," observed Dr. Maggs. "No doubt he jabbed himself, threw the syringe away, hoping it would never be looked for, and then, before he lost consciousness. climbed into the car and set light to it. A clumsy way of doing it."

"A damned ingenious way of doing it," said Wimsey. "I don't believe in that syringe, somehow." He rang up his dentist. "Lamplough, old horse," he said, "I wish you'd do something for me. I wish you'd go over those teeth again. No—not my teeth ; Prendergast's."

"Oh, blow it!" said Mr. Lamplough, uneasily.

"No, but I wish you would," said his lordship.

The body was still unburied, Mr. Lamplough, grumbling very much, went down to Wimbledon with Wimsey, and again went through his distasteful task. This time he started on the left side.

"Lower thirteen-year-old molar and second bicuspid filled amalgam. The fire's got at those a bit, but they're all right. First upper bicuspid—bicuspids are stupid sort of teeth—always the first to go. That filling looks to have been rather carelessly put in—not what I should call good work ; it seems to extend over the next tooth—possibly the fire did that. Left upper canine, cast porcelain filling on anterior face——"

"Half a jiff," said Wimsey, "Maggs' note says 'fused porcelain.' Is it the same thing?"

"No. Different process. Well, I suppose it's fused porcelain —difficult to see. I should have said it was cast, myself, but that's as may be."

"Let's verify it in the ledger. I wish Maggs had put the dates in—goodness knows how far I shall have to hunt back, and I don't understand this chap's writing or his dashed abbreviations."

"You won't have to go back very far if it's cast. The stuff only came in about 1928, from America. There was quite a rage for it then, but for some reason it didn't take on extraordinarily well over here. But some men use it."

14

"Oh, then it isn't cast," said Wimsey. "There's nothing here about canines, back to '28. Let's make sure; '27, '26, '25, '24, '23. Here you are. Canine, something or other."

"That's it," said Lamplough, coming to look over his shoulder. "Fused porcelain. I must be wrong, then. Easily see by taking it out. The grain's different, and so is the way it's put in."

"How, different?"

"Well," said Mr. Lamplough, "one's a cast, you see."

"And the other's fused. I did grasp that much. Well, go ahead and take it out."

"Can't very well; not here."

"Then take it home and do it there. Don't you see, Lamplough, how important it is? If it is cast porcelain, or whatever you call it, it *can't* have been done in '23. And if it was removed later, then another dentist must have done it. And he may have done other things—and in that case, those things ought to be there, and they're not. Don't you *see*?"

"I see you're getting rather agitato," said Mr. Lamplough; "all I can say is, I refuse to have this thing taken along to my surgery. Corpses aren't popular in Harley Street."

In the end, the body was removed, by permission, to the dental department of the local hospital. Here Mr. Lamplough, assisted by the staff dental expert, Dr. Maggs, and the police, delicately extracted the filling from the canine.

"If that," said he triumphantly, "is not cast porcelain I will extract all my own teeth without an anaesthetic and swallow them. What do you say, Benton?"

The hospital dentist agreed with him. Mr. Lamplough, who had suddenly developed an eager interest in the problem, nodded, and inserted a careful probe between the upper right bicuspids, with thir adjacent fillings.

"Come and look at this, Benton. Allowing for the action of the fire and all this muck, wouldn't you have said this was a very recent filling? There, at the point of contact. Might have been done yesterday. And—here—wait a minute. Where's the lower jaw gone to? Get that fitted up. Give me a bit of carbon. Look at the tremendous bite there ought to be here, with that big molar coming down on to it. That filling's miles too high for the job. Wimsey—when was this bottom right-hand back molar filled?"

"Two years ago." said Wimsey.

"That's impossible," said the two dentists together and Mr. Benton added:

"If you clean away the mess, you'll see it's a new filling. Never been bitten on, I should say. Look here, Mr. Lamplough, there's something odd here."

"Odd? I should say there was. I never thought about it when I was checking it up yesterday, but look at this old cavity in the lateral here. Why didn't he have that filled when all this other work was done? Now it's cleaned out you can see it plainly. Have you got a long probe? It's quite deep and must have given him jip. I say, Inspector, I want to have some of these fillings out. Do you mind?"

"Go ahead," said the Inspector, "we've got plenty of witnesses."

With Mr. Benton supporting the grisly patient, and Mr. Lamplough manipulating the drill, the filling of one of the molars was speedily drilled out, and Mr. Lamplough said: "Oh, gosh!" —which, as Lord Peter remarked, just showed you what a dentist meant when he said "Ah!"

"Try the bicuspids," suggested Mr. Benton.

"Or this thirteen-year-old," chimed in his colleague.

"Hold hard, gentlemen," protested the Inspector, "don't spoil the specimen altogether."

Mr. Lamplough drilled away without heeding him. Another filling came out, and Mr. Lamplough said "Gosh!" again.

"It's all right," said Wimsey, grinning, "you can get out your warrant, Inspector."

"What's that, my lord?"

"Murder," said Wimsey.

"Why?" said the Inspector. "Do these gentlemen mean that Mr. Prendergast got a new dentist who poisoned his teeth for him?"

"No," said Mr. Lamplough; "at least, not what you mean by poisoning. But I've never seen such work in my life. Why, in two places the man hasn't even troubled to clear out the decay at all. He's just enlarged the cavity and stopped it up again anyhow. Why this chap didn't get thundering abscesses I don't know."

"Perhaps," said Wimsey, "the stoppings were put in too recently. Hullo! what now?"

16

"This one's all right. No decay here. Doesn't look as if there ever had been, either. But one can't tell about that."

"I dare say there never was. Get your warrant out, Inspector."

"For the murder of Mr. Prendergast? And against whom?"

"No. Against Arthur Prendergast for the murder of one. Mr. Williams, and, incidentally, for arson and attempted fraud. And against Mrs. Fielding too, if you like, for conspiracy. Though you mayn't be able to prove that part of it."

It turned out, when they found Mr. Prendergast in Rouen, that he had thought out the scheme well in advance. The one thing he had had to wait for had been to find a patient of his own height and build, with a good set of teeth and few home ties. When the unhappy Williams had fallen into his clutches, he had few preparations to make. Mrs. Prendergast had to be packed off to Worthing—a journey she was ready enough to take at any time—and the maid given a holiday. Then the necessary dental accessories had to be prepared and the victim invited out to tea at Vimbledon. Then the murder—a stunning blow from behind, followed by an injection. Then, the slow and horrid process of faking the teeth to correspond with Mr. Prendergast's own. Next, the exchange of clothes and the body carried down and placed in the car. The hypodermic put where it might be overlooked on a casual inspection and yet might plausibly be found if the presence of the drug should be discovered ; ready, in the one case, to support a verdict of Accident and, in the second, of Suicide. Then the car soaked in petrol, the union loosened, the cans left about. The garage door and window left open, to lend colour to the story and provide a draught, and, finally, light set to the car by means of a train of petrol laid through the garage door. Then, flight to the station through the winter darkness and so by underground to London. The risk of being recognised on the underground was small, in Williams' hat and clothes and with a scarf wound about the lower part of the face. The next step was to pick up Williams's luggage and take the boat-train to join the wealthy and enamoured Mrs. Fielding in France. After which, Williams and Mrs. Williams could have returned to England, or not, as they pleased.

"Quite a student of criminology," remarked Wimsey, at the conclusion of this little adventure. "He'd studied Rouse and Furnace all right, and profited by their mistakes. Pity he overlooked that matter of the cast porcelain. Makes a quicker job, does it, Lamplough? Well, more haste, less speed. I do wonder, though, at what point of the proceedings Williams actually died."

"Shut up," said Mr. Lamplough, "and, by the way, I've still got to finish that filling for you."

ABSOLUTELY ELSEWHERE

A Lord Peter Wimsey Story

LORD Peter Wimsey sat with Chief-Inspector Parker, of the C.I.D., and Inspector Henley, of the Baldock police, in the library at "The Lilacs."

"So you see," said Parker, "that all the obvious suspects were elsewhere at the time."

"What do you mean by 'elsewhere'?" demanded Wimsey, peevishly. Parker had hauled him down to Wapley, on the Great North Road, without his breakfast, and his temper had suffered. "Do you mean that they couldn't have reached the scene of the murder without travelling at over 186,000 miles a second? Because, if you don't mean that, they weren't absolutely elsewhere. They were only relatively and apparently elsewhere."

"For heaven's sake, don't go all Eddington. Humanly speaking, they were elsewhere, and if we're going to nail one of them we shall have to do it without going into their Fitzgerald contractions and coefficients of spherical curvature. I think, Inspector, we had better have them in one by one, so that I can hear all their stories again. You can check them up if they depart from their original statements at any point. Let's take the butler first."

The Inspector put his head out into the hall and said: "Hamworthy."

The butler was a man of middle age, whose spherical curvature was certainly worthy of consideration. His large face was pale and puffy, and he looked unwell. However, he embarked on his story without hesitation.

"I have been in the late Mr. Grimbold's service for twenty years, gentlemen, and I have always found him a good master. He was a strict gentleman, but very just. I know he was con-

19

sidered very hard in business matters, but I suppose he had to be that. He was a bachelor, but he brought up his two nephews, Mr. Harcourt and Mr. Neville, and was very good to them. In his private life I should call him a kind and considerate man. His profession? Yes, I suppose you would call him a money-lender.

"About the events of last night, sir, yes. I shut up the house at 7.30 as usual. Everything was done exactly to time, sir,—Mr. Grimbold was very regular in his habits. I locked all the windows on the ground floor, as was customary during the winter months. I am quite sure I didn't miss anything out. They all have burglar-proof bolts and I should have noticed if they had been out of order. I also locked and bolted the front door and put up the chain."

"How about the conservatory door?"

"That, sir, is a Yale lock. I tried it, and saw that it was shut. No, I didn't fasten the catch. It was always left that way, sir, in case Mr. Grimbold had business which kept him in Town late, so that he could get in without disturbing the household."

"But he had no business in Town last night?"

"No, sir, but it was always left that way. Nobody could get in without the key, and Mr. Grimbold had that on his ring."

"Is there no other key in existence?"

"I believe"—the butler coughed—"I believe, sir, though I do not know, that there is *one,* sir,—in the possession of—of a lady, sir, who is at present in Paris."

"I see. Mr. Grimbold was about sixty years old, I believe. Just so. What is the name of this lady?"

"Mrs. Winter, sir. She lives at Wapley, but since her husband died last month, sir, I understand she has been residing abroad."

"I see. Better make a note of that, Inspector. Now, how about the upper rooms and the back door?"

"The upper-room windows were all fastened in the same way, sir, except Mr. Grimbold's bedroom and the cook's room and mine, sir; but they couldn't be reached without a ladder, and the ladder is locked up in the tool-shed."

"That's all right," put in Inspector Henley. "We went into that last night. The shed was locked and, what's more, there were unbroken cobwebs between the ladder and the wall."

"I went through all the rooms at half-past seven, sir, and there was nothing out of order."

"You may take it from me," said the Inspector, again, "that

there was no interference with any of the locks. Carry on, Hamworthy."

"Yes, sir. While I was seeing to the house, Mr. Grimbold came down into the library for his glass of sherry. At 7.45 the soup was served and I called Mr. Grimbold to dinner. He sat at the end of the table as usual, facing the serving-hatch."

"With his back to the library door," said Parker, making a mark on a rough plan of the room, which lay before him. "Was that door shut?"

"Oh, yes, sir. All the doors and windows were shut."

"It looks a dashed draughty room," said Wimsey. "Two doors and a serving-hatch and two french windows."

"Yes, my lord; but they are all very well-fitting, and the curtains were drawn."

His lordship moved across to the connecting door and opened it.

"Yes," he said; "good and heavy and moves in sinister silence. I like these thick carpets, but the pattern's a bit fierce." He shut the door noiselessly, and returned to his seat.

"Mr. Grimbold would take about five minutes over his soup, sir. When he had done, I removed it and put on the fish. I did not have to leave the room; everything comes through the serving-hatch. The wine—that is, the Chablis—was already on the table. That course was only a small portion of turbot, and would take Mr. Grimbold about five minutes again. I removed that, and put on the roast pheasant. I was just about to serve Mr. Grimbold with the vegetables, when the telephone-bell rang. Mr. Grimbold said: 'You'd better see who it is. I'll help myself.' It was not the cook's business, of course, to answer the telephone."

"Are there no other servants?"

"Only the woman who comes in to clean during the day, sir. I went out to the instrument, shutting the door behind me."

"Was that this telephone or the one in the hall?"

"The one in the hall, sir. I always used that one, unless I happened to be actually in the library at the time. The call was from Mr. Neville Grimbold in Town, sir. He and Mr. Harcourt have a flat in Jermyn Street. Mr. Neville spoke, and I recognised his voice. He said: 'Is that you, Hamworthy? Wait a moment. Mr. Harcourt wants you.' He put the receiver down and then Mr. Harcourt came on. He said: 'Hamworthy, I

want to run down tonight to see my uncle, if he's at home.'
I said: 'Yes, sir, I'll tell him.' The young gentlemen often
come down for a night or two, sir. We keep their bedrooms
ready for them. Mr. Harcourt said he would be starting at
once and expected to get down by about half-past nine. While
he was speaking I heard the big grandfather-clock up in their flat
chime the quarters and strike eight, and immediately after, our
own hall-clock struck, and then I heard the Exchange say
'Three minutes.' So the call must have come through at three
minutes to eight, sir."

"Then there's no doubt about the time. That's a comfort.
What next, Hamworthy?"

"Mr. Harcourt asked for another call and said: 'Mr. Neville
has got something to say,' and then Mr. Neville came back to
the 'phone. He said he was going up to Scotland shortly, and
he wanted me to send up a country suit and some stockings
and shirts that he had left down here. He wanted the suit sent
to the cleaner's first, and there were various other instructions,
so that he asked for another three minutes. That would be at
8.3, sir, yes. And about a minute after that, while he was still
speaking, the front-door bell rang. I couldn't very well leave the
'phone, so the caller had to wait, and at five past eight he rang
the bell again. I was just going to ask Mr. Neville to excuse
me, when I saw Cook come out of the kitchen and go through
the hall to the front door. Mr. Neville asked me to repeat his
instructions, and then the Exchange interrupted us again, so he
rang off, and when I turned round I saw Cook just closing the
library door. I went to meet her, and she said: 'Here's that
Mr. Payne again, wanting Mr. Grimbold. I've put him in the
library, but I don't like the looks of him.' So I said: 'All right;
I'll fix him,' and Cook went back to the kitchen."

"One moment," said Parker. "Who's Mr. Payne?"

"He's one of Mr. Grimbold's clients, sir. He lives about five
minutes away, across the fields, and he's been here before,
making trouble. I think he owes Mr. Grimbold money, sir, and
wanted more time to pay."

"He's here, waiting in the hall," added Henley.

"Oh?" said Wimsey. "The unshaven party with the scowl
and the ash-plant, and the blood-stained coat?"

"That's him, my lord," said the butler. "Well, sir,"—he turned
to Parker again, "I started to go along to the library, when
it come over me sudden-like that I'd never taken in the claret—

22

Mr. Grimbold would be getting very annoyed. So I went back to my pantry—you see where that is, sir,—and fetched it from where it was warming before the fire. I had a little hunt then for the salver, sir, till I found I had put down my evening paper on top of it, but I wasn't more than a minute, sir, before I got back into the dining-room. And then, sir"—the butler's voice faltered—"then I saw Mr. Grimbold fallen forward on the table, sir, all across his plate, like. I thought he must have been took ill, and I hurried up to him and found—I found he was dead, sir, with a dreadful wound in his back."

"No weapon anywhere?"

"Not that I could see, sir. There was a terrible lot of blood. It made me feel shockingly faint, sir, and for a minute I didn't hardly know what to do. As soon as I could think of anything, I rushed over to the serving-hatch and called Cook. She came hurrying in and let out an awful scream when she saw the master. Then I remembered Mr. Payne and opened the library door. He was standing there, and he began at once, asking how long he'd have to wait. So I said: "Here's an awful thing! Mr. Grimbold has been murdered!' and he pushed past me into the dining-room, and the first thing he said was: 'How about those windows?' He pulled back the curtain of the one nearest the library, and there was the window standing open. 'This is the way he went,' he said, and started to rush out. I said, 'no, you don't'—thinking he meant to get away, and I hung on to him. He called me a lot of names, and then he said: 'Look here, my man, be reasonable. The fellow's getting away all this time. We must have a look for him.' So I said, 'Not without I go with you.' And he said, 'All right.' So I told Cook not to touch anything but to ring up the police, and Mr. Payne and I went out after I'd fetched my torch from the pantry."

"Did Payne go with you to fetch it?"

"Yes, sir. Well, him and me went out and we searched about in the garden, but we couldn't see any footprints or anything, because it's an asphalt path all round the house and down to the gate. And we couldn't see any weapon, either. So then he said: 'We'd better go back and get the car and search the roads,' but I said: 'No, he'll be away by then,' because it's only a quarter of a mile from our gate to the Great North Road, and it would take us five or ten minutes before we could start. So Mr. Payne said: 'Perhaps you're right,' and came back to the house with me. Well, then, sir, the constable came from

Wapley, and after a bit, the Inspector here and Dr. Crofts from Baldock, and they made a search and asked a lot of questions, which I answered to the best of my ability, and I can't tell you no more, sir."

"Did you notice," asked Parker, "whether Mr. Payne had any stains of blood about him?"

"No sir,—I can't say that he had. When I first saw him, he was standing in here, right under the light, and I think I should have seen it if there was anything, sir. I can't say fairer than that."

"Of course you've searched this room, Inspector, for bloodstains or a weapon or for anything such as gloves or a cloth, or anything that might have been used to protect the murderer from bloodstains?"

"Yes, Mr. Parker. We searched very carefully."

"Could anybody have come downstairs while you were in the dining-room with Mr. Grimbold?"

"Well, sir, I suppose they might. But they'd have to have got into the house before half-past seven, sir, and hidden themselves somewhere. Still, there's no doubt it might have happened that way. They couldn't come down by the back stairs, of course, because they'd have had to pass the kitchen, and Cook would have heard them, the passage being flagged, sir, but the front stairs—well, I don't know hardly what to say about that."

"That's how the man got in, depend upon it," said Parker. "Don't look so distressed, Hamworthy. You can't be expected to search all the cupboards in the house every evening for concealed criminals. Now I think I had better see the two nephews. I suppose they and their uncle got on together all right?"

"Oh, yes, sir. Never had a word of any sort. It's been a great blow to them, sir. They were terribly upset when Mr. Grimbold was ill in the summer——"

"He was ill, was he?"

"Yes, sir, with his heart, last July. He took a very bad turn, sir, and we had to send for Mr. Neville. But he pulled round wonderfully, sir,—only he never seemed to be quite such a cheerful gentleman afterwards. I think it made him feel he wasn't getting younger, sir. But I'm sure nobody ever thought he'd be cut off like this."

"How is his money left?" asked Parker.

"Well, sir, that I don't know. I believe it would be divided between the two gentlemen, sir—not but what they have plenty

24

of their own. But Mr. Harcourt would be able to tell you, sir. He's the executor."

"Very well, we'll ask him. Are the brothers on good terms?"

"Oh, yes, indeed, sir. Most devoted. Mr. Neville would do anything for Mr. Harcourt—and Mr. Harcourt for him, I'm sure. A very pleasant pair of gentlemen, sir. You couldn't have nicer."

"Thanks, Hamworthy. That will do for the moment, unless anybody else has anything to ask?"

"How much of the pheasant was eaten, Hamworthy?"

"Well, my lord, not a great deal of it—I mean, nothing like all of what Mr. Grimbold had on his plate. But he'd ate some of it. It might have taken three or four minutes or so to eat what he had done, my lord, judging by what I helped him to."

"There was nothing to suggest that he had been interrupted, for example, by somebody coming to the windows, or of his having got up to let the person in?"

"Nothing at all, my lord, that I could see."

"The chair was pushed in close to the table when I saw him," put in the Inspector, "and his napkin was on his knees and the knife and fork lying just under his hands, as though he had dropped them when the blow came. I understand that the body was not disturbed."

"No sir, I never moved it—except, of course, to make sure that he was dead. But I never felt any doubt of that, sir, when I saw that dreadful wound in his back. I just lifted his head and let it fall forward again, same as before."

"All right, then, Hamworthy. Ask Mr. Harcourt to come in."

Mr. Harcourt Grimbold was a brisk-looking man of about thirty-five. He explained that he was a stockbroker and his brother Neville an official in the Ministry of Public Health, and that they had been brought up by their uncle from the ages of eleven and ten respectively. He was aware that his uncle had had many business enemies, but for his own part he had received nothing from him but kindness.

"I'm afraid I can't tell you much about this terrible business, as I didn't get here till 9.45 last night, when, of course, it was all over."

"That was a little later than you hoped to be here?"

"Just a little. My tail-lamp went out between Welwyn Garden City and Welwyn, and I was stopped by a bobby. I went to a garage in Welwyn, where they found that the lead had come

25

loose. They put it right, and that delayed me for a few minutes more." —

"It's about forty miles from here to London?"

"Just over. In the ordinary way, at that time of night, I should reckon an hour and a quarter from door to door. I'm not a speed merchant."

"Did you drive yourself?"

"Yes. I have a chauffeur, but I don't always bring him down here with me."

"When did you leave London?"

"About 8.20, I should think. Neville went round to the garage and fetched the car as soon as he'd finished telephoning, while I put my toothbrush and so on in my bag."

"You didn't hear about the death of your uncle before you left?"

"No. They didn't think of ringing me up, I gather, till after I had started. The police tried to get Neville later on, but he'd gone round to the club, or something. I 'phoned him myself after I got here, and he came down this morning."

"Well, now, Mr. Grimbold, can you tell us anything about your late uncle's affairs?"

"You mean his will? Who profits, and that kind of thing? Well, I do, for one, and Neville, for another. And Mrs.—— Have you heard of a Mrs. Winter?"

"Something, yes."

"Well, she does, for a third. And then, of course, old Hamworthy gets a nice little nest-egg, and the cook gets something, and there is a legacy of £500 to the clerk at my uncle's London office. But the bulk of it goes to us and to Mrs. Winter. I know what you're going to ask—how much is it? I haven't the faintest idea, but I know it must be something pretty considerable. The old man never let on to a soul how much he really was worth, and we never bothered about it. I'm turning over a good bit, and Neville's salary is a heavy burden on a long-suffering public, so we only had a mild, academic kind of interest in the question."

"Do you suppose Hamworthy knew he was down for a legacy?"

"Oh, yes—there was no secret about that. He was to get £100 and a life-interest in £200 a year, provided, of course, he was still in my uncle's service when he—my uncle, I mean—died."

"And he wasn't under notice, or anything?"

"N-no. No. Not more than usual. My uncle gave everybody notice about once a month, to keep them up to the mark. But it never came to anything. He was like the Queen of Hearts in *Alice*—he never executed nobody, you know."

"I see. We'd better ask Hamworthy about that, though. Now, this Mrs. Winter. Do you know anything about her?"

"Oh, yes. She's a nice woman. Of course, she was Uncle William's mistress for donkey's years, but her husband was practically potty with drink, and you could scarcely blame her. I wired her this morning and here's her reply, just come."

He handed Parker a telegram, despatched from Paris, which read: "Terribly shocked and grieved. Returning immediately. Love and sympathy. Lucy."

"You are on friendly terms with her, then?"

"Good Lord, yes. Why not? We were always damned sorry for her. Uncle William would have taken her away with him somewhere, only she wouldn't leave Winter. In fact, I think they had practically settled that they were to get married now that Winter has had the grace to peg out. She's only about thirty-eight, and it's time she had some sort of show in life, poor thing."

"So, in spite of the money, she hadn't really very much to gain by your uncle's death?"

"Not a thing. Unless, of course, she wanted to marry somebody younger, and was afraid of losing the cash. But I believe she was honestly fond of the old boy. Anyhow, she couldn't have done the murder, because she's in Paris."

"H'm!" said Parker. "I suppose she is. We'd better make sure, though. I'll ring through to the Yard and have her looked out for at the ports. Is this 'phone through to the Exchange?"

"Yes," said the Inspector. "It doesn't have to go through the hall 'phone; they're connected in parallel."

"All right. Well, I don't think we need trouble you further, at the moment, Mr. Grimbold. I'll put my call through, and after that we'll send for the next witness. . . . Give me White-hall 1212, please. . . . I suppose the time of Mr. Harcourt's call from town has been checked, Inspector?"

"Yes, Mr. Parker. It was put in at 7.57 and renewed at 8 o'clock and 8.3. Quite an expensive little item. And we've also checked up on the constable who spoke to him about his lights and the garage that put them right for him. He got into

Welwyn at 9.5 and left again about 9.15. The number of the car is right, too."

"Well, he's out of it in any case, but it's just as well to check all we can. . . . Hullo, is that Scotland Yard? Put me through to Chief-Inspector Hardy. Chief-Inspector Parker speaking."

As soon as he had finished with his call, Parker sent for Neville Grimbold. He was rather like his brother, only a little slimmer and a little more suave in speech, as befitted a Civil Servant. He had nothing to add, except to confirm his brother's story and to explain that he had gone to a cinema from 8.20 to about 10 o'clock, and then on to his club, so that he had heard nothing about the tragedy till later in the evening.

The cook was the next witness. She had a great deal to say, but nothing very convincing to tell. She had not happened to see Hamworthy go to the pantry for the claret, otherwise she confirmed his story. She scouted the idea that somebody had been concealed in one of the upper rooms, because the daily woman, Mrs. Crabbe, had been in the house till nearly dinner-time, putting camphor-bags in all the wardrobes; and, anyhow, she had no doubt but what "that Payne" had stabbed Mr. Grimbold —"a nasty, murdering beast." After which, it only remained to interview the murderous Mr. Payne.

Mr. Payne was almost aggressively frank. He had been treated very harshly by Mr. Grimbold. What with exorbitant usury and accumulated interest added to the principal, he had already paid back about five times the original loan, and now Mr. Grimbold had refused him any more time to pay, and had announced his intention of foreclosing on the security, namely, Mr. Payne's house and land. It was all the more brutal because Mr. Payne had every prospect of being able to pay off the entire debt in six months' time, owing to some sort of interest or share in something or other which was confidently expected to turn up trumps. In his opinion, old Grimbold had refused to renew on purpose, so as to prevent him from paying—what *he* wanted was the property. Grimbold's death was the saving of the situation, because it would postpone settlement till after the confidently-expected trumps had turned up. Mr. Payne would have murdered old Grimbold with pleasure, but he hadn't done so, and in any case he wasn't the sort of man to stab anybody in the back, though, if the money-lender had been a younger man, he, Payne, would have been happy to break all his bones for him. There it was, and they could take it or leave it. If that

28

old fool, Hamworthy, hadn't got in his way, he'd have laid hands on the murderer all right—if Hamworthy was a fool, which he doubted. Blood? yes, there was blood on his coat. He had got that in struggling with Hamworthy at the window. Hamworthy's hands had been all over blood when he made his appearance in the library. No. doubt he had got it from the corpse. He, Payne, had taken care not to change his clothes, because, if he had done so, somebody would have tried to make out that he was hiding something. Actually, he had not been home, or asked to go home, since the murder. Mr. Payne added that he objected strongly to the attitude taken up by the local police, who had treated him with undisguised hostility. To which Inspector Henley replied that Mr. Payne was quite mistaken.

"Mr. Payne," said Lord Peter, "will you tell me one thing? When you heard the commotion in the dining-room, and the cook screaming, and so on, why didn't you go in at once to find out what was the matter?"

"Why?" retorted Mr. Payne. "Because I never heard anything of the sort, that's why. The first thing I knew about it was seeing the butler-fellow standing there in the doorway, waving his bloody hands about and gibbering."

"Ah!" said Wimsey. "I thought it was a good, solid door. Shall we ask the lady to go in and scream for us now, with the dining-room window open?"

The Inspector departed on this errand, while the rest of the company waited anxiously to count the screams. Nothing happened, however, till Henley put his head in and asked, what about it?

"Nothing," said Parker.

"It's a well-built house," said Wimsey. "I suppose any sound coming through the window would be muffled by the conservatory. Well, Mr. Payne, if you didn't hear the screams it's not surprising that you didn't hear the murderer. Are those all your witnesses, Charles? Because I've got to get back to London to see a man about a dog. But I'll leave you with two suggestions with my blessing. One is, that you should look for a car, which was parked within a quarter of a mile of this house last night, between 7.30 and 8.15; the second is, that you should all come and sit in the dining-room tonight, with the doors and windows shut, and watch the french windows. I'll give Mr. Parker a ring about eight. Oh, and you might lend me the key of the conservatory door. I've got a theory about it."

The Chief Inspector handed over the key, and his lordship departed.

The party assembled in the dining-room was in no very companionable mood. In fact, all the conversation was supplied by the police, who kept up a chatty exchange of fishing reminiscences, while Mr. Payne glowered, the two Grimbolds smoked cigarette after cigarette, and the cook and the butler balanced themselves nervously on the extreme edges of their chairs. It was a relief when the telephone-bell rang.

Parker glanced at his watch as he got up to answer it. "Seven-fifty-seven," he observed, and saw the butler pass his handkerchief over his twitching lips. "Keep your eye on the windows." He went out into the hall.

"Hullo!" he said.

"Is that Chief-Inspector Parker?" asked a voice he knew well. "This is Lord Peter Wimsey's man speaking from his lordship's rooms in London. Would you hold the line a moment? His lordship wishes to speak to you."

Parker heard the receiver set down and lifted again. Then Wimsey's voice came through: "Hullo, old man? Have you found that car yet?"

"We've heard of *a* car," replied the Chief Inspector cautiously, "at a Road-House on the Great North Road, about five minutes' walk from the house."

"Was the number ABJ 28?"

"Yes. How did you know?"

"I thought it might be. It was hired from a London garage at five o'clock yesterday afternoon and brought back just before ten. Have you traced Mrs. Winter?"

"Yes, I think so. She landed from the Calais boat this evening. So apparently she's O.K."

"I thought she might be. Now, listen. Do you know that Harcourt Grimbold's affairs are in a bit of a mess? He nearly had a crisis last July, but somebody came to his rescue—possibly Uncle, don't you think? All rather fishy, my informant saith. And I'm told, very confidentially, that he's got badly caught over the Biggars-Whitlow crash. But of course he'll have no difficulty in raising money now, on the strength of Uncle's will. But I imagine the July business gave Uncle William a jolt. I expect——"

30

He was interrupted by a little burst of tinkling music, followed by the eight silvery strokes of a bell.

"Hear that? Recognise it? That's the big French clock in my sitting-room. . . . What? All right, Exchange, give me another three minutes. Bunter wants to speak to you again."

The receiver rattled, and the servant's suave voice took up the tale.

"His lordship asks me to ask you, sir, to ring off at once and go straight into the dining-room."

Parker obeyed. As he entered the room, he got an instantaneous impression of six people, sitting as he had left them, in an expectant semi-circle, their eyes strained towards the french windows. Then the library door opened noiselessly and Lord Peter Wimsey walked in.

"Good God!" exclaimed Parker, involuntarily. "How did you get here?" The six heads jerked round suddenly.

"On the back of the light waves," said Wimsey, smoothing back his hair. "I have travelled eighty miles to be with you, at 186,000 miles a second."

"It was rather obvious, really," said Wimsey, when they had secured Harcourt Grimbold (who fought desperately) and his brother Neville (who collapsed and had to be revived with brandy). It had to be those two; they were so very much elsewhere—almost absolutely elsewhere. The murder could only have been committed between 7.57 and 8.6, and there had to be a reason for that prolonged 'phone-call about something that Harcourt could very well have explained when he came. And the murderer had to be in the library before 7.57, or he would have been seen in the hall—unless Grimbold had let him in by the French window, which didn't appear likely.

"Here's how it was worked. Harcourt set off from town in a hired car about six o'clock, driving himself. He parked the car at the Road-House, giving some explanation. I suppose he wasn't known there?"

"No; it's quite a new place; only opened last month."

"Ah! Then he walked the last quarter-mile on foot, arriving here at 7.45. It was dark, and he probably wore goloshes, so as not to make a noise coming up the path. He let himself into the conservatory with a duplicate key."

"How did he get that?"

"Pinched Uncle William's key off his ring last July, when the
31

old boy was ill. It was probably the shock of hearing that his dear nephew was in trouble that caused the illness. Harcourt was here at the time—you remember it was only Neville that had to be 'sent for'—and I suppose Uncle paid up then, on conditions. But I doubt if he'd have done as much again—especially as he was thinking of getting married. And I expect, too, Harcourt thought that Uncle might easily alter his will after marriage. He might even have founded a family, and what would poor Harcourt do then, poor thing? From every point of view, it was better that Uncle should depart this life. So the duplicate key was cut and the plot thought out, and Brother Neville who would 'do anything for Mr. Harcourt,' was roped in to help. I'm inclined to think that Harcourt must have done something rather worse than merely lose money, and Neville may have troubles of his own. But where was I?"

"Coming in at the conservatory door."

"Oh, yes—that's the way I came tonight. He'd take cover in the garden and would know when Uncle William went into the dining-room, because he'd see the library light go out. Remember, he knew the household. He came in, in the dark, locking the outer door after him, and waited by the telephone until Neville's call came through from London. When the bell stopped ringing, he lifted the receiver in the library. As soon as Neville had spoken his little piece, Harcourt chipped in. Nobody could hear him through these sound-proof doors, and Hamworthy couldn't possibly tell that his voice wasn't coming from London. In fact, it *was* coming from London, because, as the 'phones are connected in parallel, it could only come by way of the Exchange. At eight o'clock, the grandfather clock in Jermyn Street struck—further proof that the London line was open. The minute Harcourt heard that, he called on Neville to speak again, and hung up under cover of the rattle of Neville's receiver. Then Neville detained Hamworthy with a lot of rot about a suit, while Harcourt walked into the dining-room, stabbed his uncle, and departed by the window. He had five good minutes in which to hurry back to his car and drive off—and Hamworthy and Payne actually gave him a few minutes more by suspecting and hampering one another."

"Why didn't he go back through the library and conservatory?"

"He hoped everybody would think that the murderer had come in by the window. In the meantime, Neville left London at

8.20 in Harcourt's car, carefully drawing the attention of a policeman and a garage man to the licence number as he passed through Welwyn. At an appointed place outside Welwyn he met Harcourt, primed him with his little story about tail-lights, and changed cars with him. Neville returned to town with the hired 'bus ; Harcourt came back here with his own car. But I'm afraid you'll have a little difficulty in finding the weapon and the duplicate key and Harcourt's blood-stained gloves and coat. Neville probably took them back, and they may be anywhere. There's a good, big river in London."

A SHOT AT GOAL

A Montague Egg Story

A WORKMAN put in his head at the door of the Saloon Bar.

"Is Mr. Robbins here?"

The stout gentleman who was discussing football with Mr. Montague Egg turned at the sound of his name.

"Yes? Oh, it's Warren. What is it, Warren?"

"A note, sir. Handed in at the Mills just after you left. As it was marked 'Urgent' I thought I'd best bring it down. I'd have took it up to the house, sir, only they told me in the town as you'd stepped in to the Eagle."

"Thanks," said Mr. Robbins. "Urgent only to the sender, I expect, as usual." He tore open the envelope and glanced at the message, and his face changed. "Who brought this?"

"I couldn't say, sir. It was pushed in through the letter-flap in the gate."

"Ah, very good. Thank you, Warren."

The workman withdrew, and Mr. Robbins said, after a moment's thought:

"If Mr. Edgar should look in, Bowles, will you tell him I've changed my mind and gone back to the Mill, and I'll be glad if he'd come and see me there, before he goes up to the house."

"Right you are, sir."

"I'll take a few sandwiches with me. There's a bit of work I want to put in, and it may keep me."

Mr. Bowles obligingly put up the sandwiches into a parcel, and Mr. Robbins departed, with a brief "Goodnight, all."

"That's the general manager up at the Mills," observed Mr. Bowles. "Been here five years now. Takes a great interest in the town. He's a member of the Football Committee."

"So I gathered," said Mr. Egg.

"I see you're keen on the game," went on the landlord.

"In a business capacity," replied Mr. Egg, "I'm keen on whatever the gentleman I'm talking to is keen on. As it says in *The Salesman's Handbook*, 'The haberdasher gets the golfer's trade by talking, not of buttons, but of Braid.' Isn't that right, sir?"

He appealed to a quiet, dark man in plus-fours.

"Very smart," said the latter, smiling. "And apt," he added, with a glance at his own golf clubs leaning against the counter. Mr. Egg permitted himself a modest smirk.

"Well," said Mr. Bowles, "from a business point of view, you're dead right. In a place like this you've got to keep on the right side of them you live by. And so I told Hughie Searle only yesterday."

Mr. Egg nodded. The Twiddleton Mills were a very small factory, reproducing only a limited output of the superior homespuns known as Twiddleton Tweeds; but Twiddleton was a very small town, and the Mills formed the axis about which its life revolved.

"Who's Hughie Searle?" demanded Mr. Egg.

"Best goal the Twiddleton Trojans ever had," replied Mr. Bowles. "Born and bred in the town, too. But he got across Mr. Robbins over that business about young Fletcher, and he's been dropped out of the team. I don't say it's fair, but you can't blame the committee. They're all business men and they've got to eat out of Robbins' hand, as you might say. And I told Hughie, Bill Fletcher might be a friend of his, but there's two sides to every question, and when it comes to language and threats to a gentleman in Mr. Robbins' position, you can't hardly expect him to pass it over."

"No," said Mr. Charteris, the quiet man, suddenly, "unless you take the view that footballers should be picked on their form as players, and not for personal considerations."

"Ah!" said Mr. Bowles, "but that's what Vicar would call a counsel of perfection. People talk a lot about the team spirit and let the best side win, but if you was to sit in this bar and listen to what goes on, it's all spite and jealousy, or else it's how to scrape up enough money to entice away some other team's centre-forward, or it's complaints about favouritism or wrong decisions, or something that leaves a nasty taste in the mouth. The game's not what it was when I was a lad. Too much commercialism, and enough back-biting to stock an old maids' tea-party."

"What happened to Bill Fletcher, by the way?" asked the quiet man.

"Chucked up his job and left the town," said the landlord. "I think he's gone to live with his father at Wickersby. They're still using that invention of his, whatever it was, up at the Mills, and they do say it saves them a lot of money, and he wasn't rightly done by. But Mr. Entwistle told me Fletcher hadn't a leg to stand on, according to the terms of the contract, and being a solicitor, he should know."

"The way of an inventor is hard in this country," said the quiet man.

"Very likely, sir," agreed Mr. Bowles. "I never had no turn that way myself, and perhaps it's just as well. Ah! Good evening, Mr. Edgar. Your dad was in here a few minutes back and left a message as he'd changed his mind and gone back to the Mills and he'd be obliged if you'd go and see him up there right away."

"Oh, did he?" said the young man who had just come in. He was a tall, loose-limbed, loose-lipped youngster, somewhat showily dressed, and appeared to have been drinking rather more than was good for him. "Give us a double whisky, Bowles, and look here, if anybody asks you, I didn't come in here, and I never got the Governor's message. See?"

"Very good, Mr. Edgar," said the landlord, with a surreptitious wink at Monty. He eyed Edgar Robbins thoughtfully, as though gauging his capacity, seemed to decide that he could just take a double whisky without overflowing, and fulfilled the order. Edgar put the drink down at a gulp, glanced at the clock, which marked twenty minutes to eight, muttered something and banged his way out of the bar, nearly colliding in the doorway with another young man, who scowled angrily at his retreating back.

"Did you see that?" said the newcomer. "I'd like to teach that young —— manners. Him and his —— old father are a pair, the dirty —— !"

"Now then, Hughie!" protested Mr. Bowles. An elderly man, who had been reading his paper by the fire, got up and went out with a look of disgust. "I can't allow that sort of language in my bar. You've driven that gentleman away, and him a stranger

36

to the town. A nice idea he'll get of Twiddleton. And in front of Mr. Charteris, too. I'm surprised."

"Sorry, Mr. Charteris. Sorry, Mr. Bowles. But I've had about enough of Robbinses. The old man's got his knife into me, all right. Dropping me for that fool Benson, against the Swallows! I don't mind standing aside for a better man—but Benson! Him keep goal—keeping chickens is all he's fit for. It's a damned insult. And young Edgar charging into me like a clumsy great goat and never saying so much as 'Pardon,' the insolent lout!"

"Steady," said Mr. Bowles. "'Tisn't the first time you've stood up to a charge, Hughie. Young Edgar's had one over the eight. And he's a bit put out. His dad left a message he was going up to the Mills and wanted to see him there, and Mr. Edgar wasn't having any. Told me to say he hadn't been in and didn't get the message. Spot of trouble there, I wouldn't wonder. Maybe the old gentleman's on to some of the ways he spends the money."

"Time, too," said Hughie. "Half of old-an'-mild, Mr. Bowles, if you please. Young Edgar's too much of a gentleman to work at the Mills, but he's not too grand to take the cash and spend it on skirts. Be damned to the lot of them! I haven't finished with old Robbins yet."

"The less you have to do with Mr. Robbins the better," said Mr. Bowles, severely. "You'll let that temper of yours get the better of you once too often, and say something you'll be sorry for. What's the time? Quarter to. Your chop'll be just about ready now, Mr. Egg, if you'll kindly step through to the parlour."

"I must be getting along, too," said Charteris. He picked up his clubs, bestowed a pleasant farewell upon the company and went out, leaving Hughie Searle alone before the bar, his dark eyes glowering, and his bullet head humped sulkily between his broad, square shoulders.

At half-past eight, Mr. Egg, having consumed his chop and chips, strolled back into the bar. Hughie Searle had gone, but the room had filled up and Mr. Bowles, assisted now by a barman, was doing a brisk trade. The Eagle was the only hotel of genuine importance in the little town, and all Twiddletonians of any standing passed through its hospitable door most evenings in the week. Mr. Egg had not been working that district of late, but he rediscovered several patrons and acquaintances who remembered him from six years back and were glad to see him. He was deep in conversation with Mr. Harcourt, the bank manager, when the door was hastily flung open and a man rushed in breathlessly, his eyes starting out of his head.

"Help! Murder! I want the police!"

Every head turned; every mug and glass hung suspended; Mr. Bowles, grasping the handle of the beer-engine, let half a pint of bitter overflow the pot and go frothing down the pipe.

"Why, Ted, what's up?"

The man staggered to the settle and dropped down, panting. Eager faces bent over him.

"Anything wrong up at the Mills?'

"Mr. Robbins—lying in his office—with his 'ead bashed in—all of a mask of blood. Get the police! It's murder!"

"Old Mr. Robbins!"

"Yes, the boss. A dretful sight it was."

"But 'oo done it?"

"Think I stopped to see? I come off, fast as me legs could carry me."

"Didn't you ring up the police?"

"Wot? And 'ave 'im come up behind and dot me one? Not me! There might be a gang of 'em 'anging round the place."

"Well, *you're* a fine night-watchman," said Mr. Bowles, "I don't think. Racing down here that-a-way and the murderer maybe escaping all this while. Didn't think to lock the gate after you, I suppose? 'Course you didn't. Now, you pull yourself together and take a couple of the lads and go straight on back to the Mills, and I'll ring up Inspector Weybridge. That's right, George. You give 'im a brandy and try and make a man of 'im."

"I'll run him up to the Mills," suggested Mr. Egg, to whom a murder or a mystery was very nearly as satisfying as an order for 12 dozen ports at 190s. the dozen. "My car's just out in the yard. I can start her up in two seconds."

"That's fine," said the landlord. "And I don't mind if I come myself. George, reach me my big stick, in case we meet anything, and ring up the police-station and tell the Missus I've gone out for a bit and can she come and 'elp in the bar. Now then, Ted, my lad. Up you come! Mr. Robbins murdered! That's a nice thing to 'appen."

Mr. Egg, by this time, had got his car started. Mr. Bowles climbed in beside him and Ted was accommodated in the back seat, between the banker and a young farmer, who had added themselves to the party.

A run of half a mile brought them to the Twiddleton Mills. The big gates were locked, but the small side-gate stood wide open.

"Look at that!" said Mr. Bowles. "Whoever it was, he'll have took hisself off by now, if he's any sense. Ted Baggitt ain't got no 'ead, and never 'ad, since I knew him."

They crossed a yard and came to the door leading to the offices, which also stood wide open. A light was burning in a room on the right, and through a third open door they looked into the manager's room. Slumped in his swivel chair, his head and arms sprawled over the desk, lay what had been Mr. Robbins. One side of his skull had been ferociously battered in, and the sight was horrid enough to subdue the exuberance even of Mr. Bowles. The wretched Ted sank down on a chair by the wall and began to whimper.

"He's dead, all right," said Monty. "Best not touch anything, but it can't hurt if I—eh?"

He extracted a clean handkerchief from his pocket and laid it over the dead man's head; after which it was clean no longer.

"I don't see no weapon," said Mr. Bowles, gazing vaguely first at the fireplace and then at the desk, which was strewn with scattered papers.

"There's a big brass paper-weight missing," said Mr. Harcourt. "It used to stand just here, by the blotting-pad. I've seen it scores of times.

Monty nodded. "The man will have been sitting here, in this chair at the side of the desk. They'll have talked a bit, and then he'll have jumped up, snatching the paper-weight, and caught Mr. Robbins on the head just as he was getting to his feet. The blow was struck from in front, as you'll have noticed."

"That looks," said the banker, "as though the murder was not premeditated."

"That's a fact," replied Monty. He peered gingerly at the dead man. "There's a bit of torn paper here in his left hand; perhaps that'll tell us something. No, no, Mr. Bowles. Excuse me. Best leave everything just as it is till the police come. That sounds like them now."

The noise of footsteps crossing the yard bore out his remark. A small group of men came in at the door, and Mr. Egg found himself looking, for the second time that evening, into the face of the quiet man in plus-fours.

"We meet again, Mr. Egg," said Mr. Charteris. "I'm the Chief Constable, and these are Dr. Small and Inspector Weybridge. This is a bad business. See what you can tell us about it, Doctor. Now, where's the man who found the body? What's your name? Ted Baggitt? Very well, Baggitt, what do you know about this?"

"Nothing at all, sir—only the finding him. I come on duty, sir, when the man on the gate goes off at half-past seven. Mr. Robbins had left the Mills when I came on, but about a quarter to eight, back he comes again. He lets himself in with his own key and meets me just outside the door. 'I've come up to do a bit o' private work,' he says, 'and Mr. Edgar may come along later, but don't you bother,' he says, 'I'll let him in myself.' So, I leaves him in this here office and goes off to get me bit o' supper ready. My little room's down in the other building."

"And did Mr. Edgar come?"

"Yes, sir. Leastways, the outer bell rang about 8 o'clock, but I didn't take no notice, seeing what Mr. Robbins said. I didn't hear nothing more, sir, nor see nobody, till I'd 'ad me supper and come out this way to start me first round just about 9 o'clock. Then I see this 'ere door open, and I looks in, and there's poor Mr. Robbins a-laying dead. So I says, 'O Gawd!' I says to myself, 'we'll all be murdered.' And I takes to me 'eels."

"You never actually saw Mr. Edgar?"

"No, sir." The man's face looked troubled. "No, sir—I never see 'im. You don't think it could have been 'im, sir? That would be an awful thing, to be sure."

"Mr. Edgar?" cried Mr. Bowles, in horror. "But you was there yourself, sir, when he said he wasn't coming to the Mills."

"Yes," said the Chief Constable. "Of course, he might have wanted us to think just that. It would be a very bold way to stage an alibi, but it's possible. Still, at present we've no proof that he did come. Well, Doctor, what about it?"

"Dead about an hour to an hour and a half," replied Dr. Small. "Struck with a heavy instrument with sharp edges. A paper-weight, did you say, Mr. Harcourt? Yes, it might well be something like that."

SON AND
SERVE BY RIGH
PUT IN GOAL. Y
FAIR PLAY AND
GET IT. I SHA
YOUR HOUSE
8 o'CLO
YOU HA
AND

"What's that?" asked Charteris. And when the banker had explained:

"I see. Weybridge, tell them to have a look round for the weapon. It may have been thrown away somewhere. Be careful of any possible finger-prints. Anything else, Doctor?"

"His keys are in his pocket, so the murderer didn't use them to let himself out. And here's part of a letter, tightly clenched in his left hand."

The doctor spread the crumpled scrap of paper carefully

out on the desk. The message was written in block capitals, in purple copying-pencil.

The Chief Constable and Mr. Montague Egg looked at the paper and then at one another.

"The envelope that was handed to Mr. Robbins tonight at the Eagle," said Mr. Egg, softly, "was addressed in block capitals, in purple copying-pencil."

"Yes," said Charteris. "And I think we may take it that this is it."

"H'm!" said Inspector Weybridge. "And there ain't much doubt who wrote it, sorry as I am to say it. It's what I'd call an easy dockiment to reconstruct. 'I'm a better player than Benson, and I deserve by rights to be put in goal. I want fair play and I mean to get it. I shall call at (or come to) your house tonight at 8 o'clock'—Well, it don't say tonight, actually, but it do say 8 o'clock—and then there's 'and if' at the end—looking like a threat might be coming. Has anybody seen Hughie Searle about tonight?"

Only too many people had seen Hughie Searle, and heard what he had to say.

"And to think," mourned Mr. Bowles, "that it was me told him where to find Mr. Robbins. If I'd a-kept my fat head shut, he'd a-gone up to the house, like it says in the letter, and nobody wouldn't have been able to tell him anything. Except Mr. Edgar. Gosh!" added the landlord, "of course—that's why Mr. Robbins changed his mind and came up here, and left a message to Mr. Edgar to come, thinking he might be a protection in case Hughie guessed where he'd gone and follered him up."

"That's about the size of it," agreed Weybridge. "The point is, was it Hughie who came, or was it Mr. Edgar?"

"The time would fit either of 'em," said Mr. Bowles, "for they left the Eagle within five minutes of one another, or it might be ten. If Hughie had his bicycle, he could a-got here by eight, easy. He didn't stay in the bar more nor a minute or so after you went into the parlour, Mr. Egg."

"Well," said the Chief Constable, "we must find out if anybody saw either of them in the town at 8 o'clock or thereabouts. Let's work it out. Suppose it was Mr. Edgar. His father is expecting him and lets him in. They come in here, and Mr. Robbins takes out this letter and shows it to him. Then Mr. Edgar suddenly loses his temper and strikes out, killing his father, either accidentally or of set purpose. Then what does he do? He takes the trouble to tear away as much of this letter as he can, including the signature, if there was one—on purpose to keep all the suspicion to himself. That's either very stupid or very honest of him. Then, instead of taking the keys and making his escape that way, he runs and hides somewhere, till Baggitt is fool enough to open the gate and leave the way clear for him."

"It looks more to me," said the Inspector, "as if the man that wrote that letter did the murder."

"Meaning Searle. Very well. In that case, Mr. Robbins let him in, thinking it was Mr. Edgar. Once in, he couldn't very well be turned out by a man double his age and half his strength, and Baggitt was some way away, so Mr. Robbins makes the best of a bad job and takes him into the office. They discuss this little matter of goal-keeping; Mr. Robbins says something that gets Searle's goat, and it all happens the same way as before, except that it's more natural that Searle should destroy the letter, if he wrote it, and that he shouldn't wait to look for the keys, since he wouldn't know as well as Mr. Edgar where the old man kept them."

"I can't believe, if you'll excuse me," said Mr. Bowles, "that Hughie would go to do such a thing for such a reason. It's true he's got a hot temper, and uses language—but to take a brass paper-weight to an elderly gentleman! That don't seem like Hughie."

"You'll pardon my putting my oar in," said Mr. Egg, "but even the humblest suggestion may be of use. 'When it's a question of stamps to lick, the office-boy knows most of the trick,' as it says in the *Handbook*. I wouldn't be too sure that young Searle wrote that letter. What's his job in life?"

"He's a motor-mechanic down at Hobson's garage."

"Ever been in a drawing office or advertising business? Anything of an artist, or skilled letterer? That sort of thing?"

"Nothing of that sort," replied Mr. Bowles firmly.

"I only ask," said Monty, "because this letter was written by somebody who's been accustomed to write in capitals as quick and easy as you or I would write an ordinary hand. See how the letters are joined together, and how free the movement of the pencil is. It's rough, but it's clear, and it comes natural to the writer, that's the point. It's not the printing script they teach you in the schools. And it isn't done laborlously, by way of disguise. It's the script of somebody accustomed to roughing out head-lines."

"I see what you mean," said Charteris. "That's smart."

"About this man Fletcher, who had a grievance," pursued Monty. "He's gone to live with his father. What's his father's profession?"

"I believe he's head-compositor at a small jobbing printer's," said Mr. Bowles.

"Just the man," said Monty. "And that word 'son' might very well be 'son' and not 'Benson,' mightn't it?"

"So it might," said the Chief Constable. "But if you mean to suggest that the murderer was this man Fletcher, or his father, how did he know where to find Mr. Robbins? Nobody knew he was coming up to the Mills except you and me and Bowles, and Mr. Edgar Robbins and Hughie."

"One other person, sir," replied Monty. "The elderly party who was sitting in the bar with his newspaper—the man who was a stranger to you, Mr. Bowles. He went out just after he had heard that Mr. Robbins would be up at the Mills, and that Mr. Edgar would *not* be there to protect him."

"By Jove, you're right!" Charteris thought this over for a moment. "But all this about playing in goal——"

"Ah!" said Monty, "if you bar 'gauge,' which they always spell 'guage,' that word is the biggest stumbling-block a printer can have. Trips him up every time. It's a disease with 'em. 'You've acted like a thief by my son, and deserve by right to be put in gaol.' Don't you think that sounds more natural? Personally," added Mr. Egg. "I take the soft option and write it JAIL—it mayn't look so classy, but it's safer."

DIRT CHEAP

A Montague Egg Story

MR. MONTAGUE EGG was startled out of his beauty sleep by the ugly noise next door.

"Wah! wah! wah!" in a series of crescendo roars. Then followed a long, choking gurgle.

The Griffin at Cuttlesbury was an old-fashioned and ill-kept hotel. Neither Mr. Egg nor his fellow-commercials would have dreamed of patronising it in ordinary circumstances. But the Green Man had been put temporarily out of commission by a disastrous fire; and that was how Mr. Egg, after an ill-cooked and indigestible dinner, came to be lying in a lumpy bed in this fusty, dusty bedroom, without electric light or even a bed-side candle and matches, so slovenly was the service.

As full consciousness slowly returned to him, Mr. Egg took stock of the situation. There were, he knew, only three bedrooms in this isolated corridor; his own, in the middle; on the left, No. 8, containing old Waters, of Messrs. Brotherhood, Ltd., the soft-drinks-and-confectionery firm; on the right, No. 10, allotted to that stout man who travelled in jewellery, whose name was Pringle, and who had stuffed himself up that evening with dubious mackerel and underdone pork, to the admiration of all beholders. Close behind the head of Monty's bed, the rich and rhythmical snoring of old Waters shook the thin partition like the vibration of a passing lorry. It must be Pringle who was making the uproar; mackerel and pork were the most probable explanation.

The bellowing had ceased; only a few faint grunts were now to be heard. He didn't know Pringle, and hadn't liked the look of him very much. But perhaps the man was really ill. It would be only decent to go and find out.

He swung his legs reluctantly over the side of the bed and thrust his feet into his slippers. Without troubling to search for matches and light the gloomy gas-jet with the broken mantle at the far end of the room, he felt his way to the door, unlocked it and stepped out into the corridor. At the far end, another gas-jet burned dimly on the by-pass, throwing a misleading jumble of light and shadow on the two creaking steps that separated the corridor from the main landing.

In No. 8, old Waters snored on undisturbed. Monty turned to his right and knocked at the door of No. 10.

"Who's there?" demanded a stifled voice.

"Me—Egg," said Monty. He turned the handle as he spoke, but the door was locked. "Are you all right? I heard you call out."

"Sorry" The bed creaked as though the speaker were levering himself up to a sitting position. "Nightmare. Sorry I disturbed you."

"Don't mention it," said Mr. Egg, pleased to have his diagnosis confirmed. "Sure there's nothing I can do?"

"No, thanks, quite all right." Mr. Pringle seemed to have buried his head in the blankets again.

"Good night, then," said Monty.

"G'night."

Mr. Egg slipped back to his own room. The snores in No. 8 were increasing in vehemence, and, as he shut and relocked his door, ended suddenly in a ferocious snort. All was quiet. Monty wondered what time it was, but while he was feeling in his coat-pocket for his matches, a clock began to strike with a sweet, vibrating, mellow tone that seemed to come from a considerable distance. He counted twelve strokes. It was earlier than he thought. Being tired, he had gone up to bed at half-past ten and had heard Waters pass his door only a few minutes after. There was now no sound of movement in the hotel. In the main street below, a car passed. The snoring in No. 8 began again.

Mr. Egg returned to his uncomfortable mattress and once more disposed his plump body to slumber. He hated being roused from his first, deep, delicious unconsciousness. Confound Waters! Drowsily counting the snores, he began to doze.

Click! a door in the passage had opened. Then came stealthy footsteps, interrupted by a creak and a stumble. Somebody had

same note—deep and quick and what you might call humming. Rather a pretty strike."

"H'm," said the Inspector. We'd better check that up. May have been wrong last night and right again this morning. We'll take a turn round the house and see if we can identify it. Ruggles, make Mr. Bates understand that nobody must leave the place, and tell him we'll be as quick as we can. Now, Mr. Egg."

There were only six striking clocks in the Griffin. The grandfather on the stairs was promptly eliminated; his voice was thin and high and quavering, like the voice of the very old gentleman that he was. The garage-clock, too, had quite the wrong kind of strike, while the clock in the coffee-room and the ugly bronze monster in the drawing-room were both inaudible from Monty's room, and the clock in the bar was a cuckoo clock. But when they came to the kitchen, just beneath Monty's bedroom, Monty said at once:

"That looks like it."

It was an old American eight-day wall-clock, in a rosewood veneer case, with a painted dial and the picture of a beehive on its glass door.

"I know the kind," said Monty, "it strikes on a coiled spring and gives just that sort of rich, humming tone, like a church bell, but much quicker."

The Inspector opened the clock and peered inside.

"Quite right," he said. "Now let's check him up. Twenty minutes to nine. Correct. Now, you go upstairs and I'll push the hands on to nine o'clock, and you tell us if that's what you heard."

In his bedroom, with the door shut, Monty listened again to that deep, quick, vibratory note. He hurried downstairs.

"It's exactly like it, as far as I can tell."

"Good. Then, if the clock hasn't been tampered with, we've got our time settled.

It proved unexpectedly easy to show that the clock had been right at midnight. The cook had set it by the Town Hall clock, just before going up to bed at eleven. She had then locked the kitchen door and taken away the key, as she always did, "Otherwise that there Boots would be down at all hours, sneaking food from the larder." And the Boots—an unwholesome-looking lad of sixteen—had reluctantly confirmed this statement by admitting that he had tried the kitchen door half an hour later and found it securely fastened. There was no other access to the kitchen, except by the back door and windows—all bolted on the inside.

"Very well," said the Inspector. "Now we can look into all these people's alibis. And in the meantime, Ruggles, you'd better have a good hunt for Pringle's sample-case. We know he took it to bed with him," he added, turning to Monty, whom he seemed disposed to confide in, "because the barman saw him. And it can't have been taken out of the hotel before the body was discovered, because all the outside doors were locked and the keys removed—we've verified that—and nobody went out after they were opened except your friend Waters, and on your showing, he's not the murderer. Unless, of course, he's an accomplice."

"Not Waters," said Mr. Egg stoutly. "Honest as the day, is old Waters. Won't even wangle his expense-sheet. 'Account with rigid honesty for £ and s and even d.' Waters' pet passage from *The Salesman's Handbook.*"

"Very good," replied the Inspector, "but where's that case?"

The management and staff of the Griffin being all examined and satisfactorily accounted for, Inspector Monk turned his attention to the guests. After the memorable dinner of mackerel and pork, Mr. Egg, Mr. Waters and two other commercial gentlemen named Loveday and Turnbull had played bridge till half-past ten, when Mr. Egg and Mr. Waters had retired. The other two had then gone down to the bar until it closed at eleven, after which they had gone up to Mr. Loveday's room on the other side of the house. Here they had chatted till half-past twelve and had then separated. At one o'clock, Mr. Loveday had gone in to borrow a dose of fruit salts from Mr. Turnbull, who travelled in that commodity. They thus provided alibis for one another, and there seemed to be no reason to disbelieve them.

Then came an elderly lady called Mrs. Flack, who was obviously incapable of strangling a large man single-handed. Her room was on the main landing, and she slept undisturbed till about half-past twelve, when somebody came past her door and turned on the water in the bathroom. At a little before one, this inconsiderate person had returned to his room. Otherwise she had heard nothing.

The only other guest, besides Waters and Pringle himself, was a person who had arrived with Mr. Pringle in the latter's car and said that he was a "photographic agent," answering to the name of Alistair Cobb. Inspector Monk did not like the look of him, but he was important, having spent a good part of the evening with the murdered man.

"Get it out of your heads," said Mr. Cobb, sleeking his hair, "that I know anything much about Pringle. Never set eyes on him till seven o'clock last night. I'd missed the 'bus (literally, I mean) from Tadworthy—you know it, little one-horse place about four miles out—and there wasn't another till nine. So I was starting out to leg it with my suit-case when Pringle came by and offered me a lift. Said he often gave people lifts. Companionable chap. Didn't like driving alone."

Mr. Egg (who was present at the interview, a privilege no doubt attributable to Inspector Ramage's favourable opinion of him) shuddered at this rash behaviour on the part of a traveller in jewellery, and was disagreeably reminded of the late Mr. Rouse, of burning-car celebrity.

"He was a decent old geezer," went on Mr. Cobb, reminiscently. "Quite a gay old lad. He brought me along here——"

"You had business in Cuttlesbury?"

"Sure thing. Photographs, you know. Enlarge Dad and Mother's wedding-group free. With gilt frame, twenty-five shillings. Dirt Cheap. You know the game?"

"I do," replied the Inspector, with an emphasis that made it clear that he thought the game a very doubtful one.

"Just so," said Mr. Cobb with a wink. "Well, we had dinner —and a dashed bad dinner too. Then we had a bit of a yarn in the bar-parlour. Bates and the barman saw us there. Then Bates went off to play billiards with some young fellow who dropped in, and we sat on till just about eleven. Then Pringle barged off—said he wasn't feeling the thing, and I'm not surprised. That mackerel——"

"Never mind the mackerel now," said Monk. "The barman says you and Pringle had a final drink at five to eleven, and then Pringle went off to bed, taking his bag with him. Did you go straight to the billiard-room at that point?"

"Yes, right away. We played——"

"Just a minute. Bates says you made a 'phone call first."

"So I did. At least, I went up first and found Bates and the other chap just finishing their game. So I said I'd make my call and then take Bates on. You can check the call for the time. I made it to the Bull at Tadworthy. I'd left a pair of gloves in the bar. A man answered me and said he'd found them and would send them on."

The Inspector made a note.

"And how long did you play billiards?"

"Till round about a quarter-past twelve. Then Bates said he'd had enough, as he had to get up early, so we drank the drinks I'd won off him and I pushed up to bed."

The Inspector nodded. This confirmed the landlord's evidence.

My room's on the main landing," went on Mr. Cobb. "No, not the side near the corridor where the disturbance was—the other side. But I went across and had a bath; the bathroom's near the steps that go down to the corridor. It would be about ten to one when I got back. All quiet then on the Western Front."

"What did you and Pringle talk about downstairs?"

"Oh, this and that," replied Mr. Cobb, easily. "We got swapping yarns and so on. Pringle had a hot one or two, and yours truly kept his end up. Have a fag, Inspector?"

"No, thanks. Did Pringle happen to mention—Yes, Ruggles, what is it? Excuse me one moment, gentlemen."

He stepped to the door for a word with the sergeant, returning in a minute or two with a card in his hand.

"I suppose your photographic supplies don't include this kind of thing, Mr. Cobb?"

Mr. Cobb blew out a long cloud of smoke with a whistling noise.

"No," said he, "no-ho! Where d'you get this pretty thing from?"

"Ever seen it before?"

Mr. Cobb hesitated. "Well, since you ask me, yes. The late lamented Pringle showed it me last night. Wouldn't have said anything if you hadn't asked me. Speak no ill of the dead and so on. But he *was* a bit up and coming, was Pringle."

"Sure it was the same one?"

"Looks like it. Same pretty lady—same pretty pose, anyhow."

"Where did he carry it?" asked the Inspector, taking the photograph back and attaching it to his notes with a paper-clip —but not before Mr. Egg had snatched a glimpse of it and been suitably shocked.

"In his breast-pocket," replied Mr. Cobb, after a moment's thought.

"I see. Pringle told you what his job was, I suppose. Did he happen to say anything about taking precautions against thieves, or anything of that sort?"

"He did mention that he had valuable stuff in his bag and always locked his bedroom door," returned Mr. Cobb, with an air of great frankness. "Not that I asked him. No affair of mine what he did."

"Quite so. Well, Mr. Cobb, I don't think I need trouble you further at present, but I'd be obliged if you'd stay in the hotel till I've seen you again. Sorry to inconvenience you."

"Not at all," said the obliging Mr. Cobb. "It's all the same to me." He sauntered out, smiling pleasantly.

"Pah!" said Inspector Monk. "There's a nasty piece of work for you. Cheap dirt. And a liar, too. You saw that photo? (And how anybody can print such filth beats me.) Well, that hadn't been carried round in a breast-pocket. Edges quite sharp. Fresh out of its envelope, from the look of it. Don't mind betting you'd find the rest of the series in that fellow's suit-case. But naturally he won't admit it—it's a punishable offence to sell them."

"Where was this one found?"

"Under Pringle's bed. If Cobb hadn't got an alibi—and I'm pretty sure Bates is telling the truth, and as a matter of fact, the cook's window looks on to the billiards-room window, and she saw them playing there until 12.15. Unless they're all in it together, which isn't likely. And still no sign of Pringle's bag. But we can't get over the evidence of that clock. You're sure it struck twelve?"

"Absolutely. I couldn't mistake one or two strokes for twelve."

"No, of course not." The Inspector drummed on the table and stared into vacancy. Monty took this for a dismissal. He went back into his own bedroom. The bed had not yet been made nor the slops emptied, the slatternly routine of the Griffin having been reduced to complete chaos by the catastrophe. He threw himself into a broken-springed arm-chair, lit a cigarette and meditated.

He had been brooding for ten minutes or so when he heard the town clock chime the quarters and strike eleven. Mechanically he waited, expecting to hear the answering melodious strike of the kitchen clock, but nothing came. Then he remembered that Monk had set the hands twenty minutes forward that morning, so that it must have struck some time since. And then he bounded to his feet with a loud exclamation.

"Heavens! What a fool I am! This morning at seven the town clock struck first, and the kitchen clock immediately after. *But last night I never heard the town clock strike at all.* The kitchen clock *must* have been altered somehow or other. Unless—unless—unless, by gosh! I wonder if that could be it. Yes. Yes, it's possible. *Just before that clock struck twelve, Waters stopped snoring."*

He ran from the room and plunged hastily into No. 8. Like his own room, it was in disorder. Like his own room, it did not appear to have been dusted for weeks. And on the nighttable by Waters' bed, which stood close against the thin partition between the two rooms, there was a mark in the dust, as though some object measuring about three inches by three and a half had stood there during the night.

Mr. Egg darted out of the room and along the corridor. He fell up the two ill-lighted steps with a curse, turned the corner and burst into the bathroom. Its window looked out upon a narrow side-street, communicating at one end with the main road and at the other with a lane that ran between warehouses. Rushing downstairs, Mr. Egg caught Inspector Monk just emerging from the coffee-room.

"Hold Cobb!" panted Mr. Egg. "I believe I've bust his alibi. Where's Waters gone to? I want to put a call through to him. Quick!"

"Waters said he was catching a train to Sawcaster," said Monk, rather astonished.

"Then," said Monty, calling upon his professional knowledge, "he'll put up at the Ring o' Bells, and he'll visit Hunter's, Merriman's and Hackett & Brown's. We'll get him at one place or the other."

After a hectic half-hour at the telephone, he ran his quarry to earth at one of Sawcaster's leading confectionery establishments.

"Waters," gasped Monty urgently, "I want you to answer some questions, old man, and you can ask me why afterwards. Never mind how silly they sound. Do you carry a travelling-clock? You do? What's it like? Old-fashioned repeater? Yes? About three inches square—squarish? Yes? Stood on your bedtable last night? Does it strike on a coiled spring? It does? Thank heaven for that ! Deep, quick, soft note like a church bell? Yes, yes, yes! Now, old boy, think hard. Did you wake up last night and strike that repeater? You did? You're sure?

Good man! At what time? It struck twelve? What time does that mean? *Any time between twelve and one o'clock?* Then, for God's sake, Waters, take the next train back to Cuttlesbury, because your dashed clock has nearly made you and me accomplices in a murder. Yes, MURDER. . . . Hold on a moment, Inspector Monk wants to speak to you."

"Well," said the Inspector, as he replaced the receiver, "your evidence might have landed us in a nice pickle, mightn't it? It's a good job you had that brain-wave. *Now* we'll go through Mr. Dirty Cobb's luggage and see if he's got any more juicy photos. I suppose he took 'em along to show Pringle."

"That's it. I couldn't understand how the murderer got into the room. Naturally Pringle would lock his door. But of course he'd left it open for Cobb, who'd promised to slip along later and show him something to make his hair curl—'on the strict q.t.' and all that. It must have given Cobb a shock when Pringle yelled and I knocked at the door. But he was all there, I will say that for him. He's probably a first-class salesman in his own rotten line. 'Don't let a sudden question rout you, but always keep your wits about you,' as it says in the *Handbook*."

"But look here," said the Inspector, "what did he do with Pringle's bag?"

"Dropped it out of the bathroom window to the accomplice he had summoned by 'phone from Tadworthy. Why, dash it all!" cried Monty, wiping his forehead, "I heard the car go by, just after that confounded clock struck twelve."

BITTER ALMONDS

A Montague Egg Story

"DASH it!" exclaimed Mr. Montague Egg, "there's another perfectly good customer gone west."

He frowned at his morning paper, which informed him that an inquest would be held that day on the body of Mr. Bernard Whipley, a wealthy and rather eccentric old gentleman, to whom the firm of Plummett & Rose had from time to time sold a considerable quantity of their choice vintage wines, fine old matured spirits and liqueurs.

Monty had more than once been invited by Mr. Whipley to sample his own goods, sitting in the pleasant study at Cedar Lawn—a bottle of ancient port, carried up carefully from the cellar by Mr. Whipley himself, or a liqueur brandy, brought out from the tall mahogany cabinet that stood in the alcove.

Mr. Whipley never allowed anybody but himself to handle anything alcoholic. You never, he said, could trust servants, and he had no fancy for being robbed, or finding the cook with her head under the kitchen dresser.

So Mr. Egg frowned and sighed, and then frowned still more, on seeing that Mr. Whipley had been discovered dead, apparently from prussic acid poisoning, after drinking an after-dinner glass of crème de menthe.

It is not agreeable when customers suddenly die poisoned after partaking of the drinks one has supplied to them, and it is not good for business.

Mr. Egg glanced at his watch. The town where he was at that moment reading the paper was only fifteen miles distant from the late Mr. Whipley's place of residence. Monty decided that it might be just as well to run over and attend the inquest. He was, at any rate, in a position to offer testimony as to the harmless nature of crème de menthe as supplied by Messrs. Plummett & Rose.

Accordingly he drove over there as soon as he had finished his breakfast, and by sending in his card to the coroner, secured for himself a convenient seat in the crowded little schoolroom where the inquest was being held.

The first witness was the housekeeper, Mrs. Minchin, a stout, elderly person of almost exaggerated respectability. She said she had been over twenty years in Mr. Whipley's service. He was nearly eighty years old, but very active and healthy, except that he had to be careful of his heart, as was only to be expected.

She had always found him an excellent employer. He had been, perhaps, a little close about financial matters and had kept a very sharp eye on the housekeeping, but personally she was not afraid of such, being as careful of his interests as she would be of her own. She had kept house for him ever since his wife's death.

"He was quite in his usual health on Monday evening," Mrs. Minchin went on. "Mr. Raymond Whipley had telephoned in the afternoon to say he would be down for dinner——"

"That is Mr. Whipley's son?"

"Yes—his only child." Here Mrs. Minchin glanced across at a thin, sallow, young-old man, seated near Mr. Egg on the bench reserved for witnesses, and sniffed rather meaningly. "Mr. and Mrs. Cedric were staying in the house. Mr. Cedric Whipley is Mr. Whipley's nephew. He had no other relations."

Mr. Egg identified Mr. and Mrs. Cedric Whipley as the fashionably dressed young man and woman in black who sat on the other side of Mr. Raymond. The witness proceeded.

"Mr. Raymond arrived in his car at half-past six, and went in at once to see his father in the study. He came out again when the dressing gong rang for dinner, at a quarter past seven. He passed me in the hall, and I thought he looked rather upset. As Mr. Whipley didn't come out, I went in to him. He was sitting at his writing table, reading something that looked to me like a legal paper.

"I said, 'Excuse me, Mr. Whipley, sir, but did you hear the gong?' He was sometimes a little hard of hearing, though wonderfully keen in all his faculties, considering his age. He looked up and said, 'All right, Mrs. Minchin,' and went back
57

to what he was doing. I said to myself, 'Mr. Raymond's been putting him out again.' At half-past——"

"One moment. What had you in your mind about Mr. Raymond?"

"Well, nothing much, only Mr. Whipley didn't always approve of Mr. Raymond's goings-on, and they sometimes had words about it. Mr. Whipley disliked Mr. Raymond's business.

"At half-past seven," continued the witness, "Mr. Whipley went upstairs to dress, and he seemed all right then, only his step was tired and heavy. I was waiting in the hall, in case he needed any assistance, and as he passed me he asked me to telephone to Mr. Whitehead to ask him to come over the next morning—Mr. Whitehead the lawyer. He did not say what it was for. I did as he asked me, and when Mr. Whipley came down again, about ten minutes to eight, I told him Mr. White-head had had the message, and would be with him at ten the next day."

"Did anybody else hear you say that?"

"Yes. Mr. Raymond and Mr. and Mrs. Cedric were in the hall, having their cocktails. They must all have heard me. Dinner was served at eight——"

"Were you present at dinner?"

"No. I have my meals in my own room. Dinner was over about a quarter to nine, and the parlour-maid took coffee into the drawing-room for Mr. and Mrs. Cedric, and into the study for Mr. Whipley and Mr. Raymond. I was alone in my room till 9 o'clock, when Mr. and Mrs. Cedric came in to have a little chat. We were all together till just before half-past nine, when we heard the study door slam violently, and a few minutes later, Mr. Raymond came in, looking very queer. He had his hat and coat on.

"Mr. Cedric said: 'Hullo, Ray!' He took no notice, and said to me, 'I shan't be staying the night, after all, Mrs. Minchin. I'm going back to Town at once.' I said, 'Very good, Mr. Raymond. Does Mr. Whipley know of your change of plans?' He laughed in a funny way, and said: 'Oh yes. He knows all about it.' He went out again and Mr. Cedric followed him and, I think, said something like, 'Don't lose your hair, old man.' Mrs. Cedric said to me, she was afraid Mr. Raymond might have had a quarrel with the old gentleman.

"About ten minutes later, I heard the two young gentlemen coming downstairs, and went out to see that Mr. Raymond
58

had left nothing behind him, as he was apt to be forgetful. He was just going out of the front door with Mr. Cedric. I ran after him with his scarf, which he had left on the hall-stand. He drove away in his car very quickly and I came back into the house with Mr. Cedric.

"As we passed the study door, Mr. Cedric said, 'I wonder whether my uncle——' and then he stopped, and said, 'No, better let him alone till to-morrow.' We went back to my room, where Mrs. Cedric was waiting for us. She said, 'What's the matter, Cedric?' and he answered, 'Uncle Henry's found out about Ella. I told Ray he'd better be careful.' She said, 'Oh, dear!' and after that we changed the conversation.

"Mr. and Mrs. Cedric sat with me till about eleven-thirty, when they left me to go up to bed. I put my room in order and then came out to make my usual round of the house. When I put out the light in the hall, I noticed that the light was still on in Mr. Whipley's study. It was unusual for him to be up so late, so I went to see if he had fallen asleep over a book.

"I got no answer when I knocked, so I went in, and there he was, lying back in his chair, dead. There were two empty coffee-cups and two empty liqueur glasses on the table and a half-empty flask of crème de menthe. I called Mr. Cedric at once, and he told me to leave everything exactly as it was, and to telephone to Dr. Baker."

The next witness was the parlour-maid, who had waited at table. She said that nothing unusual had happened during the dinner, except that Mr. Whipley and his son both seemed rather silent and preoccupied.

At the end of the meal, Mr. Raymond had said, "Look here, father, we can't leave it like this." Mr. Whipley had said, "If you have changed your mind you had better tell me at once," and had ordered coffee to be sent into the study. Mr. Raymond said, "I can't change my mind, but if you would only listen——" Mr. Whipley did not reply.

On going into the study with the coffee and the liqueur glasses, the parlour-maid saw Mr. Raymond seated at the table. Mr. Whipley was standing at the cabinet, with his back turned to his son, apparently getting out the liqueurs.

He said to Mr. Raymond, "What will you have?" Mr. Raymond replied, "Crème de menthe." Mr. Whipley said, "You would—that's a woman's drink." The parlour-maid then went out and did not see either gentleman again.

Mr. Egg smiled to himself as he listened. He could hear old Mr. Whipley saying it.

Then he composed his chubby face to a more serious expression, as the coroner proceeded to call Mr. Cedric Whipley.

Mr. Cedric corroborated the housekeeper's story. He said he was aged thirty-six, and was a junior partner in the publishing firm of Freeman & Toplady. He was acquainted with the circumstance of Mr. Whipley's quarrel with his son. Mr. Whipley had, in fact, asked him and his wife to the house in order that he might discuss the situation with them. The trouble had to do with Raymond's engagement to a certain lady.

Mr. Whipley had talked rather impulsively about altering his will, but he (Cedric) had urged him to think the matter over calmly. He had accompanied Raymond upstairs on the night of the tragedy and had understood from him that Mr. Whipley had threatened to cut his son off with the proverbial shilling. He had told Raymond to take things easy and the old man would "simmer down." Raymond had taken his interference in bad part.

After Raymond's departure he had thought it better to leave the old man to himself. On leaving Mrs. Minchin's room with his wife, he had gone straight upstairs without entering the study. He thought it would be about a quarter of an hour after that, that he had come down in answer to Mrs. Minchin's call, to find his uncle dead.

He had bent over the body to examine it, and had then thought he detected a faint smell of almonds about the lips. He had smelt the liqueur glasses, but without touching them and, fancying that one of them also smelt of almonds, had instructed Mrs. Minchin to leave everything exactly as it was. He had then formed the impression that his uncle might have committed suicide.

There was a rustle in the little court when Mr. Raymond Whipley took his place at the coroner's table. He was a lean, effeminate and rather unwholesome-looking person of anything between thirty and forty years of age.

He said that he was "a photographic artist" by profession. He had a studio in Bond Street. His "expressionist studies" of well-known men and women had gained considerable notice in the West End. His father had not approved of his activities. He had old-fashioned prejudices.

"I understand," said the coroner, "that prussic acid is frequently used in photography."

Mr. Raymond Whipley smiled winningly at this ominous question.

"Cyanide of potassium," he said. "Oh, dear, yes. Quite frequently."

"You are acquainted with its use for photography?"

"Oh, yes. I don't use it often. But I have some by me, if that's what you want to know."

"Thank you. Now can you tell me about this alleged difference of opinion with your father?"

"Yes. He found out that I was engaged to marry a lady connected with the stage. I don't know who told him. Probably my cousin Cedric. He'll deny it, of course, but I expect it was jolly old Cedric. My father sent for me and really cut up quite rough about it. Full of diehard prejudices, you know. We had quite a little rumpus before dinner. After dinner, I asked to see him again—thought I could talk him round. But he was really very offensive. I couldn't stand it. It upset me. So I barged off back to Town."

"Did he say anything about sending for Mr. Whitehead?"

"Oh, yes. Said if I married Ella, he'd cut me out of his will. Quite the stern parent and all that. I said, cut away, then."

"Did he say in whose favour he thought of making his new will?"

"No, he didn't say. I expect Cedric would have come in for something. He's the only other relation, of course."

"Will you describe very carefully what happened in the study after dinner?"

"We went in, and I sat down at the table near the fire. My father went to the cabinet where he keeps his spirits and liqueurs and asked me what I would have. I said I would have a crème de menthe, and he sneered at me in his usual pleasant way. He fetched out the flask and told me to help myself, when the girl brought in the glasses. I did so. I had coffee and crème de menthe. He did not drink anything while I was there. He was rather excited and walked up and down, threatening me with this and that.

"After a bit I said, 'Your coffee's getting cold, father.' Then he told me to go to hell, and I said, 'Right you are.' He added

61

a very disagreeable remark about my fiancée. I am afraid I then lost my temper and used some—shall we say, unfilial expressions. I went out and banged the door. When I left him he was standing up behind the table, facing me.

"I went to tell Mrs. Minchin that I was going back to Town. Cedric started to butt in, but I told him I knew who it was I had to thank for all this trouble, and if he wanted the old man's money he was welcome to it. That's all I know about it."

"If your father drank nothing while you were with him, how do you explain the fact that both the liqueur glasses and both the coffee-cups had been used?"

"I suppose he used his after I had gone. He certainly did not drink anything before I went."

"And he was alive when you left the study?"

"Very much so."

Mr. Whitehead, the lawyer, explained the terms of the deceased man's will. It left an income of two thousand a year to Cedric Whipley, with reversion to Raymond, who was the residuary legatee.

"Did deceased ever express any intention of altering his will?"

"He did. On the day before his death he said that he was very much dissatisfied with his son's conduct, and that unless he could get him to see reason, he would cut him off with an annuity of a thousand a year, and leave the rest of the estate to Mr. Cedric Whipley. He disliked Mr. Raymond's fiancée and said he would not have that woman's children coming in for his money. I tried to dissuade him, but I think he supposed that when the lady heard of his intentions she would break off the engagement. When Mrs. Minchin rang me up on the night in question I was convinced in my own mind that he intended to execute a new will."

"But since he had no time to do so, the will in favour of Mr. Raymond Whipley will now stand?"

"That is so."

Inspector Brown of the County Police then gave evidence about finger-prints. He said that one coffee-cup and one liqueur glass bore the finger-prints of Mr. Raymond Whipley, and the other cup and the glass which held the poison, those of Mr. Whipley, senior. There were no other prints, except, of course, those of the parlour-maid, on the cups or glasses, while the flask of crème de menthe bore those of both father and son.

Bearing in mind the possibility of suicide, the police had

made a careful search of the room for any bottle or phial which might have contained the poison. They had found nothing, either in the cabinet or elsewhere. They had, indeed, collected from the back of the fireplace the half-burnt fragment of a lead-foil capsule, which bore the letters ". . . AU . . . tier & Cie," stamped round the edge.

From its size, however, it was clear that this capsule had covered the stopper of a half-litre bottle, and it seemed highly improbable that an intending suicide would purchase prussic acid by the half-litre, nor was there any newly opened bottle to which the capsule appeared to belong.

At this point a horrible thought began to emerge from Mr. Egg's inner consciousness—a dim recollection of something he had once read in a book. He lost the remainder of Inspector Brown's evidence, which was purely formal, and only began to take notice again when, after the cook and housemaid had proved that they had been together the whole evening, the doctor was called to give the medical evidence.

He said that deceased had undoubtedly died of prussic acid poisoning. Only a very small amount of the cyanide had been found in the stomach, but even a small dose would be fatal to a man of his age and natural frailty. Prussic acid was one of the most rapidly fatal of all known poisons, producing unconsciousness and death within a very few minutes after being swallowed.

"When did you first see the body, doctor?"

"I arrived at the house at five minutes to twelve. Mr. Whipley had then been dead at least two hours, and probably a little more."

"He could not possibly have died within, say, half an hour of your arrival?"

"Not possibly. I place the death round about half-past nine and certainly not later than ten-thirty."

The analyst's report was next produced. The contents of the flask of crème de menthe and the coffee dregs in both cups had been examined and found to be perfectly harmless. Both liqueur glasses contained a few drops of crème de menthe, and in one—that which bore the finger-prints of old Mr. Whipley—there was a distinct trace of hydrocyanic acid.

Even before the coroner began his summing up it was plain that things looked very black for Raymond Whipley. There was the motive, the fact that he alone had easy access to the deadly cyanide, and the time of death, coinciding almost exactly with that of his hasty and agitated flight from the house.

Suicide seemed to be excluded; the other members of the household could prove each other's alibis; there was no suggestion that any stranger had entered the house from outside. The jury brought in the inevitable verdict of murder against Raymond Whipley.

Mr. Egg rapidly made his way out of court. Two things were troubling him—Mrs. Minchin's evidence and that half-remembered warning that he had read in a book. He went down to the village post-office and sent a telegram to his employers. Then he turned his steps to the local inn, ordered a high tea, and ate it slowly, with his thoughts elsewhere. He had an idea that this case was going to be bad for business.

In about an hour's time, the reply to his telegram was handed to him. It ran: "June 14, 1893. Freeman and Toplady, 1931," and was signed by the senior partner of Plummett & Rose.

Mr. Egg's round and cheerful face became overcast by a cloud of perplexity and distress. He shut himself into the landlord's private room alone and put through an expensive trunk call to Town. Emerging, less perlexed but still gloomy, he got into his car and set off in search of the coroner.

That official welcomed him cheerfully. He was a hearty and rubicund man with a shrewd eye and a brisk manner. Inspector Brown and the Chief Constable were with him when Monty was shown in.

"Well, Mr. Egg," said the coroner, "I'm sure you're happy to be assured that this unfortunate case conveys no imputation against the purity of the goods supplied by your firm."

"That's just what I've taken the liberty of coming to you about," said Monty. "Business is business, but, on the other hand, facts are facts, and our people are ready to face them. I've been on the 'phone to Mr. Plummett, and he authorised me to put the thing before you.

"If I didn't," added Mr. Egg, candidly, "somebody else might, and that would make matters worse. Don't wait for unpleasant disclosures to burst. If the truth must be told, see that *you* tell it first. Monty's maxim — from *The Salesman's Handbook*. Remarkable book, full of common-sense. Talking of common-sense, a spot of that commodity wouldn't have hurt our young friend, would it?"

"Meaning Raymond Whipley?" said the coroner. "That young man is a pathological case, if you ask me."

"You're right there, sir," agreed the Inspector. "I've seen a sight of foolish crooks, but he licks the lot. Barmy, I'd call him. Quarrelling with his dad, doing him in and running away in that suspicious manner—why didn't he put up an electric sign to say 'I done it'? But as you say, I don't think he's quite all there."

"Well, that may be," said Monty, "but over and above that, there's old Mr. Whipley. You see, gentlemen, I know all my customers. It's my job, as you may say, to have all their fancies by heart. No good offering an 1847 Oleroso to a gentleman that likes his sherry light and dry, or tantalising a customer that's under orders to stick to hock with bargains in vintage port.

"Now, what I'd like you to tell me is, how did the late Mr. Whipley come to be drinking crème de menthe at all? He only kept it by him for ladies; it was a flavour he couldn't do with in any shape or form. You heard what he said about it to Mr. Raymond."

"That's a point," said the chief constable. "I may say it had already occurred to us. But he must have taken the poison in something."

"Well, I only say, bear that in mind—that, and the foolishness of the murder, if it was done the way the jury brought it in. But now about this lead-foil capsule. I can tell you something about that. I didn't intrude myself at the inquest, because I hadn't got the facts, but I've got them now and here they are. You know, gentlemen, it stands to reason, if a capsule was taken off a bottle that day in the study, there must have been a bottle belonging to it. And where is it? It's got to be somewhere. A bottle's a bottle, when all's said and done.

"Now, gentlemen, Mr. Whipley dealt with my employers, Plummett & Rose, for over fifty years. It's an old-established firm. And that capsule was put out by a firm of French shippers who went into liquidation in 1900; Prelatier & Cie was their name, and we were their agents in this country. Now, that capsule came off a bottle of Noyeau sent out by them—you can see the last two letters of the word on the stamp—and we delivered a bottle of Prelatier's Noyeau to Mr. Whipley, with some other samples of liqueur, on June 14, 1893."

65

C

"Noyeau?" said the coroner, with interest.

"I see that means something to you, doctor," said Mr. Egg.

"It does, indeed," said the coroner. "Noyeau is a liqueur flavoured with oil of bitter almonds, or peach-stones—correct me if I'm wrong, Mr. Egg—and contains, therefore, a small proportion of hydrocyanic acid."

"That's it," said Monty. "Of course, in the ordinary way, there isn't enough of it to hurt anybody in a single glassful, or even two. But if you let a bottle stand long enough, the oil will rise to the top, and the first glass out of an old bottle of Noyeau has been known to cause death. I know that, because I read it in a book called *Foods and Poisons*, published a few years ago by Freeman & Toplady."

"Cedric Whipley's firm," said the inspector.

"Exactly so," said Monty.

"What, precisely, are you suggesting, Mr. Egg?" inquired the chief constable.

"Not murder, sir," said Monty. "No, not that—though I suppose it might have come to that, in a way. I'm suggesting that after Mr. Raymond had left the study, the old gentleman got fidgety and restless, the way one does when one's been through a bit of an upset. I think he started to drink up his cold coffee, and then wanted a spot of liqueur to take with it.

"He goes to the cabinet—doesn't seem to fancy anything, roots about, and comes upon this old bottle of Noyeau that's been standing unopened for the last forty years. He takes it out, removes the capsule and throws it into the fire and draws a cork with his corkscrew, as I've seen him do many a time. Then he pours off the first glass, not thinking about the danger, drinks it off as he's sitting in his chair and dies without hardly having time to call out."

"That's very ingenious," said the chief constable. "But what became of the bottle and the corkscrew? And how do you account for the crème de menthe in the glass?"

"Ah!" said Monty, "there you are. Somebody saw to that, and it wasn't Mr. Raymond, because it would have been all to his advantage to leave things as they were. But suppose, round about half-past eleven, when Mrs. Minchin was tidying her room and the other servants were in bed, another party had gone into the study and seen Mr. Whipley lying dead, with the bottle of Noyeau beside him, and had guessed what had happened.

"Supposing this party had then put the corkscrew back into the cupboard, tipped a few drops of crème de menthe from Mr. Raymond's glass into the dead gentleman's, and carried the Noyeau bottle away to be disposed of at leisure. What would it look like then?"

"But how could the party do that, without leaving prints on Mr. Raymond's glass?"

"That's easy," said Monty. "He'd only to lift the glass by taking the stem between the roots of his fingers. So. All you'd find would be a faint smudge at the base of the bowl."

"And the motive?" demanded the chief constable.

"Well, gentlemen, that's not for me to say. But if Mr. Raymond was to be hanged for murdering his father, I fancy his father's money would go to the next of kin—to that gentleman who published the book that tells you all about Noyeau."

"It's very unfortunate," said Mr. Egg, "that my firm should have supplied the goods in question, but there you are. If accidents happen and you are to blame, take steps to avoid repetition of same. Not that we should admit any responsibility, far from it, the nature of the commodity being what is it. But we might perhaps insert a warning in our forthcoming Catalogue.

"And à propos, gentlemen, let me make a note to send you our New Centenary History of the House of Plummett & Rose. It will be a very refined production, got up regardless, and worthy of a position on any library shelf."

FALSE WEIGHT

A Montague Egg Story

"HULLO!" said Mr. Montague Egg.

He knew the Royal Oak, at Pondering Parva, and it was not, in a general way, a place he would have chosen to stop at. It did but little business, its food was bad, its landlord surly, and it offered few opportunities to an enterprising traveller in high-class wines and spirits. But to find it at half-past eight in the morning the centre of an interested crowd, with a police car and an ambulance drawn up before the door, was a challenge to any man's curiosity. Mr. Egg took his foot from the accelerator, and eased the car to a standstill.

"What's up here?" he asked a bystander.

"Somebody killed. . . . Old Rudd's cut 'is missus's throat . . . no, he ain't—George done it . . . that ain't right, neither, it was thieves and they've gone off with the till . . . George, he come down and found the blood running all over the floor . . . hear that? that's Liz Rudd a-hollerin' . . . she got highsterics . . thought you said 'e'd cut 'er throat . . . no, I didn't, Jim said that, he don't know nothin'. I tell you 'tis George. . . . Ah! here's the Inspector a-comin' out; now we'll hear summat. . . ."

Mr. Egg was already out of the car and approaching the bar entrance. A uniformed Inspector of police met him on the doorstep.

"Now then, you can't come in here. Who are you, and what do you want?"

"My name's Montague Egg—travelling for Plummett & Rose, wines and spirits, Piccadilly. I've come to see Mr. Rudd."

"Well, you can't see him now, so you'd better buzz off.

Wait a minute. You say you're a commercial traveller. This your regular district?"

Mr. Egg replied that it was.

"Then you might be able to give us some information. Come in, will you?"

"Wait while I fetch my bag," said Monty. He was interested, but not to the point of forgetting that a traveller's first duty is to his samples and credentials. He fetched the heavy case from the car and carried it into the inn, to the accompaniment of cries from the crowd: "That's the photographer, see his camera?" Setting it down inside the door, he looked round the bar of the Royal Oak. At a table near the window sat a police-constable, writing in a notebook. A large, pug-faced man, whom Monty recognised as Rudd, the landlord, was leaning back against the bar in his shirt-sleeves. He was unshaven, and looked as though he had dressed hurriedly. A tousle-headed young fellow, with immense muscles and no forehead to speak of, stood scowling beside him. From a room somewhere at the back came a noise of feminine shrieking and sobbing. That was all, except that a door on the right, labelled "Bar-parlour," stood open, and through it could be seen the back of a man in an overcoat, who was bending over something on the floor.

The Inspector took Mr. Egg's papers, looked them through and returned them.

"You're on the road early," he said.

"Yes," said Monty. "I meant to get through to Pettiford last night, but the fog held me up at Madgebury. I'm making up for lost time. I slept at the Old Bell—they can tell you all about me there."

"Ah!" said the Inspector, with a glance at the constable. "Well, now, Mr. Egg. I believe all you commercial gentlemen know each other pretty well, as a rule. We'd like to see if you can identify this man in here."

"I'll try," said Monty, "though of course I don't know every traveller on the road. But surely his name will be on his papers."

"That's just it," replied the Inspector. "His papers must have been in his sample case, and that's gone. He's got some letters on him, but they don't—well, we'll go into that later on. This way, please."

He marched into the room on the right. Monty followed him. The stooping man stood up.

"No doubt about this, Birch," he observed. "Head battered

69

in. Dead eight to ten hours. Couldn't possibly have done it himself, or by accident. Weapon probably that bottle over there. Better try it for finger-prints. Anything else you want to know? Because, if not, I'll be getting back to my breakfast. I'll leave word with the coroner as I go, if you like."

"Thanks, doctor. Eight to ten hours, eh? That fits Rudd's story all right. Now, Mr. Egg, come and have a look at this, will you?"

The doctor stepped aside, and Monty saw the dead body of a man. He was a small man, dressed in a neat blue serge suit. His hair was sleek and black, and he wore a small tooth-brush moustache. The blood from an open wound on the temple had run down and caked on his smooth cheek. He appeared to be about thirty-five or forty years of age.

"Oh, yes, I know him," said Monty. "I know him quite well, as a matter of fact. His name is Wagstaffe, and he travels—travelled—for Applebaum & Moss, the big cheap jewellers."

"Oh *did* he?" said Inspector Birch, with emphasis. "That case of his would contain jewellery then, I suppose."

"Yes—and watches, and that sort of thing."

"Humph!" said the Inspector. "And can you tell me why he should be carrying letters about in his pocket addressed to a number of other people? Here's one—Joseph Smith, Esq. Here's another—Mr. William Brown. And here's a very touching one— Harry Thorne, Esq. Hot stuff, that one is."

"Do you need any telling, Inspector?" inquired Mr. Egg, softly.

"I don't know that I do, if it comes to that. Ah! you commercial gentlemen are all alike, aren't you? A wife in every port of call, eh?"

"Not me, Inspector. No wedding-bells for Monty Egg. But I'm afraid it's true about poor Wagstaffe. Well, he seems to have got what was coming to him, doesn't he?"

"You're right. He put up a bit of a struggle, though, from the looks of it." Inspector Birch glanced round the bar-parlour. It was a small room, and every piece of furniture in it seemed to have suffered violence. A small round table before the fire-place had been knocked over, and a broken whisky-bottle had distributed its contents in an odorous stream across the linoleum. Chairs had been pushed back and overturned, the glass front of a what-not was starred as though by a blow from a threshing foot, and a grandfather clock, standing near the fire-place, had been canted over sideways, so that only the edge of the mantelpiece kept it from falling. Mr. Egg's eyes wandered to the clock-face, and the Inspector's followed them. The hands stood at ten minutes past eleven.

"Yes," said Mr. Birch. "And unless he's a liar, we know pretty well when this happened and who did it. Do you know anything about a commercial called Slater?"

"I've heard of an Archibald Slater," said Monty. "Travels in lingerie."

"That's the man. Is he in a good way of business? Good screw, I mean? Comfortable, and all that?"

"I should think so. He works for a good firm." Monty named it. "But I don't know him personally. He used to work Yorkshire and Lancashire, I believe. He's taken over old Cripps' district."

"You can't say if he'd be likely to murder another chap and pinch his samples?"

Monty protested. The last thing any commercial would be likely to do. There was a freemasonry of the road.

"Hum!" said the Inspector. "Now, listen here. We'll get Rudd's story again, and have it taken down."

The landlord's account was clear enough. The first traveller—now identified as Wagstaffe—had arrived at 7.30. He had meant, he said, to push on to Pettiford, but the fog was too thick. He had ordered dinner, and had afterwards gone in to sit in the bar-parlour, which was empty. The Royal Oak did very little high-class hotel business, and there was nobody in that night except some labourers in the four-ale bar. At half-past nine, Slater had turned up, also alleging the fog as the reason for breaking his journey. He had already dined, and presently joined Wagstaffe in the bar-parlour. On entering, he had been heard to say to Wagstaffe "in a nasty sort of voice," "Oh, it's you, is it?" After that, the door had been shut, but presently Wagstaffe had knocked upon the hatch between the parlour and the bar and asked for a bottle of Scotch. At half-past ten, the bar being closed and the glasses washed up, Rudd had gone in and found the two men talking beside the fire. They both seemed flushed and angry. Rudd said that he and his wife and the barman were going to bed, as they had to get up early. Would the guests please put out the light when they came upstairs?

Here the landlord broke off to explain that there were no

71

bedrooms over the bar-parlour—only a large, empty room running over the whole front of the house and used for meetings of parish societies, and so forth. The sleeping accommodation all ran out at the back, and you could not hear, from the bedrooms, anything that went on in the ground-floor part. He then went on:

"It would be about twenty past eleven when I heard someone come up and knock at our bedroom door. I got out of bed and opened it, and there was Slater. He looked very queer and upset. He said that the weather had cleared and he'd made up his mind to push on to Pettiford. It seemed funny to me, but I looked out of the window and saw that the fog had gone and there was a sharp frost and moonlight. I said he'd have to pay for his room, and he didn't make no bones about that. I put on a dressing-gown and went with him down the back stairs into the office. That's behind the bar. I made out his bill and he paid it, and then I let him out the back way into the garage. He took his bags with him——"

"How many bags?"

"Two."

"Did he bring two with him when he came?"

"Couldn't say, I'm sure. I never see them to notice. He planked all his stuff down in the bar-parlour when he come, and when I come out of the office with his change he was standing ready with them in the passage, with his hat and coat on. I didn't go out into the yard with him, because it was bitter cold, and I weren't none too pleased to be fetched out of my bed; but I heard the car drive out a few minutes later. Then I went back to bed again, and I noticed through the office window that the light was still on in the bar-parlour, so that the door must have been open. See what I mean? There's the back door of the parlour leading into the office, and when that's open, you can see the light from the yard, through the office window. So I thinks, that other fellow's still sitting up— I'll charge him extra for burning all that light. And I goes to bed."

"You didn't go in and see that he was still there."

"No, I didn't," said Mr. Rudd. "It was too perishing cold to be hanging about. I went to bed and to sleep."

"That's a pity. Did you go to sleep at once?"

"Yes, I click."

"You didn't hear Wagstaffe come upstairs at all?"

"I didn't hear a thing. But Mrs. Rudd was awake till midnight, and he hadn't come up then. And it stands to reason he never come up at all, don't it?"

"It looks that way," agreed the Inspector cautiously. "And how about George?"

The barman confirmed Rudd's story, and added a little to it. He said that he had gone into the bar-parlour between 9.30 and 10 o'clock and had interrupted the two men in what looked like a violent quarrel. Slater had been saying, "You little rat—I've a good mind to break every bone in your body." He thought they were both drunk. He had said nothing to them, but made up the fire and gone away. He had heard no more quarrelling. After Rudd had gone up at 10.30, he had looked in again, and they were then talking quietly and appeared to be reading some letters. He had then gone to bed, and been wakened by the sound of footsteps and the departure of the car.

"And after that?" asked Inspector Birch.

George's eyes were lowered sullenly.

"Mr. Rudd came upstairs again."

"Yes?"

"Well, that's all. I went to sleep."

"You didn't hear anybody else moving about?"

"No. I went to sleep, I tell you."

"What time did Mr. Rudd come up?"

"Dunno. I didn't trouble to look."

"Did you hear twelve strike?"

"I didn't hear nothing. I was asleep."

"How many bags did this man Slater bring with him?"

"Only one."

"You're sure of that?"

"Well, I think so."

"And the other man—Wagstaffe—did he have a bag?"

"Yes, he had a bag. Took it into the parlour with him."

"Did these men sign the register?"

"Slater did when he arrived," said the landlord. "Wagstaffe didn't. I meant to remind him in the morning."

"Then Slater wasn't premeditating anything when he arrived," said Birch. "Looks like it was a casual meeting. All right, Rudd. I'll see your wife later. Now carry on, and don't go shooting your mouth off too much. We've got the number of Slater's car," he added, to nobody in particular. "If he's really gone to Pettiford, they'll pull him in."

"Just so," said Monty. "I suppose," he added, tentatively, that clock's telling the truth?""

"Thinking he might have been put back, eh?" said the Inspector. "Like in that play they've got on in town?"

"Well," admitted Monty, "it seems funny, the way the criminal carefully knocked grandpa over, just as if he was going out of his way to provide evidence against himself. It doesn't seem natural. Praise with discretion ; purchasers are quick to distrust those who lay it on too thick, as it says in *The Salesman's Handbook*."

"We'll soon see," said the Inspector, advancing upon the clock. "Wait a bit, though ; we'd better try the case for finger-prints."

The arrival of a photographer and an apparatus for bringing up and recording finger-prints led to the discovery of so many signs of handling, both on the clock and on the bottle, as to prove that the use of dusters and furniture polish must have been abandoned for a very long time at the Royal Oak. Eventually the photographs were taken, and the Inspector and a constable lifted the clock back into place. It appeared to have suffered no great shock, but only to have stopped when the pendulum came up against the side of the case, for on being righted and started it ticked away merrily. Mr. Birch lifted a thick forefinger to the minute-hand ; then he checked himself.

"No," he said, "we'll leave grandpa to himself. If there's been any jiggery-pokery, there might be something to be found on the hands, though they're a bit narrow to carry a print. But you never know. I suppose he'll run all right for an hour or two."

"Oh, yes," said Mr. Egg, opening the case and peering in. "The weights are rather near the bottom, especially one of them, but I should say he had another twelve hours or so in him. What's to-day? Saturday? They probably wind him on Sunday morning."

"Probably," agreed the Inspector. "Well, thank you, Mr. Egg. I don't think we need detain you any longer."

"No objection to me having a spot of ale in the bar, I suppose," suggested Monty, "it'll be open in half an hour or so, and I didn't have much breakfast."

"I didn't have any," said Inspector Birch, wistfully.

74

From this point, the procedure was obvious. The Inspector was just finishing a large mound of bacon and eggs when a commotion at the door announced the arrival of a police sergeant with the absconding Mr. Slater. The latter was a large, angry-looking man who, as soon as he entered the room, began to protest violently.

"Cut that out, my lad," said Mr. Birch. "How many bags did you find with him, Sergeant?"

"Only one, sir—his own."

"I tell you," said Slater, "I know nothing about all this. I left Wagstaffe here in the bar-parlour at twenty past eleven or thereabouts, and he was all right then—only drunk. I drove away at half-past, or it might be a quarter to twelve. I brought one bag and I took one bag, and here it is, and anybody who says anything else is telling a lie. If I'd been doing a murder, do you think I'd have gone straight off to Pettiford and sat eating my breakfast in the Four Bells, waiting for you to catch me?"

"You might and you mightn't," said Mr. Birch. "Did you know this man Wagstaffe?"

The angry eyes shifted uneasily.

"I'd met him," said Slater.

"They say you were quarrelling with him."

"Well—he was drunk, and made himself unpleasant. That's one reason why I pushed off."

"I see." The Inspector glanced through the correspondence taken from the dead man's pocket.

"Your name's Archibald, isn't it? Have you got a sister Edith? . . . No, you don't!"

Slater had made a quick grab at the letter in Birch's hand.

"Well," he admitted sulkily, "I don't mind telling you that that swine Wagstaffe was a dirty scoundrel. Thorne's the name we knew him by, and my sister's his wife—or thought she was, till it turned out he was married to somebody else under another name, the skunk. They got married while I was away up North, and I knew nothing about it till I came into this district, and he's been careful to keep out of my way—till last night. Not that there was anything I could do to him, except try and get maintenance for the kid, and in the end he said he'd pay. I—look here, Inspector, I quite realise that this looks bad, but——"

75

"Hi!" exclaimed Monty. "Don't forget the clock. It's just going to strike."

"Yes," said the Inspector. "Ten past eleven that clock marked when it was knocked over in the struggle. You were out of here by twenty past. If it strikes one now, we'll know it's been put back—if it strikes twelve, then it's telling the truth, and you're for it."

The case stood open. As the first stroke of the hammer fell, they watched, fascinated, while the striking weight moved slowly down from where it hung, three or four inches below the other.

The clock struck twelve.

"That's something, anyway," said Mr. Birch, grimly.

"It's not true!" cried Slater wildly. Then he added, more soberly, "The man might have been killed after I left, but still before midnight, and the hands put back three quarters of an hour."

And while the Inspector hesitated:

"Half a minute," said Monty. "If you'll excuse me, Inspector, I've just thought of something. Twelve o'clock is the longest run that weight ever does, and it's only dropped something under half an inch. Now, how does it come to hang so far below the driving weight? You see what I mean? During the long hours from six to twelve, the striking weight gets ahead of the driving weight and hangs below it, but during the short hours, the driving weight catches up on it, so that—in my experience, anyhow—there's never more than half an inch or so between them in an eight-day clock, and they finish up level. Now, how did this fellow here get all this long start of his chum?"

"Wound up carelessly," suggested the Inspector.

"Either that," said Monty, "or the clock's been *put on eleven hours*. That's the only way to put back a striking clock, unless you have the sense to take the striking weight off altogether, which most people haven't the wits to think of."

"Whew!" said Mr. Birch. "Now, who'd know about that, I wonder? Who winds this clock? We'd better ask Rudd."

"I wouldn't ask him, if you'll forgive me putting myself forward," said Mr. Egg, thoughtfully.

"Oh!" said Mr. Birch. "I see." He pulled at his moustache. "Wait a minute. I've got it."

He plunged out, and presently returned with a boy of about fourteen.

"Sonnie," said he, "who winds up the grandfather-clock?"

"Dad does, every Sunday morning."

"Did you see him do it last Sunday?"

"Oh, yes."

"Can you remember if he wound the two weights up to the same height—or were they apart, like this?"

"He always winds them up tight—fourteen winds—that's two turns for every day—and when the weight's wound up, it goes bump."

The Inspector nodded.

"That's all—run away. Mr. Egg, it looks as if you'd got hold of something right enough. Here, Sergeant!"

The sergeant gave him an understanding wink and went out. Half an hour elapsed, marked only by the almost imperceptible descent of the driving weight and the solemn ticking of the clock. Then the sergeant came in again, with a bag in his hand.

"Quite right, sir—under a heap of sacking in the hen-house. It must be either Rudd or the barman, George."

"They must both be in it," said the Inspector. "But which of them did the job, damned if I know. We'll have to wait for those finger-prints."

"Why not ask them for the key of the clock?" put in Mr. Egg.

"What for?"

"Just an idea of mine."

"All right. Send Rudd in. Rudd, we want the key of this clock."

"Oh, do you?" said the landlord. "Well, I haven't got it, see? I don't know where it's gone, and you can put that in your pipe and smoke it. A nice job this is, in a respectable house."

"All right," said the Inspector, "we'll ask George. Where's this clock-key, George?"

The barman passed a hand across his dry mouth. "It's in that there pot on the chimbley-piece," he said.

"It's not there," said the Inspector, peering into the pot.

"No," said Monty. "And how did Rudd know it wasn't there, if he wasn't hunting for it last night to wind that weight back to the right place, after he'd put the clock eleven hours forward? No wonder the place is turned upside-down."

The landlord turned a dirty green colour, and George broke out into a whimper.

"Please, sir, I never knew nothing about it till it was all over. I didn't have no hand in it."

"Put the bracelets on 'em both, Sergeant," said Inspector Birch. "And you, Slater, remember your evidence will be wanted. Much obliged to you, Mr. Egg. But it's a funny thing where that key can have gone to."

"Better ask young Hopeful," said Mr. Egg. "It's surprising how a little thing like that will trip a man up. As *The Salesman's Handbook* says: Attend to details and you'll make your sale—a little weight will often turn the scale."

THE PROFESSOR'S MANUSCRIPT

A Montague Egg Story

"SEE here, Monty," said Mr. Hopgood (travelling representative for Messrs. Brotherhood, Ltd.) to Mr. Egg (travelling representative for Messrs. Plummett & Rose); "while you're here, why don't you have a go at old Professor Pindar? I should say he was just about in your line."

Mr. Egg brought his mind back—a little unwillingly—from the headlines in his morning paper ("SCREEN STAR'S MARRIAGE ROMANCE PLANE DASH"—"CONTINENT COMB-OUT FOR MISSING FINANCIER"—"COUNTRY-HOUSE MYSTERY BLAZE ARSON SUSPICIONS"—"BUDGET INCOME-TAX REMISSION POSSIBILITY"), and inquired who Professor Pindar might be when he was at home.

"He's a funny old bird that's come and settled down at Wellingtonia House," replied Mr. Hopgood. "You know, where the Fennels used to live. Bought the place last January and moved in about a month ago. Writes books, or something. I went along yesterday to see if there was anything doing in our way. Heard he was a retired sort of old party. Thought he might be good for a case of Sparkling Pompayne or something else in the soft drinks line. Quite rude to me, he was. Called it 'gut-rot,' and spilled a piece of poetry about 'windy waters.' Shouldn't have expected such strong expressions from a brainy-looking old gent like him. Apologised for taking up his time, of course, and said to myself, 'Here's where young Monty gets in with his matured spirits and fine old fruity.' Thought I'd give you the tip, that's all—but suit yourself, of course."

Mr. Egg thanked Mr. Hopgood, and agreed that Professor Pindar sounded like a useful prospect.

"One gets to see him all right, then?" he asked.

"Yes—only you have to state your business," said Mr. Hopgood. "Housekeeper's a bit of a dragon. No good trying on the old tale of being sent round by his dear friend Mr. So-and-so, because, for one thing, he's got no friends round here and, for another, they know that one."

"In that case——" began Mr. Egg; but Mr. Hopgood did not appear to notice that he had said anything odd, and he felt it was hardly worthwhile to start an argument, especially as the morning was getting on, and he had not yet read about the film-star's marriage dash or the country-house arson suspicions. He turned his attention to these, discovered that the romance was the lady's fifth marriage and that the fire was thought to be yet another ramification of the insurance ramp, went on to ascertain that the person detained the day before in Constantinople was not, after all, the absconding head of Mammoth Industries, Ltd., and that the hope of sixpence off the income-tax was little more than the *Daily Trumpet* correspondent's dream of wish-fulfilment, and then embarked upon a juicy leader-page article headed "CAN COMMERCIAL TRAVELLERS BE CHRISTIANS?—by One of Them," which interested him, not so much because he had any doubts about commercial morality as because he fancied he knew who the author was.

Before very long, however, his own commercial conscience (which was sensitive) reminded him that he was wasting his employer's time, and he went out to inquire into a complaint received from the landlord of the Ring of Bells that the last case of Plummett & Rose's Superior Old Tawny (full body, fine masculine flavour) was not up to sample, owing to alleged faulty corking.

Having disposed of this little unpleasantness, and traced the trouble to the fact that the landlord had thoughtlessly run the main pipe of a new heating installation behind the racks housing the Superior Old Tawny, Mr. Egg asked to be directed to Wellingtonia House.

"It's about five miles out of the town," said the landlord. "Take the road to Great Windings, turn off to the left by the tower they call Grabb's Folly and then it's down the lane on the right past the old water-mill. Biggish place with a high brick wall right down in the hollow. Damp, in my opinion. Shouldn't care to live there myself. All right if you like peace and quietness, but I prefer to see a bit of life myself. So does the missis. But this old chap ain't married, so I suppose it's all right for him. Lives there alone with a housekeeper and a handy-man and about fifty million tons of books. I was sorry to hear he'd taken the house. What we want there is a family with a bit of money, to bring some trade into the town."

"Not a rich man, then?" asked Mr. Egg, mentally substituting a cheaper line for the Cockburn 1896 (a grand ancient wine thirty-five years in bottle) with which he had hoped to tempt the Professor.

"He may have," replied the landlord; "must have, I suppose, since he's bought the place freehold. But what's the odds if he don't spend it? Never goes anywhere. No entertaining. Bit of a crank, by what they tell me."

"Butcher's meat?" inquired Mr. Egg.

"Oh, yes," said the landlord, "and only the best cuts. But what's one old gentleman's steak and chop when you come to think of it? That don't make a lot of difference in the week's turn-over."

However, the thought of the steak and chops comforted Mr. Egg as he drove by Grabb's Folly and the old water-mill and turned down the little, winding lane between high hedgerows starred with dog-violets and the lesser celandine. Grilled meat and wine went together almost as certainly as nut-cutlets and home-made lemonade.

The door of Wellingtonia House was opened by a middle-aged woman in an apron, at sight of whom Mr. Egg instantly dismissed the manner he used for domestic servants and substituted the one reserved for persons "out of the top drawer," as he phrased it. A pre-War gentlewoman in a post-War job, he decided. He produced his card and stated his business frankly.

"Well," said the housekeeper. She looked Mr. Egg searchingly up and down. "Professor Pindar is a very busy man, but he may like to see you. He is very particular about his wines—especially vintage port."

"Vintage port, madam," replied Mr. Egg, "is a speciality with us."

"*Real* vintage port?" asked the housekeeper, smiling.

Mr. Egg was hurt, though he tried not to show it. He mentioned a few of Messrs. Plummett & Rose's choicer shipments, and produced a list.

"Come in," said the housekeeper. "I'll take the list to Professor Pindar. He may like to see you himself, though I can't promise. He is very hard at work upon his book, and he can't possibly spare very much time."

"Certainly not, madam," said Mr. Egg, stepping in and wiping his boots carefully. They were perfectly clean, but the ritual was part of his regular routine, as laid down by *The Salesman's Handbook.* ("Be clean and courteous; raise your hat, And wipe your boots upon the mat: Such proofs of gentlemanly feeling Are to the ladies most appealing.") "In my opinion," he added, as he followed his conductress through a handsome hall and down a long and thickly-carpeted passage, "more sales are lost through being too persistent than through not being persistent enough. There's a little verse, madam, that I try to bear in mind: 'Don't stay too long; the customer has other things to do than sitting in the parlour and listening to you; And if, through your loquacity, she lets the dinner burn, She will not soon forget it, and it does you a bad turn.' I will just show the Professor my list, and if he is not interested, I will promise to go away at once."

The housekeeper laughed. "You are more reasonable than most of them," she said, and showed him into a large and lofty room, lined from floor to ceiling with bookshelves. "Wait here a minute, and I will see what Professor Pindar says."

She was gone for some time, and Mr. Egg, being left to contemplate, with awe and some astonishment, the array of learning all about him, became restless, and even a little reckless. He walked about the library, trying to ascertain from the titles of the books what Professor Pindar was professor of. His interests, however, appeared to be catholic, for the books dealt with many subjects. One of them, a stout, calf-bound octavo in a long row of calf-bound octavos, attracted Mr. Egg's attention. It was an eighteenth-century treatise on Brewing and Distilling, and he extended a cautious finger to hook it from the shelf. It was, however, too tightly wedged between a bound collection of Pamphlets and a play by Ben Jonson to come out easily, and he abandoned the attempt. Curiosity made him next tiptoe over to the formidable great desk strewn with manuscripts. This gave more information. In the centre, near the typewriter, lay a pile of neatly-typed sheets, embellished with footnotes and a good many passages of what looked to Mr. Egg like Greek, though it might, of course, have been Russian or Arabic, or any other language with a queer alphabet. The half-finished page upon the blotter broke off abruptly with the words: "This was the opinion of St. Augustine, though Clement of Alexandria expressly declares——" Here the sentence ended, as though the writer had paused to consult his authority. The open folio on the table was, however, neither St. Augustine nor Clement of Alexandria, but Origen. Close beside it stood a metal strong-box with a combination-lock, which Mr. Egg judged to contain some rare manuscript or other.

The sound of a hand upon the door-handle caused him to start guiltily away from the table, and when the door opened he had whisked round with his back to the desk and was staring abstractedly at a shelf crammed with immense tomes, ranging from Aristotle's works to a Jacobean Life of Queen Elizabeth.

Professor Pindar was a very bent and tottery old gentleman, and the hairiest person Mr. Egg had ever set eyes upon. His beard began at his cheekbones and draped his chest as far as the penultimate waistcoat-button. Over a pair of very sharp grey eyes, heavy grey eyebrows hung like a pent-house. He wore a black skull-cap, from beneath which more grey hair flowed so as to conceal his collar. He wore a rather shabby black velvet jacket, grey trousers, which had forgotten the last time they had ever seen a trousers-press, and a pair of carpet slippers, over which grey woollen socks wreathed themselves in folds. His face (what could be seen of it) was thin, and he spoke with a curious whistle and click due to an extremely ill-fitting set of dentures.

"Hso you are the young man from the wine-merchant's, hish, click," said the Professor. "Hsit down. Click." He waved his hand to a chair some little distance away, and himself shuffled to the desk and seated himself. "You brought me a list—where have I—ah! yesh! click! here it is, hish. Let me hsee. He fumbled about himself and produced a pair of steel spectacles. "Hish! yesh! Very interesting. What made you think of calling on me, click, hey? Hish."

Mr. Egg said that he had been advised to call by Messrs. Brotherhood's representative.

"I thought, sir," he said ingenuously, "that if you disapproved so much of soft drinks, you might appreciate something more, shall we say, full-bodied."

"You did, did you?" said the Professor. "Very shrewd of you. Click! Hsmart of you, hish. Got some good hish stuff here." He waved the list. "Don't believe in high-classh wine-merchants touting for customers shthough. Infra dig. Hey?"

Mr. Egg explained that the pressure of competition had driven Messrs. Plummett & Rose to this undoubtedly rather modern expedient. "But of course, sir," he added, "we exercise our discretion. I should not dream of showing a gentleman like yourself the list we issue to licensed houses."

"Humph!" said Professor Pindar. "Well——" He entered upon a discussion of the wine-list, showing himself remarkably knowledgeable for an aged scholar whose interests were centred upon the Fathers of the Church. He was, he said, thinking of laying down a small cellar, though he should have to get some new racks installed, since the former owners had allowed that part of the establishment to fall into decay.

Mr. Egg ventured a mild witticism about "rack and ruin," and booked a useful little order for some Warre, Dow & Cockburn ports, together with a few dozen selected burgundies, to be delivered in a month's time, when the cellar accommodation should be ready for them.

"You are thinking of settling permanently in this part of the country, sir?" he ventured, as he rose (mindful of instructions) to take his leave.

"Yes. Why not, hey?" snapped the Professor.

"Very glad to hear it, sir," said Monty. "Always very glad to hear of a good customer, you know."

"Yes, of coursh," replied Professor Pindar. "Naturally. I exshpect to be here until I have finished my book, at any rate. May take years, click! *Hishtory of the Early Chrishtian Chursh*, hish, click." Here his teeth seemed to take so alarming a leap from his jaws that Mr. Egg made an instinctive dive forward to catch them, and wondered why the Professor should have hit on a subject and title so impossible of pronunciation.

"But that means nothing to *you*, I take it, hey?" concluded the Professor, opening the door.

"Nothing, I'm sorry to say, sir," said Mr. Egg, who knew where to draw the line between the pretence of interest and the confession of ignorance. "Like the Swan of Avon, if I may put it that way, I have small Latin and less Greek, and that's the only resemblance between me and him, I'm afraid."

The Professor laughed, perilously, and followed up this exercise with a terrific click.

"Mrs. Tabbitt!" he called, "show this gentleman out."

The housekeeper reappeared and took charge of Mr. Egg, who departed, full of polite thanks for esteemed favours.

"Well," thought Montague Egg, "that's a puzzler, that is. All the same, it's no business of mine, and I don't want to make a mistake. I wonder who I could ask. Wait a minute. Mr. Griffiths—he's the man. He'd know in a moment."

It so happened that he was due to return to Town that day. He attended to his business and then, as soon as he was free, went round to call upon a very good customer and friend of his, who was the senior partner in the extremely respectable Publishing firm of Griffiths & Seabright. Mr. Griffiths listened to his story with considerable interest.

"Pindar?" said he. "Never heard of him. Early Fathers of the Church, eh? Well, Dr. Abcock is the man for that. We'll ring him up. Hullo! is that Dr. Abcock? Sorry to bother you, but have you ever heard of a professor Pindar who writes your kind of stuff? You haven't? . . . I don't know. Wait a moment."

He took down various stout volumes and consulted them.

"He doesn't seem to hold any English or Scotch professorship," he observed, presently. "Of course, it might be foreign or American—did he speak with any sort of accent, Egg?— No?—Well, that proves nothing, of course. Anybody can get a professorship from those odd American universities. Well, never mind, Doctor, don't bother. Yes, a book. I rather wanted to get the thing vetted. I'll let you know again later."

He turned to Monty.

"Nothing very definite there," he said, "but I'll tell you what I'll do. I'll call on this man—or perhaps it will be better to write. I'll say I've heard about the work and would like to make an offer for it. That might produce something. You're a bit of a terror, aren't you, Egg? Have a spot of one of your own wares before you go."

It was some time before Mr. Egg heard again from Mr. Griffiths. Then a letter was forwarded to him in York, whither his travels had taken him.

"Dear Egg,

"I wrote to your Professor, and with a good bit of trouble extracted an answer and a typescript. Now, there's no doubt at all about the MS. It's first-class, of its kind. Rather unorthodox, in some ways, but stuffed as full of scholarship as an egg (sorry) is of meat. But his letter was what I should call evasive. He doesn't say where he got his professorship. Possibly he bestowed the title on himself, honoris causa. But the

85

book is so darned good that I'm going to make a stiff push to get it for G. & S. I'm writing to ask the mysterious Professor for an appointment and will send you a line if I get it."

The next communication reached Mr. Egg in Lincoln.

"Dear Egg,
"Curiouser and curiouser. Professor Pindar absolutely refuses to see me or to discuss his book with me, though he is ready to consider an offer. Abcock is getting excited about it, and has written to ask for further information on several controversial points in the MS. We cannot understand how a man of such remarkable learning and ability should have remained all this time unknown to the experts in his particular subject. I think our best chance is to get hold of old Dr. Wilverton. He knows all about everything and everybody, only he is so very eccentric that it is rather difficult to get anything out of him. But you can be sure of one thing—the man who wrote that book is a bona fide scholar, so your doubts must have been ill-founded. But I'm immensely grateful to you for putting me on to Professor Pindar, whoever he is. The work will make a big noise in the little world of learning."

Mr. Egg had returned to London before he heard from Mr. Griffiths again. Then he was rung up and requested, in rather excited tones, to come round and meet the great and eccentric Dr. Lovell Wilverton at Mr. Griffiths' house. When he got there he found the publisher and Dr. Abcock seated by the fire, while a strange little man in a check suit and steel spectacles ramped irritably up and down the room.
"It's no use," spluttered Dr. Wilverton, "it's no use to tell me. I know. I say I *know*. The views expressed—the style—the—everything points the same way. Besides, I tell you, I've seen that passage on Clement of Alexandria before. Poor Donne! He was a most brilliant scholar—*the* most brilliant scholar who ever passed through my hands. I went to see him once, at that horrible little hut on the Essex Marshes that he retired to after the—the collapse, you know—and he showed me the stuff then. Mistaken? Of course I'm not mistaken. I'm never mistaken. Couldn't be. I've often wondered since where that manuscript

went to. If only I'd been in England at the time I should have secured it. Sold with the rest of his things, for junk, I suppose, to pay the rent."

"Just a moment, Wilverton," said Dr. Abcock, soothingly. "You're going too fast for us. You say, this *History of the Early Christian Church* was written by a young man called Roger Donne, a pupil of yours, who unfortunately took to drink and went to live in very great poverty in a hut on the Essex Marshes. Now it turns up, in typescript, which you say Donne wouldn't have used, masquerading as the work of an old person calling himself Professor Pindar, of Wellingtonia House, in Somerset. Are you suggesting that Pindar stole the manuscript or bought it from Donne? Or that he is Donne in disguise?"

"Of course he isn't Donne," said Dr. Wilverton, angrily. "I told you, didn't I? Donne's dead. He died last year when I was in Syria. I suppose this old imposter bought the manuscript at the sale."

Mr. Egg smote his thigh with his palm.

"Why, of course, sir," he said. "The deed-box I saw on the table. That would have the original manuscript in it, and this old professor-man just copied it out on his own typewriter."

"But what for?" asked Mr. Griffiths. "It's a remarkable book, but it's not a thing one would get a lot of money out of."

"No," agreed Monty, "but it would be an awfully good proof that the professor really was what he pretended to be. Suppose the police made investigations—there was the professor, and there was the book, and any expert they showed it to (unless they had the luck to hit on Dr. Lovell Wilverton, of course) would recognise it for the work of a really learned gentleman."

"Police?" said Dr. Abcock, sharply. "Why the police? Who do you suppose this Pindar really is?"

Mr. Egg extracted a newspaper cutting from his pocket.

"Him, sir," he said. "Greenholt, the missing financier who absconded with all the remaining assets of Mammoth Industries, Ltd., just a week before Professor Pindar came and settled at Wellingtonia House. Here's his description: sixty years old, grey eyes, false teeth. Why, a bunch of hair and a bad set of dentures, a velvet coat and skull-cap, and there you are. There's your Professor Pindar. I did think the hair was just a bit over-done. And that Mrs. Tabbitt was a lady, all right, and here's a photo of Mrs. Greenholt. Take away the make-up and scrag her hair back in a bun, and they're as like as two peas."

87

"Great heavens!" exclaimed Mr. Griffiths. "And they've been combing Europe for the fellow. Egg, I shouldn't wonder if you're right. Give me the 'phone. We'll get on to Scotland Yard. Hullo! Give me Whitehall 1212."

"You seem to be something of a detective, Mr. Egg," said Dr. Lovell Wilverton, later in the evening, when word had come through of the arrest of Robert Greenholt at Wellingtonia House. "Do you mind telling me what first put this idea into your head?"

"Well, sir," replied Mr. Egg, modestly, "I'm not a brainy man, but in my line one learns to size a party up pretty quickly. The first thing that seemed odd was that this Professor wouldn't see my friend, Hopgood, of Brotherhood, Ltd., till he knew where he came from, and then, when he did see him, told him he couldn't stick soft drinks. Now, you know, sir, as a rule, a busy gentleman won't see a commercial at all if he's not interested in the goods. It's one of our big difficulties. It looked as though the Professor wanted to be seen, in his character as a professor, by anybody and everybody, provided that it wasn't anybody who knew too much about books and so on. Then there was the butcher. He supplied steaks and chops to the household, which looked like a gentleman with good teeth ; but when I got there, I found a hairy old boy whose dental plate was so wonky he could hardly have chewed scrambled eggs with it. But the thing that really bothered me was the books in that library. I'm no reader, unless it's a crook yarn or something of that kind, but I visit a good many learned gentlemen, and I've now and again cast my eye on their shelves, always liking to improve myself. Now, there were three things in that library that weren't like the library of any gentleman that uses his books. First, the books were all mixed up, with different subjects alongside one another, instead of all the same subject together. Then, the books were too neat, all big books in one place and all small ones in another. And then they were too snug in the shelves. No gentleman that likes books or needs to consult them quickly keeps them as tight as that—they won't come out when you want them and besides, it breaks the bindings. That's true, I know, because I asked a friend of mine in the second-hand book business. So you see," said Mr. Egg, persuasively, "Greek or no Greek, I couldn't believe that gentleman ever read any of his books. I expect he just bought up somebody's library—

or you can have 'em delivered by the yard; it's often done by rich gentlemen who get their libraries done by furnishing firms."

"Bless my soul," said Dr. Lovell Wilverton, "is Saul also among the Prophets? You seem to be an observant man, Mr. Egg."

"I try to be," replied Mr. Egg. "Never miss a chance of learning for that word spells '£' plus 'earning.'—You'll find that in *The Salesman's Handbook*. Very neat, sir, don't you think?"

THE MILK-BOTTLES

MR. HECTOR PUNCHEON, of the *Morning Star*, concluded his interview with the gentleman who had won the £5,000 Football Crossword and walked rapidly away along the street. Not so rapidly, however, that he failed to note a pair of pint bottles, filled with milk, standing at the head of some area-steps. Having a deductive turn of mind, he half-consciously summed up to himself the various possibilities suggested by this phenomenon; a new baby; a houseful of young children; a houseful of cats; a week-end absence from home.

Hector was still young and enthusiastic enough to look for a "story" in almost anything. There might be one in milk-bottles. Tragedies in lonely houses, first brought to light by accumulated milk-bottles. Queer, solitary spinsters living in shuttered gloom. The Sauchiehall Street murder, and old James Fleming taking in the milk while the servant's corpse lay in the back room. What the milkman knows. Something might be made of it: why not?

He mulled the matter over in his mind, went back to the office and, having turned in his Crossword story sat down to spin out a breezy half-column about milk-bottles.

The Editor of the Literary Page, who always had more material than he could use, glanced at it, sniffed at it, endorsed it in blue pencil and sent it down to the Home Page Editor. The latter skimmed through it carelessly and tossed it into a basket labelled "Waiting," where it remained for three months. Hector Puncheon, who had never had very much hope of it, forgot it and carried on with his usual duties.

One day in August, however, the lady who usually did the little Special Article for the Home Page was struck down by a motor-bus and taken to hospital, leaving her "copy" unwritten.

The Home Page Editor, at a loss for 400 words, tossed out the contents of "Waiting" on his desk, picked out Hector Puncheon's article at random and pushed it to the Sub-editor, saying, "Cut this down and shove it in."

The Sub-editor looked rapidly through it, struck out the first and last paragraphs, removed Hector's more literary passages, ran three sentences into one, gratuitously introducing two syntactical errors in the process, re-cast the story from the third person into the first, headed it "By a Milk-Roundsman," and sent it down to the printers. In this form it appeared the next morning, and Hector Puncheon, not recognising his mutilated offspring, muttered bitterly that somebody had pinched his idea.

Two days later, the Editor of the *Morning Star* received a letter:

"DEAR SIR,
  "Being interested to read a piece by a milk-roundsman in your paper would wish to state that there is something queer on my round and would be pleased to give any information. I as not been to the police as they do not pay attention to a working man and do not pay for same but sir I see as you printed an article by a milk-roundsman and your great paper would be fair to one as earns his living. Sir there are five milk bottles starting last Sunday morning and a couple as not been seen since. Hopeing this finds you as it leaves me,
                    Yours respectfully,
                                "J. HIGGINS."

In any other month of the year, Mr. Higgins' letter would probably have received no attention, but in August all news is good news. The Editor passed the letter to the News Editor, who rang a bell and sent for a subordinate, who rang a bell for another subordinate, who consulted the files of the paper. Thus, by devious methods, the matter was referred back to Hector Puncheon, who was sent to look for Mr. Higgins and get his story at the price of a few shillings if it seemed promising.

Mr. Higgins had a milk round in and about the Clerkenwell Road. He welcomed Hector Puncheon, and gladly undertook to show him for a consideration the mysterious milk-bottles. He accordingly conducted him to an obscure street and there plunged into a dark entrance beside a greengrocer's shop. They made their way up a dark and rickety staircase, smelling of cats.

At the top was a gloomy little door, with a dirty visiting-card tacked on to it which bore the name: "Hugh Wilbraham." On the threshold stood five half-pint bottles filled with milk. Hector thought he had never seen anything so utterly desolate.

There was a window on the landing, through which he could see a wide vista of roofs and chimneys, scorching in the hot sun. The window was not open and apparently not made to open. Up the narrow staircase—well, the sour and fetid air seemed to press upward intolerably, like the fumes from a gas-stove.

"Who is this man, Wilbraham?" demanded Hector, trying to control his disgust at the place.

"I dunno," said the milkman. "They been living here three months. Milk-bill paid regular every Saturday by the young woman. Shabby-looking lot, but speak decent. Come down in the world, if you ask me."

"Just the two of them?"

"Yes."

"When did you see them last?"

"Saturday morning, when she paid up. Been crying, she had. What I want to know is, have they 'opped it? Because if so, what about this week's milk?"

"I see," said Hector.

"I'm responsible, in a manner of speaking," said Mr. Higgins, "but the parties having paid regular and my orders being to deliver milk, I'd like to know what I ought to do about it—see?"

"Don't the neighbours know anything about it?" suggested Hector.

"Not a lot, they don't," said Mr. Higgins, "but there ain't no furniture gone out, and that's something. You better have a word with Mrs. Bowles."

Mrs. Bowles lived on the floor below and took in washing. She did not know much about the Wilbrahams, she explained, punctuating her remarks with thumps of the iron. Kept themselves to themselves. Thought they were too good for the likes of her, she supposed, though she had always kept herself respectable, which was more than you could say of some. They had taken the top room unfurnished, beginning of last June. She had seen their furniture go up. Nothing to write home about, it wasn't. Now Mrs. Bowles' double-bedstead, that was good, it was—real brass, and as good a feather-bed as you could wish to see. The Wilbrahams hadn't so much as a decent chair or table. Rubbishing stuff. No class—not worth a couple of pounds, the whole lot of it. She thought the young man did writing or something of that, because he had once complained that the noise made by the young Bowleses disturbed his work. If he was so high and mighty, why did he come to live here? About thirty, he might be, with a nasty, sulky, spiteful look about him. She'd heard Mrs. Wilbraham—if she *was* Mrs. Wilbraham—crying time and time again, and him going on at her ever so.

When, asked Hector, had she seen them last?

Mrs. Bowles straightened her lean back, put her iron down to the fire, and took off another, which she held close to her perspiring cheek. The close room swam in heat.

"Well now," she said, " 'er—I can't call to mind *when* I seen 'er last. Saturday dinner-time 'e came in and run upstairs and I 'ears them talking 'ammer and tongs. An' Saturday evening I meets 'im coming downstairs with a suitcase. 'Bout six o'clock that 'ud be—jest as I was coming in from taking Mrs. Jepson's washing 'ome. Funny in 'is manner 'e was, too, and in an awful 'urry. Nearly knocked me down, 'e did, and not so much as said 'pardon.' That's the last time I seen 'im, and he ain't been back, nor 'er either, or I'd 'ave 'eard them over me ceiling. Cruel it was, the way 'e useter tramp up and down at nights when we was trying to get to sleep, and then to complain of my boys on top of it!"

"Then you don't know when Mrs. Wilbraham left?"

"I do not, but gone they is, and if you ask me, they don't intend to come back. I says to young 'Iggins, if you go on leaving the milk there, I says, that's your look-out. I daresay if their sticks was to be sold up it 'ud pay a week's milk, I says, but that's about all if you ask me."

Hector thanked Mrs. Bowles, adding a small present of money, and made his way down to the floor below. This was inhabited by an aged man who seemed to have seen better days. He shook his head at Hector's inquiry.

"No, sir," he said, "I'm afraid I couldn't tell you anything. It seems strange to me, sometimes, to think how lost a man may be in this great wilderness of London. That's what Charles Dickens called it and, by heavens, sir, he was right. If I was to die tomorrow, and my health is not what it was, who could be the wiser? I buy my own little bits of food and such, you see, and pick up a bit of a living where I can with fetching taxis and such. It's hard to think I used to have a nice little shop of my own. I was well-respected, sir, where I came from, but if I was to go out now, there's nobody would miss me."

"The rent-collector, perhaps?" said Hector.

"Well, yes, to be sure. But if he came once or twice and found I was out, he wouldn't press me for a week or two. He isn't a hard man, and he knows I pay when I can. After two or three weeks he might make inquiries. Oh, yes. He'd make inquiries, to be sure. And the gas-company, when they came to empty the slot-meter, but that mightn't be for a long time."

"I suppose not," said Hector, rather struck. He had not realised the casualness of life in London.

"Then you really know nothing about these Wilbrahams?"

"Very little, sir. Not since I took it upon me to speak to the young man about the way he treated his wife."

"Oh?" said Hector.

"A young man shouldn't speak harsh to a woman," said the old man, "for she has a lot to put up with at the best of times. And men are thoughtless. I know that—oh, yes, I know that. And she was fond of him, you could see that by her face. But they were in difficulties, I think, and often when a man doesn't know which way to turn to make ends meet, he's apt to speak sharp and quick, not meaning to hurt."

"When did this happen?"

"About a month ago. Not here. In St. Pancras Churchyard—that's where they were sitting. It's a pleasant place on a summer's day, with the grass and the children playing about. 'It's a pity you ever married me, isn't it?' he said, with an ugly look on his face. It upset her, poor thing. They didn't know it was me sitting next them till I spoke to him."

"And what did he say?"

"Told me to mind my own business. And I daresay he was right, too. It's a mistake to interfere between married people, but I was sorry for her."

Hector nodded.

"You didn't see anything of them last Saturday?"

"No, sir, but then I was out all day."

The greengrocer on the ground floor knew nothing. He had occasionally sold a few vegetables to Mrs. Wilbraham, but he did not live on the premises and had no information about the movements of the couple. After a little more research, which led to nothing, Hector gave the matter up. It did not seem to him that there was much in it—however, he had expended some time and a few shillings on the business and must have something to show for it. Accordingly, he concocted a brief paragraph:

FIVE MYSTERY MILK-BOTTLES

What has become of Mr. and Mrs. Hugh Wilbraham of 14B Buttercup Road, Clerkenwell? The fact that the milk had not been taken in for five days attracted the attention of Mr. J. Higgins, a roundsman, who had read the article "Milk-bottle Mysteries" published in our Home Page on Tuesday. Mr. Wilbraham, who is said to be a literary man, was seen to leave the house with a suitcase last Saturday; neither he nor his wife, with whom he is alleged to be on bad terms, has been seen since.

The News-Editor, who happened to want half a dozen lines to fill up the foot of a column, handed this to the Sub-editor, who dexterously boiled the first two sentences into one, altered the heading to "MYSTERY 5 MILK-BOTTLES" and sent it to press.

On Friday evening, the *Evening Wire*, which had obviously been doing a little investigation of its own, came out with an expanded version of the story, occupying half a column on the news-page.

MILK-BOTTLE MYSTERY

WILD-EYED MAN WITH SUITCASE

TAXI-DRIVER'S STORY

Six unopened milk-bottles outside the door of a room in a tenement house in Clerkenwell, present to-day a mystery which has several disquieting features. The room, which was taken three months ago by a man, said to be a novelist, and his wife, giving the names of Mr. and Mrs. Hugh Wilbraham, is situated on the top floor of No. 14B Buttercup Road, and has remained locked for six days, while nothing has been seen of the tenants since last Saturday night, when Wilbraham was seen by Mrs. Bowles, the resident on the floor below, leaving the house in a suspicious manner with a suit-case.

A taxi-driver named Hodges, remembers that on Saturday night about 6 o'clock his taxi was standing outside the adjacent public-house, the Star & Crown, when he was hailed by a man, carrying a suitcase, and corresponding to the description of Wilbraham. The man's eyes had a wild appearance, and he seemed to be under the influence of drink or violent excitement. He directed Hodges to drive him as fast as possible to Liverpool Street Station, and seemed urgently anxious to catch the train.

It is alleged by the other residents in the house that Mr. and Mrs. Wilbraham were frequently seen and heard quarrelling and that the man had been heard to say it was a pity they had ever got married. The woman was last seen, crying bitterly, when the milkman called on Saturday morning.

A strange and sinister feature of the case is the gradual spread of a heavy and unpleasant odour proceeding from behind the locked door. It is understood that the police have been communicated with.

The news-editor of the *Morning Star* sent for Hector Puncheon.

"Here, this is your story, isn't it?" he said. "The *Wire* seems to have got ahead of you. Go round and get on to it."

Hector Puncheon, trudging through the sultry squalor of the August evening, felt a strong repugnance to plunging into the dark entry and up those sickly stairs. Dusty newspapers blew about his feet as he passed the greengrocer's stall. Round the entry, half a dozen loiterers were gathered.

" 'Orrible, it is," said Mrs. Bowles, "wuss than when they took up the old cat from under the boards what the gas-fitter's men 'ad nailed down. I 'ad to come out to get a breath of air."

"Why don't the police do something, that's what I'd like to know?" asked a slatternly girl with a made-up face.

" 'As to get a warrant, dear, afore they can break in. Damaging property, that's what it is, and the landlord——"

"Well, 'e ought to do something 'imself. Wot 'e ever want to let to such as them for——"

"It's easy to talk. One person's money is as good as another's."

"All very well, but you could see by that fellow's face 'e was up to no good."

"Well, wot I say is, I'm sorry for 'er."

Hector pushed his way through them and boldly tackled the climb to the top floor. The air, stewed and thickened in the dark chimney of the staircase, caught him by the throat. It grew worse as he ascended.

The smell was perceptible on the first floor, mingled with the familiar odours of cats and cabbage. On the second floor it was stronger ; on the top floor it was overpowering. The six bottles of milk stood, sour and dusty, outside the locked door. There was a letter-slit, Hector noticed. Lifting it, he tried to peer through. At once the stench seemed to pour out at him, nauseating, unbearable. He retreated, feeling sick. He was not sure whether it was his own head that was buzzing. No—it was not. A couple of fat black flies had come heavily through the slit. They clung to the woodwork, and crawled with satiated slowness over the blistered paint.

"Fit to turn you up, ain't it?" said a voice behind him. A man had followed him up.

"It's ghastly," said Hector.

Suddenly the squalid place seemed to heave about him He turned and ran hurriedly down the stairs out into the street. To his horror he found a great fly, somnolently clinging to his collar.

Hector went home. He had had enough of the place. But early the next morning he remembered his duty to his news-paper. Come what might, he must get that story. He returned to Buttercup Road.

Andrews of the *Wire* was already there. He grinned when he saw Puncheon.

"Come to be in at the death?" said he.

Hector nodded, and lit a cigarette.

"Copper's just coming along," said Andrews.

The narrow passage was packed with people. Presently two stout official forms in blue came shouldering their way through.

" 'Ere," said the foremost, "wot's all this about? Pass along here, pass along."

"Press," said Hector and Andrews in unison.

"Oh, *all* right," said the policeman. "Now then, missus, let's get along up. We've got the warrant. Where is it? Third floor. Right you are."

D

The procession tramped heavily up. On the top floor stood Mr. J. Higgins, with the seventh milk-bottle in his hand.

The policemen gave a huge concerted sniff.

"Somethink in there all right," said the larger of the two. "Ere, missus, take them kids along out o' the way. No place for them."

He strode to the door and beat upon it, summoning that which lay behind it to open in the name of the law.

There was no answer. How could there be any answer?

"Gimme that crow-bar."

The policeman set the bar to the lock and heaved. There was a crack. He heaved again. The lock shuddered and gave. As the door swung slowly back, a huge crowd of flies rose, zooming, from something close behind it.

In a pleasant hotel coffee-room at Clacton, a young man smiled at his wife over the breakfast table.

"Better than Buttercup Road, eh, Helen?" he said.

"It's marvellous. Oh, Hugh! I think I should have gone cracked in that ghastly place. Isn't it luck? Isn't it luck your getting that cheque? Just in time."

"Yes, just in time. I was about at the last gasp, old girl. Afraid I was a bit. I was a fool to get so hysterical. My nerves were all to pieces."

"I know, dear. It doesn't matter a bit. I was a fool to get so hysterical. It was a wonderful idea just to come away and get out of it all. Do you know, when you brought the news, and I could run out and buy new clothes—oh, Hugh! it was heavenly. That was the most marvellous bit. And when I was sitting at Liverpool Street waiting for you to come, I had to keep pinching the parcels to be sure it wasn't all a dream."

"Yes, I know. I didn't know if I was on my head or my heels either. I nearly missed the train as it was—I had just to stay and finish up that last chapter."

"I know. But you did catch it."

"I did. But—I've never told you. I clean forgot about stopping the milk, as you told me."

"Blow the milk. We needn't count pennies now."

"Hear, hear!"

The young man opened his paper. Then his face suddenly became convulsed.

"My God! Look at this!"

98

The girl stared at the headlines.

"Oh, *Hugh*! How *awful*! That horrible Mrs. Bowles! And that silly old Nosey-Parker from downstairs! Wild-eyed man with a suspicious appearance—good gracious, Hugh! We'll never dare to go back. But, I say, dear, what's all this about a smell?"

"Smell?"

The young man slowly flushed a deep crimson.

"*Hugh*!" said his wife. "You *don't* mean to say you left that haddock on the table!"

DILEMMA

I HAVE no idea who started the imbecile discussion. I think it must have been Timpany. At any rate, it is just the futile and irritating sort of topic that Timpany *would* start at the end of a long day's fishing. By the time I had settled with the landlord about a boat for the next morning and had come back to the smoking-room, they were hard at it, and had got to the problem about the Chinaman.

You know that one. If you could get a million pounds, without any evil consequences to yourself, by merely pressing a button which would electrocute a single unknown Chinaman ten thousand miles away—would you press the button? Everybody seemed to have an opinion on the point, except the sallow-faced Stranger who was not of our party.

He was modestly hidden behind a book, and I was rather sorry for him, hemmed in as he was in a corner by Timpany and his friend Popper, who are the world's champion talkers. The Colonel said Woof! of course he'd press the button. Too many damned Chinamen in the world anyway—too many damned people altogether.

And I said most people would do a lot for a million pounds.

And the Padre said (as of course he had to) that nothing could justify taking the life of a fellow-creature. And Timpany said, Think of the good one could do with a million pounds, and old Popper said it all depended on the character of the Chinaman—he might have lived to be another Confucius—and from that the talk drifted to still sillier problems, such as, if you had the choice between rescuing a diseased tramp or the Codex Sinaiticus, which would you save?

Timpany said that it was all very well to say that no decent man would hesitate for a moment (I was the silly ass who had committed myself to this sentiment). Didn't we remember that something very like that had happened once, and the awful fuss there was about it? He meant, he said, that old affair of the Davenant-Smith manuscripts.

The Padre remembered Davenant-Smith was the man who lost his life in Bunga-Bunga, researching into the cause and treatment of sleeping sickness. He was a martyr to science, if ever there was one.

Timpany agreed and went on to describe how Davenant-Smith's papers, containing all his valuable results, were sent home to his widow. There was a whole trunkful of them, not yet sorted or classified or even read. Mrs. Davenant-Smith had got hold of a bright young medico to prepare them for publication. And that night a fire broke out in her house.

I remembered then and exclaimed, "Oh yes; a drunken butler and a paraffin lamp, wasn't it?"

Timpany nodded. It had all happened in the middle of the night—a thatch and timber house, no water and the local fire-brigade ten miles off. To cut a long story short, the young medico had had to choose between saving the papers or the sodden old fool of a butler. He'd chucked the papers out first, and when he went back for the butler, the roof fell in and he couldn't get through to him.

I heard the Padre murmur "Terrible!" and noticed that though the Stranger in the corner pretended to turn over a page of his book, he kept his melancholy dark eyes fixed on Timpany.

"All this came out at the inquest," Timpany went on. "The medico got a pretty stiff gruelling. He explained that he believed the manuscripts to be of immense value to humanity, whereas he knew no particular good of the butler.

"He was severely reprimanded by the coroner, and but for the fact that the fire had started in the butler's bedroom, he might have found himself in a very unpleasant position. As it was, the jury decided that the butler was probably dead of suffocation before the alarm was given.

"But it broke the medico, of course. Nobody would think of calling in a doctor who took realistic views about human life, and thought a few thousand sick niggers in the bush more important than a butler in the hand. What happened to the poor devil I don't know. I believe he changed his name and went abroad. Anyway, somebody else did the work on the manuscripts, which form as you probably know, the basis for

101

our whole modern practice with regard to sleeping sickness. I suppose the Davenant-Smith treatment must have saved innumerable lives. Now, Padre, was that young medico a martyr or a murderer?"

"God knows," said the Padre. "But I think, in his place, I should have tried to rescue the butler."

"Woof!" said the Colonel. "Damned awkward. Drunken old ruffian's no loss. Too many of 'em about—no good to anybody. But all the same, damned unpleasant thing, letting a man burn to death."

"Sleeping sickness is pretty unpleasant, too," observed the Stranger. "I've seen a lot of it."

"And what is your own opinion, sir?" inquired the Padre.

"The young doctor was a fool," said the Stranger, with bitter emphasis. "He should have known that the world is run by sentimentalists. He deserved everything he got."

Old Popper turned and considered the Stranger with a slow and thoughtful eye.

"The terms of that problem were comparatively simple," he observed. "The papers were undoubtedly valuable and the butler undoubtedly worthless. Now *I* could tell you of a problem that really *was* a problem. The thing actually happened to *me*—years ago, many years ago. And even now—especially now—it gives me the jim-jams to think about it."

The Colonel grunted, and Timpany said:

"Go on, Popper; tell us the story."

"I don't know that I can," said Popper. "I've tried not to dwell upon it. I've never mentioned it from that day to this. I don't think——"

"Perhaps if you told us now," said the Padre, "it might relieve your mind."

"I rather doubt it," said Popper. "Of course, I know I can count upon your sympathy. But perhaps that's the worst part of it."

We made suitable noises, and the Stranger said, rather primly, but with a queer kind of eagerness:

"I should very much like to hear your experience."

Old Popper looked at him again. Then he rang the bell and ordered a double whisky.

"Very well," he said, when he had put it down, "I'll tell you. I won't mention names, but you may possibly remember the case. It happened when I was quite a youngster, and was working as a clerk in a solicitor's office. We were instructed for the defence of a certain man—a commercial traveller—who was accused of murdering a girl. The evidence against him looked pretty formidable, but we were convinced, from his manner, that he was innocent, and we were, naturally, extremely keen to get him off. It would be a feather in our caps, and besides—well, as I say, we believed he was an innocent man.

"The case came up before the magistrate, and things didn't look any too good for our client. The defence was an alibi, but unfortunately he could bring no evidence at all to prove it. His story was that after having a row with the girl (which he admitted) he had left her in a country lane—where she was afterwards found dead, you understand—and had driven away without noticing where he was going.

"He said he remembered going into some pub or other and getting exceedingly drunk and then driving on and on till he came to a wood, where he got out and went to sleep for a bit. He said he thought he must have woken up again about three o'clock in the morning, when it was still dark.

"He had no idea where he was, but after going through a lot of side-roads and small villages which he couldn't put a name to, he had fetched up, round about six o'clock, in a town which we will call Workingham. He had spoken to nobody after leaving the pub earlier in the evening, and the only other bit of help he could give us was that he thought he had lost a pair of woollen gloves at some time during his wanderings.

"The police theory, of course, was that after leaving the pub, he had gone back and strangled the girl and had then driven straight through to Workingham. The murder hadn't taken place till after midnight, if one could trust the medical evidence, but there was plenty of time for him to do the job and get to Workingham by six. The case went up for trial, and we didn't feel any too happy about it, though there was something about the man that made us believe he was telling the truth.

"Well, two days after the first hearing, we got a letter from a man living in a village about twenty miles from Workingham, who said he had some information for us, and I was sent up to interview him. He turned out to be a shifty-looking person of the labouring class, and after a good deal of argument and a ten-bob note had passed between us, he more or less admitted that he got his living by poaching. His story was that on the night of the murder, he had been setting snares in a wood near his village. He said that he had visited one particular snare just after 10 o'clock and again at one in the morning. He had seen no man and no car, but on his second visit to the snare, he had found a pair of woollen gloves lying close beside it. He had taken the gloves home and said nothing about them to anybody, but after reading the report of the magistrate's inquiry, he had thought it his duty to communicate with us. He also made it pretty obvious that he expected a reward for his testimony.

"He showed me the gloves, which corresponded fairly closely to the description given by our client. Not that that proved very much, because they had been described in court and might have been purchased for the occasion. Still, there they were, and if they did belong to our client, and he had left them in a wood near Workingham before one a.m., he couldn't possibly have been doing a murder at midnight eighty miles away. It did seem as though we might be able to get them identified, either by somebody who knew our man or through the manufacturer. I took down a statement from the poacher and set off home, carrying the gloves in my handbag.

"I had no car in those early days, and had to return by rail—a nasty cross-country journey in a ramshackle local train with no corridor. It was a dark November night, with a thick fog, and everything running late.

"I don't remember the crash. We found out afterwards that the London express had somehow over-run the signals and rammed us from behind just before we cleared the points. All I knew was that something hit me with a noise like Doomsday, and that, after what seemed an endless age, I was crawling out from under a pile of wreckage, with blood running into my mouth from a bad cut on my head. I had been snoozing with my feet up on the seat, otherwise I should have been cut clean in two, for when I did get clear, I could see that the three rear coaches of the local had been telescoped. The engine of the express had turned over and set fire to the wreckage, and the place was an inferno. The dead and injured were sprawled about everywhere, and the survivors were working like navvies to extricate the unfortunate devils who were trapped in the blazing coaches. The groaning and screaming were simply ghastly. Booh!! I won't dwell on that, if you

104

don't mind. You might touch the bell, Timpany. George, bring me another whisky. Same as before.

"As soon as I got my wits about me," continued Popper, "I remembered the gloves in my handbag. I *must get them* out, I thought. I couldn't find anyone to help me, and the flames were already licking up the side of the coach. Where the bag had got to I had no idea, but somewhere underneath all that mass of twisted iron and broken woodwork was the evidence that might save our client's life.

"I was just starting in to hunt for it, when I felt a clutch on my arm. It was a woman.

"'My baby,' she said. 'My little boy! In there!'

"She pointed to the compartment next to mine. The fire was just beginning to take hold, and when I peered in I could see the child in the light of the flames. It was lying on the underside of the overturned coach, pinned in by some timbers which had saved it from being crushed to death, but I didn't see how we were going to shift all that stuff before the fire got to it. The woman was shaking me in a kind of frenzy. 'Be quick!' she said. 'Be quick! It's too heavy—I can't lift it. Be quick!' Well, there was only one thing to do. I had another shot at getting help, but everybody seemed to have their hands full already. I clambered through the window and clawed about in the wreckage till I could reach down and satisfy myself that the boy was still alive.

"All the time I was doing it, you know, I could smell and hear the fire crackling and crunching the bones of my own compartment—eating up my bag and my papers and the gloves and everything. Each minute spent in saving the child was a nail in my client's coffin. And—do remember this—I felt certain that the man was absolutely innocent.

"And yet, you see, it was a pretty slender chance. The gloves might not be his, and even if they were, the evidence might not save him. Or, take it the other way. Even without the gloves, the jury might believe his story.

"And there was no doubt about the baby. There it was, alive and howling. And its mother was working frantically beside me, tugging at blazing planks and cutting herself on broken window glass, and calling out to the child all the time. What could I do? Though, you know, I had serious doubts whether we shouldn't lose both the child and the evidence.

"Well, anyhow, just when I was giving up hope, two men

came along to lend a hand and we managed to lift the wreckage free and get the boy out. It was touch and go. His frock was alight already.

"And by that time my own compartment was nothing but a roaring furnace. There was nothing left. Not a thing. When we hunted through the red-hot ashes in the morning, all we could find was the brass lock of my handbag.

"We did our best, of course. We got the poacher to court, but he didn't stand up very well under cross-examination. And the whole thing was so vague. You can't identify a pair of gloves from a description, and we failed absolutely to find anybody who had seen the car near the wood that night. Perhaps, after all, there never was a car.

"Rightly or wrongly, we lost the case. Of course, we might have lost it anyway. The man may even have been guilty— I hope he was. But I can see his face now, as it looked when I told my story. I can see the foreman giving his verdict, with his eyes everywhere but on the prisoner."

Popper stopped speaking, and put his hands over his face.

"Was the fellow hanged?" asked the Colonel.

"Yes," said Popper in a stifled tone, "yes, he was hanged."

"And what," inquired the Padre, "became of the baby?"

Popper lowered his hands in a hopeless gesture.

"He was hanged too. Last year. For the murder of two little girls. It was a pretty revolting case."

There was a long silence. Popper finished his drink and stood up.

"But you couldn't have foreseen that," ventured the Padre at length.

"No," said Popper, "I couldn't have foreseen it. And I know you will say that I did the right thing."

The Stranger got up in his turn and laid his hand on Popper's shoulder. "These things cannot be helped," he said. "I am the man who saved the Davenant-Smith manuscripts and I have my nightmares too."

"Ah! but you've paid your debt," said Popper quickly. "I've never had to pay, you see."

"Yes," said the other man thoughtfully, "I've paid, and time has justified me. One does what one can. What happens afterwards is no business of ours."

But as he followed Popper out of the room, he held his head erect and moved with a new assurance.

"That is a very dreadful story," said the Padre.

"Very," said I, "and there are some rather odd points about it. Did commercial travellers dash about in motor-cars when Popper was a youngster? And why didn't he take that evidence straight to the police?"

Timpany chuckled.

"Of course," he said, "Popper attended the inquest on Davenant-Smith's butler. He must have spotted that doctor bloke the minute he set eyes on him. Popper's the kindest-hearted old bluffer going, but you mustn't believe a word of those stories of his. He was in great form to-night, was old Popper."

AN ARROW O'ER THE HOUSE

"THE FACT IS, Miss Robbins," said Mr. Humphrey Podd, that we don't go the right way about it. We are too meek, too humdrum. We write—that is, I write—a story that is a hair-raiser, a flesh-creeper, a blood-curdler, calculated to make stony-eyed gorgons howl in their haunted slumbers. And what do we do with it?"

Miss Robbins, withdrawing from the typewriter the final sheet of *The Time Will Come!* by Humphrey Podd, fastened it to the rest of the chapter with a paper clip and gazed timidly at her employer.

"We send it to a publisher," she hazarded.

"Yes," repeated Mr. Podd, bitterly, "we send it to a publisher. How? Tied up in brown paper, with a servile covering note, begging to submit it for his consideration. Does he consider it? Does he even read it? No! He keeps it in a dusty basket for six months and then sends it back with hypocritical thanks and compliments."

Miss Robbins glanced involuntarily towards a drawer, in which, as she too well knew, lay entombed the still-born corpses of *Murder Marriage*, *The Deadly Elephant*, and *The Needle of Nemesis*, battered with travel and melancholy with neglect. Tears came into her eyes, for, though Heaven had denied her brains, she was as devoted to her work as any typist can be, and cherished, moreover, a secret and passionate attachment to Mr. Podd.

"Do you think a personal call——?" she began.

"That's no good," said Mr. Podd. "The beasts are never in. Or if they are, they are always in conference with somebody of importance, ha ha! No. What we want to do is to take a leaf out of the advertiser's book—create a demand—rouse expectation. The 'Watch This Space' stunt, and all that sort of thing. We must plan a campaign."

"Oh, *yes*, Mr. Podd?"

"We must be up to date, dynamic, soul-shattering," pursued the author. He swept back the lock of fair hair which was trained to tumble into his eyes at impressive moments, and assumed the air of a Napoleon. "Whom shall we select as our objective? Not Sloop—he is too well-fed. Nothing could make that swill-fatted carcase quiver. Nor Gribble and Tape, because they are both dead and you cannot hope to stagger a bone-headed Board of Directors. Horace Pincock is vulnerable, but I would rather starve in a garret than become a Horace Pincock author." (Not that there was any chance of Mr. Podd's starving, for he had an ample allowance from his widowed mother, but the expression sounded well.) "Nor Mutters and Stalk—I've met Algernon Mutters and he reminded me of a lop-eared rabbit. John Paragon is out of the question—his own advertising is pitiable, and he wouldn't appreciate us. I think we will concentrate on Milton Ramp. For a publisher he is intelligent and go-ahead, and my friends tell me he is highly strung. Go and get me a broad pen, a bottle of scarlet ink, and some of that revolting bright green paper you buy from the sixpenny bazaar."

"Oh, *yes*, Mr. Podd," breathed Miss Robbins.

The campaign against Mr. Milton Ramp opened that day with an emerald missive marked "Private and Confidential." Inside the paper bore only the words: THE TIME WILL COME! executed in scarlet letters an inch high. Miss Robbins posted this at the West Central Post Office.

"They must all be posted from different places," said Mr. Podd, "for fear of discovery."

The second message (posted in Shaftesbury Avenue) had no wording; it consisted merely of an immense scarlet arrow with a venomous-looking barb. The third (posted in Fleet Street) showed the arrow again, together with the mysterious caption: "Time has an arrow—see Eddington—its mark is ruin and desolation." The fourth drove home this ambiguous remark with a quotation from Mr. Podd's latest work: "Ruin may seem far distant, but—THE TIME WILL COME!" At this point the week-end intervened, and Mr. Podd rested on his oars. He spent Sunday morning in picking out choice bits from his novel. The story lent itself to this, being concerned with the activities of an indignant gentleman wrongfully condemned to penal servitude by the machinations of a company promoter, and devoting his remaining years to a long-drawn-out series of threats and revenges. On Sunday night, Mr. Podd posted the next letter with his own hand. It was an excerpt from Chapter IV, where the hero, in a great scene, defies his oppressor, and ran:

"Guilty as you are, you cannot escape for ever. Truth shall prevail. THE TIME WILL COME!"

On Monday he was assailed by the thought that Mr. Ramp might take the whole thing as a joke. This worried him. He made researches into the life-history of a more celebrated author, and wrote:

"You laugh now—but THE TIME WILL COME when you *will* hear me!—see Disraeli."

This pleased him until the moment when he found Miss Robbins throwing a letter into the waste-paper basket.

"Only an advertising circular, Mr. Podd," explained Miss Robbins.

"Woman!" cried Mr. Podd, "you alarm me! How if the hippopotamus-skinned Ramp has protected himself with a bulwark of women like you? Perhaps he has never even seen our well-thought-out nerve-shatterers! Damnable thought. But stay! Did not that idea also occur to the injured Rupert Pentecost?"

"Oh, yes, Mr. Podd. In Chapter XV. I'll look it up for you."

"A quotation to suit every situation," said Mr. Podd. "Ah! thank you, Miss Robbins. Yes. 'Remember the woman whose life you laid waste! If you persist in your obduracy, the warnings will go to your private address.' That will do nicely. Pass me the red ink. Post this in Hampstead on your way home and find out where the unspeakable Ramp has his detested lair."

The task was not a hard one, for Mr. Ramp's lair was quite openly entered in the telephone directory, and the next letter was posted (from a pillar-box in Piccadilly) to that address:

"Nemesis sits on the ruined hearth. THE TIME WILL COME!"

This was embellished by a clock-face, in which arrow-shaped hands pointed to half-past eleven.

"We will move the time five minutes on every day," said Mr. Podd. "In another week's time the fellow ought to be twittering. We'll show him what advertising means. Talking about it's paying to advertise, oughtn't we to make some suggestion about advance royalties? Five hundred would be mild for a book of this quality, but these fellows are all hard-fisted misers. Let us say £250 to start with."

"There's nothing about that in the book," said Miss Robbins.

"No, not in the book," agreed Mr. Podd, "because Jeremy Vanbrugh is supposed to be a sympathetic character—I didn't want to turn him into a blackmailer. The public can get fond of a mere murderer and doesn't mind if the detective lets him off at the end, but a blackmailing murderer *must* be hanged. It's one of the rules."

"But," said Miss Robbins, "mightn't Mr. Ramp think we were blackmailers if we asked for money?"

"That's different," replied Mr. Podd, rather irritably. "We are only asking for our due reward. He'll think so when he sees the book. Let's see: 'A first payment of £250'—no, hang it! that sounds like hire-purchase. Wait a minute. 'I only ask for £250—now—but THE TIME WILL COME when you will pay me more'—no—'pay up in full'—that's crisper. We'll push this round to both addresses."

He wrote the letters and dictated a chapter of a new book. "It will be wanted quickly when the first one gets going," he observed. "We shall hardly be able to turn them out fast enough. It will be a great strain, no doubt."

"Oh, but you have so many wonderful ideas, Mr. Podd. And I don't mind working extra."

"Thank you, Miss Robbins," said Mr. Podd, condescendingly. "You are a good girl. I don't know what I should do without you." He tossed back the Napoleon lock. "Have you got your note-book? Take down this. *The Corpse in the Sewer*. Chapter I. The Smell in the Scullery. 'Anne,' said Mrs. Fletcher to the cook, 'have you been throwing cabbage-water down the sink?' 'No, ma'am,' replied the girl, pertly, 'I should hope I know better than that——' That gives the right domestic touch for the opening, I think."

"Oh, *yes*, Mr. Podd."

Mr. Podd was lunching with a literary friend named Gamble. He did not very much like Gamble, who was one of those people who are quite spoilt by a trifling success. Gamble's novel *Waste of Shame* had, for some reason, achieved a sort of fluky popularity, and the incense had gone to his head. He was frequently seen at publishers' parties, had made a witty speech before Royalty at a literary dinner, and now made a foolish pretence of possessing inside knowledge of everyone in the publishing world. One could not afford not to know Gamble, but he was very trying to his friends. Humphrey Podd looked forward to the day when he would be able to patronize Gamble in his turn.

"Look!" said Gamble, "there's Ramp just come in. That fellow's cracking up. Got the willies. You can see it in his face."

Mr. Podd gazed at the publisher—a thin, dark, fretted face and a pair of nervous hands that picked unceasingly at a roll of bread.

"Why?" asked Mr. Podd. "He's all right, isn't he? His stuff sells, doesn't it?"

"Oh, there's nothing wrong with the *business,*" said Gamble. "You're all right there, if you're thinking of placing anything with him. No—it's something quite different. Don't let this go any further, but I shouldn't be surprised if there was an explosion in that quarter before very long."

"Explosion?" repeated Mr. Podd.

"Well, yes—but I oughtn't to say anything. I just happen to know, that's all. One gets to hear these things somehow."

Mr. Podd was annoyed. He would have liked to hear more, but he was determined not to encourage Gamble.

"Oh, well," he said, "as long as the firm's all right, that's the main thing. Chap's private life is none of my business."

"Private—ah! there you are," said Gamble, darkly. "From what I hear, it won't stay private very long. If some of the letters come into court—whew!"

"Letters?" asked Mr. Podd suddenly interested.

"Hell!" said Gamble. "I oughtn't to have said anything about that. It was told me in confidence. Forget it, will you old boy?"

"Oh, certainly," said Humphrey Podd, annoyed with himself and with Gamble.

"He's beginning to sit up and take notice," announced Mr. Podd to Miss Robbins. And he repeated Mr. Gamble's conversation.

"Oh, Mr. *Podd!*" exclaimed Miss Robbins. She fiddled nervously with her typewriter ribbon. "Mr. Podd!" she burst out, uncontrollably, "you don't suppose he—I mean, you never know, do you? And he might be angry."

"He'll forget it, once he sees the book," said Mr. Podd.

"Yes, but—just imagine! I mean, he might have really done something. Perhaps he's getting frightened—I mean—you'll think I'm awfully silly."

"Not at all, Miss Robbins," said Humphrey Podd.

"Well, I mean—suppose there's a dark secret in his past life——"

"That would be an idea," cried Mr. Podd, excitedly. "Wait a minute—wait a minute! Miss Robbins, you've given me the plot for a new book. Here! take this down. Title: *A Bow at a Venture.* No, dash it! I've an idea that's been used before. I've got it: *An Arrow o'er the House.* Quotation from *Hamlet*: 'That I have shot my arrow o'er the house and hurt my brother.' Plot begins. Somebody—call him Jones—writes threatening letters to—say, Robinson. Jones means it for a joke, but Robinson is frightened to death because, unknown to Jones, he really has—call it, murdered somebody. Make it a woman—female victims always go down well. Robinson commits suicide and Jones is prosecuted for blackmail and murder. I'm not sure if frightening a man to death would be brought in murder, but I expect it would. Blackmail is a felony, and if you accidentally kill somebody while you're engaged in felony, the killing is murder, so it might come in that way. I say, this idea of mine is going to be good. Wash out *The Corpse in the Sewer*—I never thought a lot of that. We'll get going straight away on this one. Jones thinks he has covered his tracks, but the police—no, not the police—they're baffled, of course. The detective. Let's see; I think we'd better use Major Hawke again for this one. He's my best detective, and if readers get keen on him in *The Time will come* they'll want to hear about him again—Hawke gets on the scene of the letters. It's difficult, because of course they've all been posted in different places, but——"

Miss Robbins, her pencil staggering over the paper as she
113

struggled to follow Humphrey Podd's disjointed speech, gave a little gasp.

"Hawke traces the paper, of course—where purchased, and so on. And the ink. Oh, yes—and we can have a thumb-print on one of the envelopes. Not Jones's—his *fiancée's*, I think, who has posted the letters for him. She—yes, she's a good character, but hopelessly under the influence of Jones. We'll think that out. Better marry her off to somebody nicer in the end. Not Major Hawke—somebody else. We'll invent a decent chap for her. There'll be a good scene when she is frantically burning the evidence while the police hammer at the door. We must make her overlook something, of course, or Jones would never get detected—never mind, I can think that out later. Court scene—that'll be good——"

"Oh, Mr. Podd! But does poor Jones get hanged? I mean, it seems very hard lines on him, when he only meant it for a joke."

"That's where the irony comes in," said Mr. Podd, ruthlessly. "Still, I see what you mean. The public will want him saved. All right—we'll stack that. We'll make him a bad character—one of those men who trample over women's hearts and laugh at their sufferings. He gets away with all his real crimes and then—here's your irony—does himself in over this one harmless joke on a man he quite likes. Make a note, 'Jones laughs once too often.' Must get a better name than Jones. Lester is a good name. Everybody calls him 'Laughing Lester.' Fair, curly hair—put that down—but his eyes are set a little too close together. I say, this is shaping splendidly."

"And about the letter to Mr. Ramp," suggested Miss Robbins, with some hesitation, when the main lines of *An Arrow o'er the House* had been sucessfully laid down. "Perhaps you'd rather I didn't post it?"

"Not post it?" said Mr. Podd, amazed. "Why, it's a beauty. 'THE TIME WILL COME—and it is later than you think' Post it, of course. Ramp's got to be roused."

Miss Robbins obediently posted the letter—with gloves on.

It was not till the arrow-headed hands on Mr. Podd's clock-face had reached 11.45, and the message had taken the form, "To-morrow, and to-morrow, and to-morrow," that it occurred to him to test the victim's reaction personally. The idea came to him at 11.45 precisely, in the middle of Piccadilly Circus. With a hoarse chuckle, which caused a passing messenger-boy to turn round and stare at him in amazement, he plunged headlong down the subway and into a public call-box in the rotunda. Here he obtained the number of Mr. Ramp's office.

The female voice that answered said that Mr. Ramp was engaged, and inquired the name of the caller. Mr. Podd was prepared for this, and said that the matter was strictly private and very urgent. Further, that he would not feel justified in giving his name to anybody but Mr. Ramp. The girl seemed less surprised and less obdurate than Mr. Podd might have expected. She put him through. A sharp, worried voice said: "Yes? yes? yes? Who's that?"

Mr. Podd lowered his naturally rather high tones to an impressive croak.

"THE TIME WILL COME," he said. There was a pause.

"*What* did you say?" demanded the sharp voice, irritably.

"THE TIME WILL COME," repeated Mr. Podd. Then, prompted by a sudden inspiration, he added: "*Shall we send the proofs to the Public Prosecutor?*"

There was another pause. Then the voice said: "I don't know what you are talking about. Who is it speaking, please?"

Mr. Podd laughed fiendishly, and rang off.

"And why not?" said Mr. Podd to Miss Robbins. "People are always sending advance proofs to Prime Ministers and literary critics. The Public Prosecutor's opinion ought to be as good as anybody's. Make a note of it.

Two days passed. The daily missive now bore only the ominous word: "TO-MORROW." Mr. Podd dictated three chapters of *An Arrow o'er the House* right off the reel and went out to tea with a friend, leaving Miss Robbins to pack up the top copy of *The Time Will Come* and dispatch it, per post, to Mr. Milton Ramp.

It was a raw and foggy day. Cold, too—Miss Robbins stoked up the stove in Humphrey Podd's studio, for her fingers were numb with note-taking. As she stepped out into the Square, with the manuscript under her arm, she shivered, and pulled her fur more closely about her neck

On her way to the post-office she had to pass the news-vendor at the corner of the Square. The scarlet lettering on the placards he held made a splash of brightness in the gloom and caught Miss Robbins' eye. With a sudden leap of the heart she read the words: LONDON PUBLISHER SHOT.

The manuscript slipped from her grasp. She picked it up,

fumbled hurriedly in her bag for a penny, and bought a copy of the *Evening Banner*. She opened it, standing by the Square railings. A heavy splash of soot-laden water dripped from an overhanging tree upon the crown of her hat. At first she could not find what she was looking for. Eventually she discovered a few smudged lines in the Stop Press column.

"Mr. Milton Ramp, the well-known publisher, was found shot dead in his office to-day when his secretary returned from lunch. A discharged revolver lay on the floor beside him. Mr. Ramp is said to have been worried of late by domestic troubles, and by the receipt of anonymous letters. The police are making investigations"

The manuscript under Miss Robbins's arm seemed to have grown to colossal size. She looked up, and caught the eye of the newsvendor. It was an unnaturally bright eye, like a hawk's. It made her think of the chapter in *Murder Marriage* where Major Hawke had disguised himself as a newsvendor in order to watch a suspected house. She hurried back to the studio. As she bolted up the front steps, she glanced nervously back. Through the fog, she made out a dim and bulky shape advancing along the other side of the Square. It wore a helmet and a water-proof cape.

Humphrey Podd's studio flat was on the top floor. Miss Robbins took the three flights at a run, dashed to cover and locked the door after her. Peeping out from behind the window-curtain, she saw the policeman speaking to the newsvendor

"Thank goodness," thought Miss Robbins, "I hadn't posted the manuscript." She tore off the brown paper and gaspingly extracted the covering letter that bore Humphrey Podd's name and address. The top sheet of the manuscript followed it into the fire. Then she sat trembling. But not for long. There was the carbon copy. There were her shorthand notes. There was the story itself, which bore the unmistakable marks of Humphrey Podd's authorship. With a sick presentiment of disaster, Miss Robbins remembered that Major Hawke—that inspired detective—figured, not only in *The Time Will Come,* but also in *Murder Marriage*, which had been submitted to Mr. Milton Ramp only three months ago. Mr. Podd had said that publishers never read his manuscripts—but could one count on that? Some secretary, some hired reader, might have

116

glanced at it, and nobody who had ever encountered Major Hawke could possibly forget him and his eccentricities.

Miss Robbins looked out of the window again. The policeman was advancing with his stately tread along the near side of the Square, and glancing up at the windows. He approached the house. He stopped. With a terrified squeak, Miss Robbins rushed to the roaring stove and crammed the manuscript in—top copy—carbon—note-book—pulling the chapters hurriedly apart to make the mass of paper burn faster. What else was there? The plot-book—that must go too. Her hand shook as she wrenched the pages out. And—oh, she had nearly forgotten the most damning evidence of all—the green paper. Mr. Podd had said that detectives could always trace the purchase of paper. She fed it desperately to the leaping flame, flinging the pen and the bottle of red ink after it for good measure, and piling fresh coal and coke on top of it.

She was still bending. hot and flushed, over the stove, when she heard footsteps coming up the stair. She dashed to the typewriter and began to pound nervously at the keys. A hand shook the door-handle.

"Hell!" said the voice of Humphrey Podd. Then came the noise of a key entering the lock. "Damn the girl—she's still out."

Mr. Podd walked in.

"You're here!" he said, astonished. "What the devil are you doing with the door locked? Look here, here's a dashed nuisance! That ass, Ramp, has gone and blown his brains out, if he ever had any, and all our advance publicity has been wasted. We'll have to start all over again."

"Oh, Mr. Podd!" cried Miss Robbins. "I'm so thankful you're here. When I saw the policeman I was afraid he'd catch you, and I didn't know where you were, to warn you——"

"No wonder Ramp looked white about the gills," pursued Mr. Podd, unheeding. "His wife's been carrying on with some man or other. Ramp got wind of it through some anonymous letters from a discharged servant, and there was a frightful bust-up last night and his wife's bolted. And now the fool's gone and shot himself. I got hold of that infuriating chap, Gamble, and wrung the whole thing out of him. He might have told me earlier, blast him! It's no good sending anything there now. I hope you didn't post that manuscript. If you did, we must get it back and try it on Sloop——What on earth's

117

the matter with you, Miss Robbins?"

"Oh, Mr. Podd!" cried Miss Robbins. "We can't—we—I thought—oh, Mr. Podd, I've burnt the manuscripts!"

Police-constable E 999 withdrew his wistful gaze from the lighted area. Somebody in the basement was stewing tripe, and the smell came up comfortingly. He hoped there would be something equally good waiting for him at home. As he ambled along the pavement, he heard a crash and tinkle of glass, and a typewriter came hurtling out of an upper window, just missing his helmet.

"Hullo!" said P.C. E 999.

A loud shriek followed. Then a shrill female voice cried, "Help! help! murder!"

"Gor lumme!" said the constable. "They *would* go and start something just when I was getting away to my supper."

He climbed the steps and knocked thunderously upon the door.

SCRAWNS

THE gate, on whose peeled and faded surface the name SCRAWNS was just legible in the dim light, fell to with a clap that shook the rotten gate-post and scattered a shower of drops from the drenched laurels. Susan Tabbit set down the heavy suit-case which had made her arm ache, and peered through the drizzle towards the little house.

It was a curious, lop-sided, hunch-shouldered building, seeming not so much to preside over its patch of wintry garden as to be eavesdropping behind its own hedges. Against a streak of watery light in the west, its chimney-stacks—one at either end—suggested pricked ears, intensely aware; the more so, that its face was blind.

Susan shivered a little, and thought regretfully of the cheerful bus that she had left at the bottom of the hill. The conductor had seemed just as much surprised as the station porter had been when she mentioned her destination. He had opened his mouth as though about to make some comment, but had thought better of it. She wished she had had the courage to ask him what sort of place she was coming to. Scrawns. It was a queer name; she had thought so when she had first seen it on Mrs. Wispell's notepaper. Susan Tabbit, care of Mrs. Wispell, Scrawns, Roman Way, Dedcaster.

Her married sister had pursed up her lips when Susan gave her the address, reading it aloud with an air of disapproval. "What's she like, this Mrs. Wispell of Scrawns?" Susan had to confess that she did not know; she had taken the situation without an interview.

Now the house faced her, aloof, indifferent, but on the watch. No house should look so. She had been a fool to come; but it had been so evident that her sister was anxious to get her out of the house. There was no room for her, with all her brother-in-law's family coming. And she was short of money.

119

She had thought it might be pleasant at Scrawns. House-parlourmaid, to work with married couple; that had sounded all right. Three in family; that was all right, too. In her last job there had been only herself and eight in family; she had looked forward to a light place and a lively kitchen.

"And what am I thinking about?" said Susan, picking up the suit-case. "The family'll be out, as like as not, at a party or something of that. There'll be a light in the kitchen all right, I'll be bound."

She plodded over the sodden gravel, between two squares of lawn, flanked by empty beds and backed by a huddle of shrubbery; then turned along a path to the right, following the front of the house with its blank unwelcoming windows. The side-walk was as dark as the front. She made out the outline of a French window, opening upon the path and, to her right, a wide herbaceous border, where tin labels, attached to canes, flapped forlornly. Beyond this there seemed to be a lawn, but the tall trees which surrounded it on all three sides drowned it in blackness and made its shape and extent a mystery. The path led on, through a half-open door that creaked as she pushed it back, and she found herself in a small, paved court-yard, across which the light streamed in a narrow beam from a small, lighted window.

She tried to look in at this window, but a net curtain veiled its lower half. She could only see the ceiling, low, with black rafters, from one of which there hung a paraffin lamp. Passing the window she found a door and knocked.

With the first fall of the old-fashioned iron knocker, a dog began to bark, loudly, incessantly, and furiously. She waited, her heart hammering, but nobody came. After a little, she summoned up resolution to knock afresh. This time she thought she could distinguish, through the clamour, a movement within. The barking ceased, she heard a key turn and bolts withdrawn, and the door opened.

The light within came from a doorway on the left, and out-lined against it, she was only aware of an enormous bulk and a dim triangle of whiteness, blocking her entrance to the house.

"Who is it?"

The voice was unlike any she had ever heard; curiously harsh and husky and sexless, like the voice of something strangled.

"My name's Tabbit—Susan Tabbit."

"Oh, you're the new girl!" There was a pause, as though the speaker were trying, in the uncertain dusk, to sum her up and reckon out her possibilities.

"Come in."

The looming bulk retreated, and Susan again lifted her suitcase and carried it inside.

"Mrs. Wispell got my letter, saying I was coming?"

"Yes; she got it. But one can't be too careful. It's a lonely place. You can leave your bag for Jarrock. This way."

Susan stepped into the kitchen. It was a low room, not very large but appearing larger than it was because of the shadows thrown into the far corners by the wide shade of the hanging lamp. There was a good fire, which Susan was glad to see, and over the mantelpiece an array of polished copper pans winked reassuringly. Behind her she again heard the jarring of shot bolts and turned key. Then her jailer—why did that word leap uncalled into her mind?—came back and stepped for the first time into the light.

As before, her first overwhelming impression was of enormous height and size. The flat, white, wide face, the billowing breasts, the enormous girth of white-aproned haunch seemed to fill the room and swim above her. Then she forgot everything else in the shock of realizing that the huge woman was cross-eyed.

It was no mere cast; not even an ordinary squint. The left eye was swivelled so horribly far inward that half the iris was invisible, giving to that side of the face a look of blind and cunning malignity. The other eye was bright and dark and small, and fixed itself acutely on Susan's face.

"I'm Mrs. Jarrock," said the woman in her odd, hoarse voice.

It was incredible to Susan that any man who was not blind and deaf should have married a woman so hideously disfigured and with such a raven croak. She said: "How do you do?" and extended a reluctant hand, which Mrs. Jarrock's vast palm engulfed in a grasp unexpectedly hard and masculine.

"You'll like a cup of tea before you change," said Mrs. Jarrock. "You can wait at table, I suppose?"

"Oh, yes, I'm used to that."

"Then you'd better begin to-night. Jarrock's got his hands full with Mr. Alistair. It's one of his bad days. We was both

121

upstairs, that's why you had to wait." She again glanced sharply at the girl, and the swivel eye rolled unpleasantly and uncontrollably in its socket. She turned and bent to lift the kettle from the range, and Susan could not rid herself of the notion that the left eye was still squinting at her from its ambush behind the cook's flat nose.

"Is it a good place?" asked Susan.

"It's all right," said Mrs. Jarrock, "for them as isn't nervous. *She* don't trouble herself much, but that's only to be expected as things are, and *he's* quiet enough if you don't cross him. Mr. Alistair won't trouble you, that's Jarrock's job. There's your tea. Help yourself to milk and sugar. I wonder if Jarrock——"

She broke off short; set down the teapot and stood with her large head cocked sideways, as though listening to something going on above. Then she moved hastily across the kitchen, with a lightness of step surprising in so unwieldy a woman, and disappeared into the darkness of the passage. Susan, listening anxiously, thought she could hear a sound like moaning and a movement of feet across the raftered ceiling. In a few minutes, Mrs. Jarrock came back, took the kettle from the fire and handed it out to some unseen person in the passage. A prolonged whispering followed, after which Mrs. Jarrock again returned and, without offering any comment, began to make buttered toast.

Susan ate without relish. She had been hungry when she left the bus, but the atmosphere of the house disconcerted her. She had just refused a second slice of toast when she became aware that a man had entered the kitchen.

He was a tall man and powerfully built, but he stood in the doorway as though suspicious or intimidated; she realised that he had probably been standing there for some time before she observed him. Mrs. Jarrock, seeing Susan's head turn and remain arrested, looked round also.

"Oh, there you are, Jarrock. Come and take your tea."

The man moved then, skirting the wall with a curious, crablike movement, and so coming by reluctant degrees to the opposite side of the fire, where he stood, his head averted, shooting a glance at Susan from the corner of his eye.

"This here's Susan," said Mrs. Jarrock. "It's to be hoped she'll settle down and be comfortable with us. I'll be glad to have her to help with the work, as *you* know, with one thing and another."

"We'll do our betht to make things eathy for her," said the man. He lisped oddly and, though he held out his hand, he still kept his head half averted, like a cat that refuses to take notice. He retreated into an arm-chair, drawn rather far back from the hearth, and sat gazing into the fire. The dog which had barked when Susan knocked had followed him into the room, and now came over and sniffed at the girl's legs, uttering a menacing growl.

"Be quiet, Crippen," said the man. "Friends."

The dog, a large brindled bull-terrier, was apparently not reassured He continued to growl, till Jarrock, hauling him back by the collar, gave him a smart cuff on the head and ordered him under the table, where he went, sullenly. In bending to beat the dog, Jarrock for the first time turned his full face upon Susan, and she saw, with horror, that the left side of it, from the cheek-bone downwards, could scarcely be called a face, for it was seamed and puckered by a horrible scar, which had dragged the mouth upwards into the appearance of a ghastly grin, while the left-hand side of the jaw seemed shapeless and boneless, a mere bag of wrinkled flesh.

"Is everybody in this house maimed and abnormal?" she thought, desperately. As though in answer to her thoughts, Mrs. Jarrock spoke to her husband.

"Has he settled down now?"

"Oh, he's quiet enough," replied the man, lisping through his shattered teeth. "He'll do all right." He retired again to his corner and began sucking in his buttered toast, making awkward sounds.

"If you've finished your tea," said Mrs. Jarrock, "I'd better show you your room. Have you taken Susan's bag up, Jarrock?"

The man nodded without speaking, and Susan, in some trepidation, followed the huge woman, who had lit a candle in a brass candlestick.

"You'll find the stairs awkward at first," said the hoarse voice, "and you'll have to mind your head in these passages. Built in the year one, this place was, and by a crazy builder at that, if you ask me."

She glided noiselessly along a narrow corridor and out into a square flagged hall, where a small oil-lamp, heavily shaded, seemed to make darkness deeper; then mounted a flight of black oak stairs with twisted banisters of polished oak and shining oak treads, in which the candlelight was reflected on wavering yellow pools.

"There's only the one staircase," said Mrs. Jarrock. "Unhandy, I calls it, but you'll have to do your best. You'll have to wait till he's shut himself up of a morning before you bring down the slops; he don't like to see pails about. This here's their bedroom and that's the spare and this is Mr. Alistair's room. Jarrock sleeps in with him, of course, in case——" She stopped at the door, listening; then led the way up a narrow attic staircase.

"You're in here. It's small, but you're by yourself. And I'm next door to you."

The candle threw their shadows, gigantically distorted, upon the sloping ceiling, and Susan thought, fantastically: "If I stay here, I shall grow the wrong shape, too."

"And the big attic's the master's place. You don't have nothing to do with that. Much as your place or ours is worth to poke your nose round the door. He keeps it locked, anyway." The cook laughed, a hoarse, throaty chuckle. "Queer things he keeps in there, I must say. I've seen 'em—when he brings' em downstairs, that is. He's a funny one, is Mr. Wispell. Well, you'd better get changed into your black, then I'll take you to the mistress."

Susan dressed hurriedly before the little, heart-shaped mirror with its old, greenish glass that seemed to absorb more of the candlelight than it reflected. She pulled aside the check window-curtain and looked out. It was almost night, but she contrived to make out that the attic looked over the garden at the side of the house. Beneath her lay the herbaceous border, and beyond that, the tall trees stood up like a wall. The room itself was comfortably furnished, though, as Mrs. Jarrock had said, extremely small and twisted into a curious shape by the slanting flue of the great chimney, which ran up on the left-hand side and made a great elbow beside the bed-head. There was a minute fireplace cut into the chimney, but it had an unused look. Probably, thought Susan, it would smoke.

At the head of the stairs she hesitated, candle in hand. She was divided between a dread of solitude and a dread of what she was to meet below. She tiptoed down the attic stair and emerged upon the landing. As she did so, she saw the back of Jarrock flitting down the lower flight, and noticed that he had left the door of "Mr. Alistair's" room open behind him. Urged by a curiosity powerful enough to overcome her uneasiness, she crept to the door and peeped in.

Facing her was an old-fashioned tester bed with dull green hangings; a shaded reading-lamp burned beside it on a small table. The man on the bed lay flat on his back with closed eyes; his face was yellow and transparent as wax, with pinched, sharp nostrils; one hand, thin as a claw, lay passive upon the green counterpane; the other was hidden in the shadows of the curtains. Certainly, if Jarrock had been speaking of Mr. Alistair, he was right; this man was quiet enough now.

"Poor gentleman," whispered Susan, "he's passed away. And while the words were still on her lips a great bellow of laughter burst forth from somewhere on the floor below. It was monstrous, gargantuan, fantastic; it was an outrage upon the silent house. Susan started back, and the snuffer, jerking from the candlestick, leaped into the air and went ringing and rolling down the oak staircase to land with a brazen clang on the flags below.

Somewhere a door burst open and a loud voice, with a hint of that preposterous mirth still lurking in its depths, bawled out:

"What's that? What the devil's that? Jarrock! Did you make that filthy noise?"

"I beg your pardon, sir," said Susan, advancing in some alarm to the stairhead. "It was my fault, sir. I shook the candlestick and the snuffer fell down. I am very sorry, sir."

"You?" said the man. "Who the devil are you? Come down and let's have a look at you. Oh!" as Susan's black dress and muslin apron came into his view at the turn of the stair, "the new housemaid, hey! That's a pretty way to announce yourself. A damned good beginning! Don't you do it again, that's all. I won't have noise, d'you understand? All the noise in this house is made by me. That's my prerogative, if you know what the word means. Hey? Do you understand?"

"Yes, sir. I won't let it happen again, sir."

"That's right. And look here. If you've made a dent in those boards, d'you know what I'll do? Hey? I'll have the insides out of you, d'you hear?" He jerked back his big, bearded head, and his great guffaw seemed to shake the old

125

house like a gust of wind. "Come on, girl, I won't eat you this time. Let's see your face. Your legs are all right, anyway. I won't have a housemaid with thick legs. Come in here and be vetted. Sidonia, here's the new girl, chucking the furniture all over the place the minute she's in the house. Did you hear it? Did you ever hear anything like it? Hey? Ha, ha!"

He pushed Susan in front of him into a sitting-room furnished in deep orange and rich blues and greens like a peacock's tail, and with white walls that caught and flung back the yellow lamplight. The windows were closely shuttered and barred.

On a couch drawn up near the fire a girl was lying. She had a little, white, heart-shaped face, framed and almost drowned in a mass of heavy red hair, and on her long fingers were several old and heavy rings. At her husband's boisterous entry she rose rather awkwardly and uncertainly.

"Walter, dear, don't shout so. My head aches, and you'll frighten the poor girl. So you're Susan. How are you? I hope you had a good journey. Are Mr. and Mrs. Jarrock looking after you?"

"Yes, thank you, madam."

"Oh! then that's all right." She looked a little helplessly at her husband, and then back to Susan. "I hope you'll be a good girl, Susan."

"I shall try to give satisfaction, madam."

"Yes, yes, I'm sure you will." She laughed, on a high, silver note like a bird's call. "Mrs. Jarrock will put you in the way of things. I hope you'll be happy and stay with us." Her pretty, aimless laughter tinkled out again.

"I hope Susan won't disappear like the last one," said Mr. Wispell. Susan caught a quick glance darted at him by his wife, but before she could decide whether it was one of fear or of warning, they were interrupted. A bell pealed sharply, with a jangling of wires, and in the silence that followed the two Wispells stared uneasily at each other.

"What the devil's that?" said Mr. Wispell. "I only hope to heaven——"

Jarrock came in. He held a telegram in his hand. Wispell snatched it from him and tore it open. With an exclamation of distaste and alarm he handed it to his wife, who uttered a sharp cry.

"Walter, we can't! She mustn't. Can't we stop her?"

126

"Don't be a fool, Sidonia. How can we stop her?"

"Yes, Walter. But don't you understand? She'll expect to find Helen here."

"Oh, lord!" said Mr. Wispell.

Susan went early to bed. Dinner had been a strained and melancholy meal. Mrs. Wispell talked embarrassed nothings at intervals; Mr. Wispell seemed sunk in a savage gloom, from which he only roused himself to bark at Susan for more potatoes or another slice of bread. Nor were things much better in the kitchen, for it seemed that a visitor was expected.

"Motoring down from York," muttered Mrs. Jarrock. "Goodness knows when they'll get here. But that's her all over. No consideration, and never had. I'm sorry for the mistress, that's all."

Jarrock's distorted mouth twisted into a still more ghastly semblance of a grin.

"Rich folks must have their way," he said. "Four years ago it was the same thing. A minute's notice and woe betide if everything's not right. But we'll be ready for her, oh! we'll be ready for her, you'll see." He chuckled gently to himself.

Mrs. Jarrock gave a curious, sly smile. "You'll have to help me with spare room, Susan," she said.

Later, coming down into the scullery to fill a hot-water bottle, Susan found the Jarrocks in close confabulation beside the sink.

"And see you make no noise about it," the cook was saying. "These girls have long tongues, and I wouldn't trust——"

She turned and saw Susan.

"If you've finished," she said, taking the bottle from her, "you'd best be off to bed. You've had a long journey."

The words were softly spoken, but they had an undertone of command. Susan took up her candlestick from the kitchen. As she passed the scullery on her way upstairs, she heard the Jarrocks whispering together and noticed, just inside the back door, two spades standing, with an empty sack beside them. They had not been there before, and she wondered idly what Jarrock could be wanting with them.

She fell asleep quickly, for she was tired; but an hour or two later she woke with a start and a feeling that people were talking in the room. The rain had ceased, for through the window she could see a star shining, and the attic was lit by

127

the diffused greyness of moonlight. Nobody was there, but the voices were no dream. She could hear their low rumble, close beside her head. She sat up and lit her candle; then slipped out of bed and crept across to the door.

The landing was empty; from the room next her own she could hear the deep and regular snoring of the cook. She came back and stood for a moment, puzzled. In the middle of the room she could hear nothing, but as she returned to the bed, she heard the voices again, smothered, as though the speakers were at the bottom of a well. Stooping, she put her ear to the empty fireplace. At once the voices became more distinct, and she realised that the great chimney was acting as a speaking-tube from the room below. Mr. Wispell was talking. ". . . better be getting on with it . . . here at any time . . ."

"The ground's soft enough." That was Jarrock speaking. She lost a few words, and then:

". . . bury her four feet deep, because of the rose-trees."

There came a silence. Then came the muffled echo of Mr. Wispell's great laugh; it rumbled with a goblin sound in the hollow chimney.

Susan crouched by the fireplace, feeling herself grow rigid with cold. The voices dropped to a subdued murmur. Then she heard a door shut and there was complete silence. She stretched her cramped limbs and stood a moment listening. Then, with fumbling haste she began to drag on her clothes. She must get out of this horrible house.

Suddenly a soft step sounded on the gravel beneath her window; it was followed by the chink of iron. Then a man's voice said: "Here, between Betty Uprichard and Evelyn Thornton." There followed the thick sound of a spade driven into heavy soil.

Susan stole to the window and looked out. Down below, in the moonlight, Mr. Wispell and Jarrock were digging, fast and feverishly, flinging up the soil about a shallow trench. A rose-tree was lifted and laid to one side, and as she watched them, the trench deepened and widened to a sinister shape.

She huddled on the last of her clothing, pulled on her coat and hat, sought for and found the handbag that held her money and set the door gently ajar. There was no sound but the deep snoring from the next-door room.

She picked up her suitcase, which she had not unpacked before tumbling into bed. She hesitated a moment; then, as swiftly and silently as she could, she tiptoed across the landing and down the steep stair. The words of Mr. Wispell came back to her with sudden sinister import. "I hope she won't disappear like the last one." Had the last one, also, seen that which she was not meant to see, and scuttled on trembling feet down the stair with its twisted black banisters? Or had she disappeared still more strangely, to lie forever four feet deep under the rose-trees? The old boards creaked beneath her weight; on the lower landing the door of Mr. Alistair's room stood ajar, and a faint light came from within it. Was he to be the tenant of the grave in the garden? Or was it meant for her, or for the visitor who was expected that night?

Her flickering candle-flame showed her the front door chained and bolted. With a caution and control inspired by sheer terror, she pulled back the complaining bolts, lowered the chain with her hand, so that it should not jangle against the door, and turned the heavy key. The garden lay still and sodden under the moonlight. Drawing the door very gently to behind her, she stood on the threshold, free. She took a deep breath and slipped down the path as silently as a shadow.

A few yards down the hill road she came to a clump of thick bushes. Inside this she thrust the suitcase. Then, relieved of its weight, she ran.

At four o'clock the next morning a young policeman was repeating a curious tale to the police-sergeant at Dedcaster.

"The young woman is pretty badly frightened," he said, "but she tells her story straight enough. Do you think we ought to look into it?"

"Sounds queerish," said the sergeant. "Maybe you'd better go and have a look. Wait a minute, I'll come with you myself. They're odd people, those Wispells. Man's an artist, isn't he? Loose-living gentry they are, as often as not. Get the car out, Blaycock; you can drive us."

"What the devil is all this?" demanded Mr. Wispell. He stood upright in the light of the police lantern, leaning upon his spade, and wiped the sweat from his forehead with an earthy hand. "Is that our girl you've got with you? What's wrong with her? Hey? Thief, hey? If you've been bagging the silver, you young besom, it'll be the worse for you."

"This young woman's come to us with a queer tale, Mr. Wispell," said the sergeant. "I'd like to know what you're a-digging of here for."

Mr. Wispell laughed. "Of here for? What should I be digging of here for? Can't I dig in my own garden witthout your damned interference?"

"Now, that won't work, Mr. Wispell. That's a grave, that is. People don't dig graves in their gardens in the middle of the night for fun. I want that there grave opened. What've you got inside it? Now, be careful."

"There's nobody inside it at the moment," said Mr. Wispell, "and I should be obliged if you'd make rather less noise. My wife's in a delicate state of health, and my brother-in-law, who is an invalid with an injured spine, has had a very bad turn. We've had to keep him under morphia and we've only just got him off into a natural sleep. And now you come bellowing round——"

"What's that there in that sack?" interrupted the young policeman. As they all pressed forward to look, he found Susan beside him, and reassured her with a friendly pat on the arm.

"That?" Mr. Wispell laughed again. "That's Helen. Don't damage her, I implore you—if my aunt——"

The sergeant had bent down and slit open the sacking with a pen-knife. Soiled and stained, the pale face of a woman glimmered up at him. There was earth in her eyelids.

"Marble!" said the sergeant. "Well, I'll be hanged!"

There was the sound of a car stopping at the gate.

"Heaven almighty!" ejaculated Mr. Wispell. "We're done for! Get this into the house quickly, Jarrock."

"Wait a bit, sir. What I want to know——"

Steps sounded on the gravel. Mr. Wispell flung his hands to heaven. "Too late!" he groaned.

An elderly lady, very tall and upright, was coming round the side of the house.

"What on earth are you up to out here, Walter?" she demanded, in a piercing voice. "Policemen? A nice welcome for your aunt, I must say. And what—*what* is my wedding-present doing in the garden?" she added, as her eye fell on the naked marble figure.

"Oh, Lor'!" said Mr. Wispell. He flung down the spade and stalked away into the house.

"I'm afraid," said Mrs. Wispell, "you will have to take your month's money and go, Susan. Mr. Wispell is very much annoyed. You see, it was such a hideous statue, he wouldn't have it in the house, and nobody would buy it, and besides, Mrs. Glassover might turn up at any time, so we buried it and when she wired, of course we had to dig it up. But I'm afraid Mrs. Glassover will never forgive Walter, and she's sure to alter her will and—well, he's very angry, and really I don't know how you could be so silly."

"I'm sure I'm very sorry, madam. I was a bit nervous, some-how——"

"Maybe," said Mrs. Jarrock in her hoarse voice, "the poor girl was upset-like, by Jarrock. I did ought to have explained about him and poor Mr. Alistair getting blown up in the war and you being so kind to us—but there! Being used to his poor face myself I didn't think, somehow—and what with being all upset and one thing and another . . ."

The voice of Mr. Wispell came booming down the staircase. "Has that fool of a girl cleared off?"

The young policeman took Susan by the arm. He had pleasant brown eyes and curly hair, and his voice was friendly.

"Seems to me, miss," he said, "Scrawns ain't no place for you. You'd better come along of us and eat your dinner with mother and me.

NEBUCHADNEZZAR

You have played "Nebuchadnezzar," of course—unless you are so ingenuous as never to have heard of any game but Yo-yo, or whatever the latest fad may be. "Nebuchadnezzar" is so old-fashioned that only the sophisticated play it. It came back with charades, of which, of course, it is only a variation. It is called "Nebuchadnezzar," I suppose, because you could not easily find a more impossible name with which to play it.

You choose a name—and unless your audience is very patient, it had better be a short one—of some well-known character. Say, Job. Then you act in dumb show a character beginning with J, then one beginning with O, then one beginning with B. Then you act Job, and the spectators guess that Job is what you mean, and applaud kindly. That is all. Light-hearted people, with imagination, can get a lot of fun out of it.

Bob Lester was having a birthday party—his mother and sister and about twenty intimate friends squashed into the little flat at Hammersmith. Everybody was either a writer or a painter or an actor of sorts, or did something or the other quite entertaining for a living, and they were fairly well accustomed to amusing themselves with sing-songs and games. They could fool wittily and behave like children, and get merry on invisible quantities of claret-cup, and they were all rather clever and all knew each other extremely well. Cyril Markham felt slightly out of it, though they were all exceedingly nice to him and tried to cheer him up. It was nearly six months since Jane had died, and though they all sympathised terribly with him for her loss (they had all loved Jane), he felt that he and they were, and ever would be, strangers and aliens to one another. Dear Jane. They had found it hard to forgive him for marrying her and taking her away to Cornwall. It was terrible that she should have died—

132

only two years later—of gastro-enteritis. Jane would have entered into all their jokes. She would have played absurd games with them and given an exquisite personal grace to the absurdest. Markham could never do that. He felt stiff, awkward, cruelly self-conscious. When Bob suggested "Nebuchadnezzar," he courteously asked Markham to make one of his team of actors. Too kind; too kind. Markham said he preferred to look on, and Bob, sighing with relief, went on to pick up a side of trusted veterans.

The two front rooms of the flat had been thrown into one by the opening of the folding doors. Though it was November, the night was strangely close, and one of the three tall balconied windows overlooking the river had been thrown open. Across the smoke-filled room and over the heads of the guests, Markham could see the lights of the Surrey side dance in the river like tall Japanese lanterns. The smaller of the two rooms formed a stage for the players, and across the dividing doorway a pair of thick purple curtains had been hung. Outside, in the passage, the players scuffled backwards and forwards amid laughter. Waiting for the game to begin, Markham stared at the curtains. They were familiar. They were surely the curtains from his own Cornish cottage. Jane had hung them across the living room to screen off the dining part from the lounge part. How odd that Bob should have got them here. No, it wasn't. Bob had given Jane her curtains for a wedding-present, and this must be another pair. They were old ones, he knew. Damask of that quality wasn't made today.

Bob drew back the curtains, thrust out a dishevelled head, announced: "The Nebuchadnezzar has four letters," and disappeared again. In the distance was heard a vigorous bumping, and a voice called out, "There's a clothes-line in the kitchen!" Somebody standing near the door of the room switched off the lights, and the damask curtains were drawn aside for the acting of the first letter.

A Japanese screen at the back of the stage, above which appeared the head of Lavinia Forbes, elegantly attired in a silk scarf, bound round the forehead with a cricket-belt, caused Mrs. Lester, always precipitate, to exclaim, "Romeo and Juliet—balcony scene!" Everybody said "Hush," and the supposed Juliet, producing from behind the screen a mirror and lipstick, proceeded to make up her face in a very lavish manner. In the middle of this, her attention appeared to be distracted by something in the distance. She leaned over the screen and pointed eagerly in the direction of the landing, whence, indeed, some remarkable noises were proceeding. To her, amid frenzied applause, entered, on hands and knees, the twins, Peter and Paul Barnaby, got up regardless of expense in fur coats worn with the hair outside, and champing furiously upon the clothes-line. Attached to them by stout luggage-straps was a basket-chair, which, after ominous hesitation and creaking between the door-posts, was propelled vigorously into the room by unseen hands, so that the charioteer—very gorgeous in scarlet dressing-gown, striped sash and military sabre, with a large gravy-strainer inverted upon his head—was nearly shot on to the backs of his steeds, and was heard to mutter an indignant "Steady on!" through his forest of crêpe beard. The lady, from behind the screen, apeared to harangue the driver, who replied with a vulgar and regrettable gesture. A further brief exchange of pantomime led to the appearance of two stout parties in bath-robes and turbans, who proceeded to hoist the lady bodily over the screen. Somebody said, "Look out!", the screen rocked and was hastily held up by one of the horses, and the victim was deposited on the floor with a thud, and promptly died with a considerable amount of twitching and gasping. The charioteer cracked his umbrella across the backs of his horses and was drawn round the room and off again in a masterly manner. A loud barking from the wings heralded the arrival of three savage door-mats, who, after snuffling a good deal over the corpse, started to devour it in large gulps as the curtain fell.

This spirited presentation was loudly cheered, and offered little difficulty to the spectators.

"Jezebel, of course," said Tony Withers.

"Or Jehu," said Miss Holroyd.

"I do hope Lavvie wasn't hurt," said Mrs. Lester. "She came down an awful bump."

"Well, the first letter's J, anyhow," said Patricia Martin. "I liked the furious driving."

"Bob looked simply marvellous," added Bice Taylor, who was sitting just behind Mrs. Lester. Then, turning to Markham:

"But one does so miss darling Jane. She loved acting and dressing-up, didn't she? She was the gayest wee bit of a thing."

Markham nodded. Yes, Jane had always been an actress. And her gaiety had been somehow proof against the solitude of their cottage and his own morose temper. She always would sing

134

as she went about the house, and it had got so terribly on his nerves that he had snarled at her. He had always wondered what she found to sing about. Until, of course, he had found those letters, and then he had known.

He wished he had not come to this party. He was out of place here, and Tom Deering knew it and was sneering at him. He could see Tom's dark, sardonic face in the far corner against the door. He must be remembering things too, the sleek devil. Well he, Markham, had put a spoke in Deering's wheel anyhow, that was one comfort.

In spite of the open window, the room was stifling. What did they need with that enormous fire? The blood was pumping violently through his brain—he felt as though the top of his head would lift off. There were far too many people for the place. And they made so much noise. Something fearfully elaborate must be in preparation, to judge by the long wait and the running of feet on the landing. This was a tedious game.

The lights clicked off once more, and a voice announced "Second letter," as the curtains drew apart.

The apparition of Betty Sander in an exiguous pair of pale pink cami-bockers, with her hair down her back, embracing the deeply-embarrassed George P. Brewster in a tight-fitting gent's union suit, was hailed with happy laughter.

"The bedroom scene!" exclaimed Mrs. Lester, prematurely as usual. After an affecting exchange of endearments, the couple separated, George retiring to the far side of the piano to dig industriously with the coal-scoop, while Betty seated herself on the sofa and combed her hair with her fingers. Presently there advanced through the door the crimson face of Peter Barnaby, worming along at ground-level, with energetically working tongue. Behind it trailed an endless length of green table-cloth, whose slow, humping progress proclaimed the presence within it of yet another human engine—probably the second Barnaby twin. This procession advanced to the sofa and rubbed itself against Betty's leg—then reared itself up rather awkwardly in its mufflings and jerked its head at the aspidistra on the occasional table. Betty registered horror and refusal, but presently yielded and took from amid the leaves of the aspidistra a large apple, which she proceeded to eat with expressions of enjoyment, while the combined Barnabys retired behind the sofa. At this moment, George, wiping the honest sweat from his brow, returned from his labours, with the coal-scoop over his shoulder.

On seeing what Betty was about, he dropped the scoop and flung his arms to heaven. After some solicitation, however, he accepted his share of the feast, carefully polishing the apple first on his union suit. After this, he appeared to be suddenly struck by the indelicacy of the union suit and, moreover, proceeded to point the finger of scorn and reprimand at the cami-bockers. Betty, dissolved in tears, rushed to the aspidistra, tore off two large leaves ("Oh, the poor plant!" cried Mrs. Lester) and attached them severally, with string, about the waists of George and herself. Then, from behind the Japanese screen appeared the awful presence of Bob, in the scarlet dressing-gown and a bright blue table-cloth, and wearing a large saucepan-lid tied to the back of his head. An immense beard of cotton-wool added majesty to his countenance. The delinquents fell flat on their faces, and the curtains were flung to amid rejoicings.

"Now, was that Adam or Eve?" demanded Miss Holroyd.

"I think it was Eve," said somebody. "Then the whole word might be Jehu."

"But we've had Jehu."

"No, we haven't, that was Jezebel."

"But they can't be giving us Jehu and Jezebel again."

"JE, JA, JE, JA . . ."

The lights were on again now. Queer, how white and unnatural all their faces looked. Like masks. Markham's fingers pulled at his collar. Jezebel, Adam—wanton woman, deluded man. J, A, Jane. So long as the whoredoms of thy mother Jezebel and her witchcrafts are so many. If Deering had known that those letters had been found, would he be smiling like that? He did know. That was why he was smiling that dark smile. He knew, and he had put Bob up to this. Let the galled jade wince. Jade; J, A, Jade. J, A, Jane. Jade, Jane, Jezebel. The dogs shall eat Jezebel in the portion of Jezreel. Dogs. Dogging his footsteps. The Hound of Heaven with a saucepan-lid on his head. Jehovah. JAH. J, A, Jane. . . .

The lights went out.

They had draped a sheet over some chairs to form a little tent. At the door sat Bob, in the dressing-gown and the white beard, but without the saucepan-lid. Paul Barnaby, wearing a handkerchief over his head and a short tunic with a sash round the waist, presented him with frugal meal of two dried figs on a plate. In front of the tent stood a tin bath full of water and surrounded with aspidistras.

A noise of mingled instruments heralded the approach of George, in an Oriental costume of surpassing magnificence and a head-dress made of a gilt waste-paper basket. Attended by a train of Oriental followers, he approached Bob, and indicated, with gestures of distress, some livid patches of flour on his face and arms. Bob examined him carefully, clapped him cordially on the shoulder and indicated the tin bath, going through a pantomime of washing. George seemed to be overcome with indignation and contempt. He kicked the bath scornfully and spat vulgarly into the aspidistras. Then, shaking his fist at Bob, he stalked away in high dudgeon in the direction of the piano.

"Hi!" shouted Tony Withers, "where's your chariot, old man?"

"Shut up!" returned George, disconcerted, "we can't do that horse business over again."

Lavinia, modestly attired in a kind of yashmak, now took the stage. Kneeling at George's feet, she gently expostulated with him. The other Oriental followers joined their petitions to hers, and presently his frown relaxed. Returning to the tin bath, and being solemnly supplied with a piece of soap and a loofah, he scrubbed the flour from his face. On observing the effect in a shaving-mirror, he was transported with joy, prostrated himself before Bob, and offered him a handsome collection of cushion-covers and drawing-room ornaments. These being refused, he went away rejoicing, followed, surreptitiously, by Paul Barnaby. Bob appeared gratified by this result, and was just sitting down to read the *Evening News* in his tent when he observed Paul slinking back through the door with an armful of cushion-covers. Overcome with righteous anger he rose to his feet and, dexterously drawing from behind the newspaper a bag of flour, flung it over Paul's face, thus closing the episode.

Markham vaguely heard the applause, but his eyes were fixed on the purple curtains. He knew them so well. They were heavy and swung into thick, rich folds. Jane had adored those curtains. He had always said they were dark and gloomy, but she would hear nothing against them. Nowadays people lived so publicly, behind thin casement cloth and stuff like that; but that old-fashioned damask was made for concealment. Curtains like those kept their secrets for ever.

Bice Taylor spoke almost in his ear.

"I don't believe it's either Naaman or Elisha. I think it's Abigail, don't you? The little maid, you know. Not so obvious.

It might be J, E, A, something. Jean somebody. Or the French Jean."

J for Jezebel, A for Adam, N for Naaman the leper. J, A, N, Jane, Janitor, January. This was November. Jane died in June.

"What nonsense—Abigail was somebody quite different. It's Gehazi, of course."

"Gehazi? My dear child—there's no name in four letters beginning JEG or JAG."

"Yes, there is. There's JAGO."

"Who's Jago?"

"I don't know. Somebody wrote a book called *John Jago's Ghost*. I do know that."

"It isn't a book. It's a short story by Wilkie Collins."

"Oh! is it? I only remember the title."

"But who was Jago, anyway?"

"I don't know, except that he had a ghost. And what was the point of bringing Gehazi in if it isn't Gehazi?"

"Oh, that's just to make it more difficult."

Gehazi—Naaman—He went out from before him a leper as white as snow. One felt like a leper among all these people who hated one. Leper. See the leopard-dog-thing something at his side, a leer and a lie in every eye. It was so queer that nobody would look a him. They looked round and over him at each other. That was because he was a leper—but they need never know that unless he told them. He had never noticed the pattern on the curtains before, but now the strong light showed it up—damask, damascened like a sword, damn the lot of them. How hot it was, and what a stupid oaf Bob Lester looked, playing childish games. But it was really horrible, the way these people pretended not to know that it was J, A, N, Jane. They did know, really, all the time and were wondering how long he would stick it. Let them wonder! All the same, he must think out what to do when it came to the complete word. J, A, N. Of course, if the last letter wasn't E . . . but it was bound to be E. Well, it would be a relief in a way, because then he would know that they knew.

The fourth scene was, for a change, mediaeval and brief. Betty in white robes, her long hair loosed, oared on the spare-room mattress across the parquet to where Arthur's Court stood grouped by the piano. Bob, simply but effectively armed in corrugated cardboard, weeping fat tears out of a sponge.

138

"Well, *that's* obvious," said Mrs. Lester. "The Lady of Shal-lott. Now, dear me, what can the word be?"

"Oh, *dear* Mrs. Lester. Not. Shallott. It's Lancelot and Thingummy."

"Oh, Lancelot, is it?"

"Or, of course, Thingummy."

"Especially Thingummy," said Deering.

"Have you guessed it, Tom?"

"Yes, of course. Haven't you?"

"Well, I *think* so, but I'm not absolutely certain."

"You mustn't say until the end."

"No, all right."

Oh, yes, thought Markham. Deering would have guessed it, of course. Lancelot and Elaine. Elaine the lovable. Jane, Elaine. J, A, N, E, Jane. But it was all wrong, because Elaine was pure and faithful and died of love. Died. That was the point. Elaine was dead. Jane was dead. Jane, Elaine as Jane had lain.

He fixed his eyes on the damask curtains. There was one point where they did not quite meet, and the light from the stage showed through. Somebody called "Are you ready?" and turned off the switch on the side of the spectators. Markham could not see them any longer, but he could hear them breath-ing and rustling about him, packed close like wolves, pressing in upon him. The point of light still shone between the curtains. It grew larger, and glowed more intensely, yet as though from an enormous distance.

Then, very slowly this time, and in absolute silence, the curtains parted. The whole word at last.

They had done a wonderful piece of staging this time. He recognised every object, though the blaze of the electric globe had been somehow subdued. There was the bed and the dressing-table and the wardrobe with its tall glass door, and the low casement on the right. It was hot, and the scent of the syringa —philadelphus, the books said, but Jane called it syringa—came billowing in from the garden in thick puffs. The girl on the bed was asleep. Her face was hidden, turned to the wall. Dying people always turned to the wall. Too bad to have to lie in June, with the scent of the syringa coming in through the window and the nightingale singing so loudly. Did they do that with a bird-whistle, or was it a gramophone record?

Somebody was moving in the shadows. He had opened the door very gently. There was a glass of lemonade on the table by the bed. It chinked against the bottle as he picked it up, but the girl did not move. He walked right forward till he stood directly beneath the light. His head was bent down as he shot the white powder into the glass and stirred it with a spoon. He went back to the bedside, walking like Agag, delicately. A, G, A, G, Adam and Gehazi. Jezebel, Adam, Naaman, Elaine, J, A, N, E. He touched the girl on the shoulder and she stirred a little. He put one arm behind her shoulders and held the glass to her lips. It clinked again as he set it down empty. Then he kissed her. He went out, shutting the door.

He had never known such silence. He could not even hear the wolf-pack breathing. He was alone in the room with the girl who lay on the bed. And now she was moving. The sheet slipped from her shoulders to her breast, from her breast to her waist. She was rising to her knees, lifting herself up to face him over the footboard of the bed—gold hair, sweat-streaked forehead, eyes dark with fear and pain, black hollow of the mouth, and the glittering line of white teeth in the fallen jaw.

JANE!

Had he cried out, or had they? The room was full of light and noise, but his voice rose above it.

"Jane, Jezebel! I killed her. I poisoned her. Jane, jade, Jezebel. The doctor never knew, but she knew, and he knew, and now you all know. Get out! damn you! curse you! Let me go!"

Chairs were falling, people were shouting, clutching at him. He smashed a fist into a silly, gaping face. He was on the balcony. He was fighting for the balustrade. The lights on the Surrey side were like tall Japanese lanterns. He was over. The black water leapt to meet him. Cataracts, roaring.

It had all happened so quickly that the actors knew nothing about it. As Tom Deering pulled off his coat to dive after Markham and Mrs. Lester rushed to telephone the river police George's voice announced "The Whole Word," and the curtains were flung open to display the tent of JAEL.

THE INSPIRATION OF MR. BUDD

" £500 REWARD

"THE 'EVENING MESSENGER,' ever anxious to further the ends of justice, has decided to offer the above reward to any person who shall give information leading to the arrest of the man, William Strickland, alias Bolton, who is wanted by the police in connection with the murder of the late Emma Strickland at 59 Acacia Crescent, Manchester.

"DESCRIPTION OF THE WANTED MAN.

"The following is the official description of William Strickland: Age 43; height 6 ft. 1 or 2 in.; complexion rather dark; hair silver-grey and abundant, may dye same; full grey moustache and beard, may now be clean-shaven; eyes light grey, rather close-set; hawk nose; teeth strong and white, displays them somewhat prominently when laughing, left upper eyetooth stopped with gold; left thumb-nail disfigured by a recent blow.

"Speaks in rather loud voice; quick, decisive manner. Good address.

"May be dressed in a grey or dark blue lounge suit, with stand-up collar (size 15) and soft felt hat.

"Absconded 5th inst., and may have left, or will endeavour to leave, the country."

Mr. Budd read the description through carefully once again and sighed. It was in the highest degree unlikely that William Strickland should choose his small and unsuccessful saloon, out of all the barbers' shops in London, for a haircut or a shave, still less for "dyeing same"; even if he was in London, which Mr. Budd saw no reason to suppose.

Three weeks had gone by since the murder, and the odds were a hundred to one that William Strickland had already left a country too eager with its offer of free hospitality. Nevertheless, Mr. Budd committed the description, as well as he could, to memory. It was a chance—just as the Great Crossword Tournament had been a chance, just as the Ninth Rainbow Ballot had been a chance, and the Bunko Poster Ballot, and the Monster Treasure Hunt organised by the *Evening Clarion*. Any headline with money in it could attract Mr. Budd's fascinated eye in these lean days, whether it offered a choice between fifty thousand pounds down and ten pounds a week for life, or merely a modest hundred or so.

It may seem strange, in an age of shingling and bingling, Mr. Budd should look enviously at Complete Lists of Prizewinners. Had not the hairdresser across the way, who only last year had eked out his mean ninepences with the yet meaner profits on cheap cigarettes and comic papers, lately bought out the greengrocer next door, and engaged a staff of exquisitely coiffed assistants to adorn his new "Ladies' Hairdressing Department" with its purple and orange curtains, its two rows of gleaming marble basins, and an apparatus like a Victorian chandelier for permanent waving?

Had he not installed a large electric sign surrounded by a scarlet border that ran round and round perpetually, like a kitten chasing its own cometary tail? Was it not his sandwich-man even now patrolling the pavement with a luminous announcement of Treatment and Prices? And was there not at this moment an endless stream of young ladies hastening into those heavily-perfumed parlours in the desperate hope of somehow getting a shampoo and a wave "squeezed in" before closing-time?

If the reception clerk shook a regretful head, they did not think of crossing the road to Mr. Budd's dimly-lighted window. They made an appointment for days ahead and waited patiently, anxiously fingering the bristly growth at the back of the neck and the straggly bits behind the ears that so soon got out of hand.

Day after day Mr. Budd watched them flit in and out of the rival establishment, willing, praying even, in a vague, ill-directed manner, that some of them would come over to him; but they never did.

And yet Mr. Budd knew himself to be the finer artist. He had seen shingles turned out from over the way that he would never have countenanced, let alone charged three shillings and sixpence for. Shingles with an ugly hard line at the nape, shingles which were a slander on the shape of a good head or brutally emphasised the weak points of an ugly one; hurried, conscienceless shingles, botched work, handed over on a crowded afternoon to a girl who had only served a three years' apprenticeship and to whom the final mysteries of "tapering" were a sealed book.

And then there was the "tinting"—his own pet subject, which he had studied *con amore*—if only those too-sprightly matrons would come to him! He would gently dissuade them from that dreadful mahogany dye that made them look like metallic Robots—he would warn them against that widely advertised preparation which was so incalculable in its effects; he would use the cunning skill which long experience had matured in him —tint them with the infinitely delicate art which conceals itself.

Yet nobody came to Mr. Budd but the navvies and the young loungers and the men who plied their trade beneath the naphthaflares in Wilton Street.

And why could not Mr. Budd also have burst out into marble and electricity and swum to fortune on the rising tide?

The reason is very distressing, and, as it fortunately has no bearing on the story, shall be told with merciful brevity.

Mr. Budd had a younger brother, Richard, whom he had promised his mother to look after. In happier days Mr. Budd had owned a flourishing business in their native town of Northampton, and Richard had been a bank clerk. Richard had got into bad ways (poor Mr. Budd blamed himself dreadfully for this). There had been a sad affair with a girl, and a horrid series of affairs with bookmakers, and then Richard had tried to mend bad with worse by taking money from the bank. You need to be very much more skilful than Richard to juggle successfully with bank ledgers.

The bank manager was a hard man of the old school: he prosecuted. Mr. Budd paid the bank and the bookmakers, and saw the girl through her trouble while Richard was in prison, and paid for their fares to Australia when he came out, and gave them something to start life on.

But it took all the profits of the hairdressing business, and he couldn't face all the people in Northampton any more, who had known him all his life. So he had run to vast London, the refuge of all who shrink from the eyes of their neighbours, and bought this little shop in Pimlico, which had done fairly well, until the

143

new fashion which did so much for other hairdressing businesses killed it for lack of capital.

That is why Mr. Budd's eye was so painfully fascinated by headlines with money in them.

He put the newspaper down, and as he did so, caught sight of his own reflection in the glass and smiled, for he was not without a sense of humour. He did not look quite the man to catch a brutal murderer single-handed. He was well on in the middle forties—a trifle paunchy, with fluffy pale hair, getting a trifle thin on top (partly hereditary, partly worry, that was), five feet six at most, and soft-handed, as a hairdresser must be.

Even razor in hand, he would hardly be a match for William Strickland, height six feet one or two, who had so ferociously battered his old aunt to death, so butcherly hacked her limb from limb, so horribly disposed of her remains in the copper. Shaking his head dubiously, Mr. Budd advanced to the door, to cast a forlorn eye at the busy establishment over the way, and nearly ran into a bulky customer who dived in rather precipitately.

"I beg your pardon, sir," murmured Mr. Budd, fearful of alienating ninepence; "just stepping out for a breath of fresh air, sir. Shave, sir?"

The large man tore off his overcoat without waiting for Mr. Budd's obsequious hands.

"Are you prepared to die?" he demanded abruptly.

The question chimed in so alarmingly with Mr. Budd's thoughts about murder that for a moment it quite threw him off his professional balance.

"I beg your pardon, sir," he stammered, and in the same moment decided that the man must be a preacher of some kind. He looked rather like it, with his odd, light eyes, his bush of fiery hair and short, jutting chin-beard. Perhaps he even wanted a subscription. That would be hard, when Mr. Budd had already set him down as ninepence, or, with tip, possibly even a shilling.

"Do you do dyeing?" said the man impatiently.

"Oh!" said Mr. Budd, relieved, "yes, sir, certainly, sir."

A stroke of luck, this. Dyeing meant quite a big sum—his mind soared to seven-and-sixpence.

"Good," said the man, sitting down and allowing Mr. Budd to put an apron about his neck. (He was safely gathered in now—he could hardly dart away down the street with a couple of yards of white cotton flapping from his shoulders.)

"Fact is," said the man, "my young lady doesn't like red hair. She says it's conspicuous. The other young ladies in her firm make jokes about it. So, as she's a good bit younger than I am, you see, I like to oblige her, and I was thinking perhaps it could be changed into something quieter, what? Dark brown, now—that's the colour she has a fancy to. What do *you* say?"

It occurred to Mr. Budd that the young ladies might consider this abrupt change of coat even funnier that the original colour, but in the interests of business he agreed that dark brown would be very becoming and a great deal less noticeable than red. Besides, very likely there was no young lady. A woman, he knew, will say frankly that she wants different coloured hair for a change, or just to try, or because she fancies it would suit her, but if a man is going to do a silly thing he prefers, if possible, to shuffle the responsibility on to someone else.

"Very well, then," said the customer, "go ahead. And I'm afraid the beard will have to go. My young lady doesn't like beards."

"A great many young ladies don't, sir," said Mr. Budd. "They're not so fashionable nowadays as they used to be. It's very fortunate that you can stand a clean shave very well, sir. You have just the chin for it."

"Do you think so?" said the man, examining himself a little anxiously. "I'm glad to hear it."

"Will you have the moustache off as well, sir?"

"Well, no—no, I think I'll stick to that as long as I'm allowed to, what?" He laughed loudly, and Mr. Budd approvingly noted well-kept teeth and a gold stopping. The customer was obviously ready to spend money on his personal appearance.

In fancy, Mr. Budd saw this well-off and gentlemanly customer advising all his friends to visit "his man"—"wonderful fellow—wonderful—round at the back of Victoria Station—you'd never find it by yourself—only a little place, but he knows what he's about—I'll write it down for you." It was imperative that there should be no fiasco. Hair-dyes were awkward things —there had been a case in the paper lately.

"I see you have been using a tint before, sir," said Mr. Budd with respect. "Could you tell me——?"

"Eh?" said the man. "Oh, yes—well, fact is, as I said, my fiancée's a good bit younger than I am. As I expect you can see I began to go grey early—my father was just the same—all our family—so I had it touched up—streaky bits restored, you see.

145

But she doesn't take to the colour, so I thought, if I have to dye it at all, why not a colour she *does* fancy while we're about it, what?"

It is a common jest among the unthinking that hairdressers are garrulous. This is their wisdom. The hairdresser hears many secrets and very many lies. In his discretion he occupies his unruly tongue with the weather and the political situation, lest, restless with inaction, it plunge unbridled into a mad career of inconvenient candour.

Lightly holding forth upon the caprices of the feminine mind, Mr. Budd subjected his customer's locks to the scrutiny of trained eye and fingers. Never—never in the process of nature could hair of that texture and quality have been red. It was naturally black hair, prematurely turned, as some black hair will turn, to a silvery grey. However that was none of his business. He elicited the information he really needed—the name of the dye formerly used, and noted that he would have to be careful. Some dyes do not mix kindly with other dyes.

Chatting pleasantly, Mr. Budd lathered his customer, removed the offending beard, and executed a vigorous shampoo, preliminary to the dyeing process. As he wielded the roaring drier, he reviewed Wimbledon, the Silk-tax and the Summer Time Bill—at that moment threatened with sudden strangulation—and passed naturally on to the Manchester murder.

"The police seem to have given it up as a bad job," said the man.

"Perhaps the reward will liven things up a bit," said Mr. Budd, the thought being naturally uppermost in his mind.

"Oh, there's a reward, is there? I hadn't seen that."

"It's in tonight's paper, sir. Maybe you'd like to have a look at it."

"Thanks, I should."

Mr. Budd left the drier to blow the fiery bush of hair at its own wild will for a moment, while he fetched the *Evening Messenger*. The stranger read the paragraph carefully and Mr. Budd, watching him in the glass, after the disquieting manner of his craft, saw him suddenly draw back his left hand, which was resting carelessly on the arm of the chair, and thrust it under the apron.

But not before Mr. Budd had seen it. Not before he had taken conscious note of the horny, misshapen thumb-nail. Many people had such an ugly mark, Mr. Budd told himself hurriedly

146

—there was his friend, Bert Webber, who had sliced the top of his thumb right off in a motor-cycle chain—his nail looked very much like that.

The man glanced up, and the eyes of his reflection became fixed on Mr. Budd's face with a penetrating scrutiny—a horrid warning that the real eyes were steadfastly interrogating the reflection of Mr. Budd.

"Not but what," said Mr. Budd, "the man is safe out of the country by now, I reckon. They've put it off too late."

The man laughed.

"I reckon they have," he said. Mr. Budd wondered whether many men with smashed left thumbs showed a gold left upper eye-tooth. Probably there were hundreds of people like that going about the country. Likewise with silver-grey hair ("may dye same") and aged about forty-three. Undoubtedly.

Mr. Budd folded up the drier and turned off the gas. Mechanically he took up a comb and drew it through the hair that never, never in the process of Nature had been that fiery red.

There came back to him, with an accuracy which quite unnerved him, the exact number and extent of the brutal wounds inflicted upon the Manchester victim—an elderly lady, rather stout, she had been. Glaring through the door, Mr. Budd noticed that his rival over the way had closed. The streets were full of people. How easy it would be——

"Be as quick as you can, won't you?" said the man, a little impatiently, but pleasantly enough. "It's getting late. I'm afraid it will keep you overtime."

"Not at all, sir," said Mr. Budd. "It's of no consequence—not the least."

No—if he tried to bolt out of the door, his terrible customer would leap upon him, drag him back, throttle his cries, and then with one frightful blow like the one he had smashed in his aunt's skull with——

Yet surely Mr. Budd was in a position of advantage. A decided man would do it. He would be out in the street before the customer could disentangle himself from the chair. Mr. Budd began to edge round towards the door.

"What's the matter?" said the customer.

"Just stepping out to look at the time, sir," said Mr. Budd, meekly pausing. (Yet he might have done it then, if he only had the courage to make the first swift step that would give the game away.)

147

"It's five-and-twenty past eight," said the man, "by tonight's broadcast. I'll pay extra for the overtime."

"Not on any account," said Mr. Budd. Too late now, he couldn't make another effort. He vividly saw himself tripping on the threshold—falling—the terrible fist lifted to smash him into a pulp. Or perhaps, under the familiar white apron, the disfigured hand was actually clutching a pistol.

Mr. Budd retreated to the back of the shop, collecting his materials. If only he had been quicker—more like a detective in a book—he would have observed that thumb-nail, that tooth, put two and two together, and run out to give the alarm while the man's beard was wet and soapy and his face buried in the towel. Or he could have dabbed lather in his eyes—nobody could possibly commit a murder or even run away down the street with his eyes full of soap.

Even now—Mr. Budd took down a bottle, shook his head and put it back on the shelf—even now, was it really too late? Why could he not take a bold course? He had only to open a razor, go quietly up behind the unsuspecting man and say in a firm, loud, convincing voice: "William Strickland, put up your hands. Your life is at my mercy. Stand up till I take your gun away. Now walk straight out to the nearest policeman." Surely, in his position, that was what Sherlock Holmes would do.

But as Mr. Budd returned with a little trayful of requirements, it was borne in upon him that he was not of the stuff of which great man-hunters are made. For he could not seriously see that attempt "coming off." Because if he held the razor to the man's throat and said: "Put up your hands," the man would probably merely catch him by the wrists and take the razor away. And greatly as Mr. Budd feared his customer unarmed, he felt it would be a perfect crescendo of madness to put a razor into his hands.

Or, supposing he said, "Put up your hands," and the man just said, "I won't." What was he to do next? To cut his throat then and there would be murder, even if Mr. Budd could possibly have brought himself to do such a thing. They could not remain there, fixed in one position, till the boy came to do out the shop in the morning.

Perhaps the policeman would notice the light on and the door unfastened and come in? Then he would say, "I congratulate you, Mr. Budd, on having captured a very dangerous criminal." But supposing the policeman didn't happen to notice—and Mr.

Budd would have to stand all the time, and he would get exhausted and his attention would relax, and then——

After all, Mr. Budd wasn't called upon to arrest the man himself. "Information leading to arrest"—those were the words. He would be able to tell them the wanted man had been there, that he would now have dark brown hair and moustache and no beard. He might even shadow him when he left—he might—

It was at this moment that the Great Inspiration came to Mr. Budd.

As he fetched a bottle from the glass-fronted case he remembered, with odd vividness, an old-fashioned wooden paper-knife that had belonged to his mother. Between sprigs of blue forget-me-not, hand-painted, it bore the inscription "Knowledge is Power."

A strange freedom and confidence were vouchsafed to Mr. Budd; his mind was alert; he removed the razors with an easy, natural movement, and made nonchalant conversation as he skilfully applied the dark-brown tint.

The streets were less crowded when Mr. Budd let his customer out. He watched the tall figure cross Grosvenor Place and climb on to a 24 bus.

"But that was only his artfulness," said Mr. Budd, as he put on his hat and coat and extinguished the lights carefully, "he'll take another at Victoria, like as not, and be making tracks from Charing Cross or Waterloo."

He closed the shop door, shook it, as was his wont, to make sure that the lock had caught properly, and in his turn made his way, by means of a 24, to the top of Whitehall.

The policeman was a little condescending at first when Mr. Budd demanded to see "somebody very high up," but finding the little barber insist so earnestly that he had news of the Manchester murderer, and that there wasn't any time to lose, he consented to pass him through.

Mr. Budd was interviewed first by an important-looking inspector in uniform, who listened very politely to his story and made him repeat very carefully about the gold tooth and the thumb-nail and the hair which had been black before it was grey or red and was now dark-brown.

The inspector then touched a bell, and said, "Perkins, I think Sir Andrew would like to see this gentleman at once," and he was taken to another room, where sat a very shrewd, genial gentleman in mufti, who heard him with even greater attention,

149

and called in another inspector to listen too, and to take down a very exact description of—yes, surely the undoubted William Strickland as he now appeared.

"But there's one thing more," said Mr. Budd—"and I'm sure to goodness," he added, "I hope, sir, it is the right man, because if it isn't it'll be the ruin of me——"

He crushed his soft hat into an agitated ball as he leant across the table, breathlessly uttering the story of his great professional betrayal.

"Tzee—z-z-z—tzee—tzee—z-z—tzee—z-z——"
"Dzoo—dz-dz-dz—dzoo—dz—dzoo—dzoo—dz——"
"Tzee—z—z."

The fingers of the wireless operator on the packet *Miranda* bound for Ostend moved swiftly as they jotted down the messages of the buzzing mosquito-swarms.

One of them made him laugh.

"The Old Man'd better have this, I suppose," he said.

The Old Man scratched his head when he read and rang a little bell for the steward. The steward ran down to the little round office where the purser was counting out his money and checking it before he locked it away for the night. On receiving the Old Man's message, the purser put the money quickly into the safe, picked up the passenger list and departed aft. There was a short consultation, and the bell was rung again—this time to summon the head steward.

"Tzee—z-z—tzeez-z-z—tzee—tzee—z—tzee."

All down the Channel, all over the North Sea, up to the Mersey Docks, out into the Atlantic soared the busy mosquito-swarms. In ship after ship the wireless operator sent his message to the captain, the captain sent for the purser, the purser sent for the head steward and the head steward called his staff about him. Huge liners, little packets, destroyers, sumptuous private yachts—every floating thing that carried aerials—every port in England, France, Holland, Germany, Denmark, Norway, every police centre that could interpret the mosquito message, heard, between laughter and excitement, the tale of Mr. Budd's betrayal. Two Boy Scouts at Croydon, practising their Morse with a home-made valve set, decoded it laboriously into an exercise book.

"Cripes," said Jim to George, "what a joke? D'you think they'll get the beggar?"

The *Miranda* docked at Ostend at 7 a.m. A man burst hurriedly into the cabin where the wireless operator was just taking off his headphones.

"Here!" he cried; "this is to go. There's something up and the Old Man's sent over for the police. The Consul's coming on board."

The wireless operator groaned, and switched on his valves.

"Tzee—z—tzee——" a message to the English police.

"Man on board answering to description. Ticket booked name of Watson. Has locked himself in cabin and refuses to come out. Insists on having hairdresser sent out to him. Have communicated Ostend police. Await instructions."

The Old Man with sharp words and authoritative gestures cleared a way through the excited little knot of people gathered about First Class Cabin No. 36. Several passengers had got wind of "something up." Magnificently he herded them away to the gangway with their bags and suitcases. Sternly he bade the stewards and the boy, who stood gaping with his hands full of breakfast dishes, to stand away from the door. Terribly he commanded them to hold their tongues. Four or five sailors stood watchfully at his side. In the restored silence, the passenger in No. 36 could be heard pacing up and down the narrow cabin, moving things, clattering, splashing water.

Presently came steps overhead. Somebody arrived, with a message. The Old Man nodded. Six pairs of Belgian police boots came tip-toeing down the companion. The Old Man glanced at the official paper held out to him and nodded again.

"Ready?"

"Yes."

The Old Man knocked at the door of No. 36.

"Who it is?" cried a harsh, sharp voice.

"The barber is here, sir, that you sent for."

"Ah!!" There was relief in the tone. "Send him in alone, if you please. I—I have had an accident."

"Yes, sir."

At the sound of the bolt being cautiously withdrawn, the Old Man stepped forward. The door opened a chink, and was slammed to again, but the Old Man's boot was firmly wedged against the jamb. The policemen surged forward. There was a yelp and a shot which smashed harmlessly through the window of the first-class saloon, and the passenger was brought out.

151

"Strike me pink!" shrieked the boy, "strike me pink if he ain't gone green in the night!"

Green!!

Not for nothing had Mr. Budd studied the intricate mutual reactions of chemical dyes. In the pride of his knowledge he had set a mark on his man, to mark him out from all the billions of this overpopulated world. Was there a port in all Christendom where a murderer might slip away, with every hair on him green as a parrot—green moustache, green eyebrows, and that thick, springing shock of hair, vivid, flaring mid-summer green?

Mr. Budd got his £500. The *Evening Messenger* published the full story of his great betrayal. He trembled, fearing this sinister fame. Surely no one would ever come to him again.

On the next morning an enormous blue limousine rolled up to his door, to the immense admiration of Wilton Street. A lady, magnificent in musquash and diamonds, swept into the saloon.

"You *are* Mr. Budd, aren't you?" she cried. "The *great* Mr. Budd? Isn't it *too* wonderful? And now, *dear* Mr. Budd, you *must* do me a favour. You must dye my hair green, *at once*. *Now*. I want to be able to say I'm the *very first* to be done by *you*. I'm the Duchess of Winchester, and that awful Melcaster woman is chasing me down the street—the cat!"

If you want it done, I can give you the number of Mr. Budd's parlours in Bond Street. But I understand it is a terribly expensive process.

BLOOD SACRIFICE

IF things went on at this rate, John Scales would be a very rich man. Already he was a man to be envied, as any ignoramus might guess who passed the King's Theatre after 8 o'clock. Old Florrie, who had sat for so many years on the corner with her little tray of matches, could have given more than a guess, for what she didn't know about the King's was hardly worth knowing. When she had ceased to adorn its boards (thanks to a dreadful accident with a careless match and gauze draperies, that had left her with a scarred face and a withered arm) she had taken her stand near the theatre for old sake's sake, and she watched over its fortunes, still, like a mother. She knew, none better, how much money it held when it was playing to capacity, what its salary list was like, how much of its earnings went in permanent charges, and what the author's share of the box-office receipts was likely to amount to. Besides, everybody who went in or out by the stage-door came and had a word with Florrie. She shared good times and bad at the King's. She had lamented over lean days caused by slumps and talkie competition, shaken her head over perilous experiments into highbrow tragedy, waxed tearful and indignant over the disastrous period (now happily past) of the Scorer-Bitterby management, which had ended in a scandal, rejoiced when the energetic Mr. Garrick Drury, launching out into management after his tremendous triumph in the name-part of *The Wistful Harlequin*, had taken the old house over, reconditioned it inside and out (incidentally squeezing two more rows into the reconstructed pit) and voiced his optimistic determination to break the run of ill-luck ; and since then she had watched its steady soaring into prosperity on the well-tried wings of old-fashioned adventure and romance. Mr. Garrick Drury (Somerset House knew him as Obadiah Potts, but he was none the less good-looking for that) was an actor-manager of the sort Florrie understood; he followed his calling in the good old way, building his successes about his own glamorous personality, talking no nonsense about new schools of dramatic thought, and paying only lip-service to "team-work." He had had the luck to embark on his managerial career at a moment when the public had grown tired of gloomy Slav tragedies of repressed husbands, and human documents about drink and diseases, and was (in its own incoherent way) clamouring for a good, romantic story to cry about, with a romantic hero suffering torments of self-sacrifice through two-and-three-quarter acts and getting the girl in the last ten minutes. Mr. Drury (forty-two in the daylight, thirty-five in the lamplight and twenty-five or what you will in a blond wig and the spotlight) was well fitted by nature to acquire girls in this sacrificial manner, and had learnt the trick of so lacing nineteenth-century sentiment with twentieth-century nonchalance that the mixture went to the heads equally of Joan who worked in the office and Aunt Mabel up from the country.

And since Mr. Drury, leaping nightly from his Rolls saloon with that nervous and youthful alacrity that had been his most engaging asset for the past twenty years, always had time to bestow at least a smile and a friendly word on old Florrie, he affected her head and heart as much as anybody else's. Nobody was more delighted than Florrie to know that he had again found a winner in *Bitter Laurel*, now sweeping on to its 100th performance. Night by night she saluted with a satisfied chuckle each board as it appeared: "Pit Full," "Gallery Full," "Dress Circle Full," "Upper Circle Full," "Stalls Full," "Standing Room Only," "House Full." Set to run for ever, it was, and the faces that went in by the stage door looked merry and prosperous, as Florrie liked to see them.

As for the young man who had provided the raw material out of which Mr. Drury had built up this glittering monument of success, if he wasn't pleased, thought Florrie, he ought to be. Not that, in the ordinary way, one thought much about the author of a play—unless, of course, it was Shakespeare, who was different; compared with the cast, he was of small importance and rarely seen. But Mr. Drury had one day arrived arm-in-arm with a sulky-looking and ill-dressed youth whom he had introduced to Florrie, saying in his fine, generous way: "Here, John, you must know Florrie. She's our mascot—we

154

couldn't get on without her. Florrie, this is Mr. Scales, whose new play's going to make all our fortunes." Mr. Drury was never mistaken about plays; he had the golden touch. Certainly, in the last three months, Mr. Scales, though still sulky-looking, had become much better dressed.

On this particular night—Saturday, 15th April, when *Bitter Laurel* was giving its 96th performance to a full house after a packed matinée—Mr. Scales and Mr. Drury arrived together, in evening dress and, Florrie noted with concern, rather late. Mr. Drury would have to hurry, and it was tiresome of Mr. Scales to detain him, as he did, by arguing and expostulating upon the threshold. Not that Mr. Drury seemed put out. He was smiling (his smile, one-sided and slightly elfin in quality, was famous), and at last he said, with his hand (Mr. Drury's expressive hands were renowned) affectionately upon Mr. Scales's shoulder, "Sorry, old boy, can't stop now. Curtain must go up, you know. Come round and see me after the show—I'll have those fellows there." Then he vanished, still smiling the elfin smile and waving the expressive hand; and Mr. Scales, after hesitating a moment, had turned away and came down past Florrie's corner. He seemed to be still sulky and rather preoccupied, but, looking up, caught sight of Florrie and grinned at her. There was nothing elfin about Mr. Scales's smile, but it improved his face very much.

"Well, Florrie," said Mr. Scales, "we seem to be doing pretty well, financially speaking, don't we?"

Florrie eagerly agreed. "But there," she observed, "we're getting used to that. Mr. Drury's a wonderful man. It doesn't matter what he's in, they all come to see him. Of course," she added, remembering that this might not sound very kind, "he's very clever at picking the right play."

"Oh, yes," said Mr. Scales. "The play. I suppose the play has something to do with it. Not much, but something. Have you seen the play, Florrie?"

Yes, indeed, Florrie had. Mr. Drury was so kind, he always remembered to give Florrie a pass early on in the run, even if the house was ever so full.

"What did you think of it?" enquired Mr. Scales.

"I thought it was lovely," said Florrie. "I cried ever so. When he came back with only one arm and found his fiancée gone to the bad at a cocktail party——"

"Just so," said Mr. Scales.

155

"And the scene on the Embankment—lovely, I thought that was, when he rolls up his old army coat and says to the bobby, 'I will rest on my laurels'—that was a beautiful curtain line you gave him there, Mr. Scales. And the way he put it over——"

"Yes, rather," said Mr. Scales. "There's nobody like Drury for putting over that kind of a line."

"And when she came back to him and he wouldn't have her any more and then Lady Sylvia took him up and fell in love with him——"

"Yes, yes," said Mr. Scales. "You found that part moving?"

"Romantic," said Florrie. "And the scene between the two girls—that was splendid. All worked-up, it made you feel. And then in the end, when he took the one he really loved after all——"

"Sure-fire, isn't it?" said Mr. Scales. "Goes straight to the heart. I'm glad you think so, Florrie. Because, of course, quite apart from anything else, it's very good box-office."

"I believe you," said Florrie. "Your first play, isn't it? You're lucky to have it taken by Mr. Drury."

"Yes," said Mr. Scales, "I owe him a lot. Everybody says so, and it must be true. There are two fat gentlemen in astrakhan coats coming along tonight to settle about the film-rights. I'm a made man, Florrie, and that's always pleasant, particularly after five or six years of living hand-to-mouth. No fun in not having enough to eat, is there?"

"That there isn't," said Florrie, who knew all about it. "I'm ever so glad your luck's turned at last, dearie."

"Thank you," said Mr. Scales. "Have something to drink the health of the play." He fumbled in his breast-pocket. "Here you are. A green one and a brown one. Thirty bob. Thirty pieces of silver. Spend it on something you fancy, Florrie. It's the price of blood."

"What a thing to say!" exclaimed Florrie. "But you writing gentlemen will have a bit of a joke. And I know poor Mr. Milling, who wrote the book for *Pussycat, Pussycat* and *The Lipstick Girl* always used to say he sweated blood over every one of 'em."

A nice young gentleman, thought Florrie, as Mr. Scales passed on, but queer and, perhaps, a little bit difficult in his temper, for them that had to live with him. He had spoken very nicely about Mr. Drury, but there had been a moment when she had fancied that he was (as they said) registering sarcasm. And she

156

didn't quite like that joke about the thirty pieces of silver—that was New Testament, and New Testament (unlike Old) was blasphemous. It was like the difference between saying, "Oh, God!" (which nobody minded) and "Oh, Christ!" (which Florrie had never held with). Still, people said all kinds of things nowadays, and thirty bob was thirty bob; it was very kind of Mr. Scales.

Mr. John Scales, slouching along Shaftesbury Avenue and wondering how he was going to put in the next three hours or so, encountered a friend just turning out of Wardour Street. The friend was a tall, thin young man, with a shabby overcoat and a face, under a dilapidated soft hat, like a hungry hawk's. There was a girl with him.

"Hullo, Mollie!" said Scales. "Hullo, Sheridan!"

"Hullo!" said Sheridan. "Look who's here! The great man himself. London's rising dramatist. Sweet Scales of Old Drury."

"Cut it out," said Scales.

"Your show seems to be booming," went on Sheridan. "Congratulations. On the boom, I mean."

"God!" said Scales, "have you seen it? I did send you tickets."

"You did—it was kind of you to think of us amid your busy life. We saw the show. In these bargain-basement days, you've managed to sell your soul in a pretty good market."

"See here, Sheridan—it wasn't my fault. I'm just as sick as you are. Sicker. But like a fool I signed the contract without a controlling clause, and by the time Drury and his producer had finished mucking the script about——"

"He didn't sell himself," said the girl, "he was took advantage of, your worship."

"Pity," said Sheridan. "It was a good play—but he done her wrong. But," he added, glancing at Scales, "I take it you drink the champagne that she sends you. You're looking prosperous."

"Well," said Scales, "what do you expect me to do? Return the cheque with thanks?"

"Good lord, no," said Sheridan. "It's all right. Nobody's grudging you your luck."

"It's something, after all," said Scales defensively, "to get one's foot in at all. One can't always look a gift horse in the mouth."

157

"No," said Sheridan. "Good lord, I know that. Only I'm afraid you'll find this thing hang round your neck a bit if you want to go back to your own line. You know what the public is—it likes to get what it expects. Once you've made a name for sob-stuff, you're labelled for good—or bad."

"I know. Hell. Can't do anything about it, though. Come and have a drink."

But the others had an appointment to keep, and passed on their way. The encounter was typical. Damnation, thought Scales, savagely, turning in to the Criterion Bar, wasn't it enough to have had your decent play cut about and turned into the sort of thing that made you retch to listen to it, without your friends supposing you had acquiesced in the mutilation for the sake of making money?

He had been a little worried when he knew that George Philpotts (kindly, officious George, who always knew everybody) had sent *Bitter Laurel* to Drury. The very last management he himself would have selected; but also the very last management that would be likely to take so cynical and disillusioned a play. Miraculously, however, Drury had expressed himself as "dead keen" about it. There had been an interview with Drury, and Drury, damn his expressive eyes, had—yes, one had to admit it—Drury had "put himself across" with great success. He had been flattering, he had been charming. Scales had succumbed, as night by night pit and stalls and dress circle succumbed to the gracious manner and the elfin smile. "A grand piece—grand situations," Garrick Drury had said. "Of course, here and there it will need a little tidying up in production." Scales said modestly that he expected that—he knew very little about writing for the stage—he was a novelist—he was quite ready to agree to alterations, provided, naturally, nothing was done to upset the artistic unity of the thing. Mr. Garrick Drury was pained by the suggestion. As an artist himself, he should, of course, allow nothing inartistic to be done. Scales, overcome by Drury's manner, and by a flood of technicalities about sets and lighting and costing and casting poured out upon him by the producer, who was present at the interview, signed a contract giving the author a very handsome share of the royalties, and hardly noticed that he had left the management with full power to make any "reasonable" alterations to fit the play for production.

It was only gradually in the course of rehearsal, that he

discovered what was being done to his play. It was not merely that Mr. Drury had succeeded in importing into the lines given to him, as the war-shattered hero, a succulent emotionalism which was very far from the dramatist's idea of that embittered and damaged character. So much, one had expected. But the plot had slowly disintegrated and reshaped itself into something revoltingly different. Originally, for example, the girl Judith (the one who had "gone to the bad at a cocktail party") had not spurned the one-armed soldier (Mr. Drury). Far from it. She had welcomed him and several other heroes home with indiscriminate, not to say promiscuous enthusiasm. And the hero, instead of behaving (as Mr. Drury saw to it that he did in the acted version) in a highly sacrificial manner, had gone deliberately and cynically to the bad in his turn. Nor had "Lady Sylvia," who rescued him from the Embankment, been (as Mr. Drury's second leading lady now represented her to be) a handsome and passionate girl deeply in love with the hero, but a nauseous, rich, elderly woman with a fancy for a gigolo, whose attentions the hero (now thoroughly deteriorated as a result of war and post-war experience) accepted without shame or remorse in exchange for the luxuries of life. And finally, when Judith, thoroughly shocked and brought to her senses by these developments, had tried to recapture him, the hero (as originally depicted) had so far lost all sense of decency as to prefer— though with a bitter sense of failure and frustration—to stick to Lady Sylvia, as the line of least resistance, and had ended, on Armistice Day, by tearing away the public trophies of laurel and poppy from the Cenotaph and being ignominiously removed by the police after a drunken and furious harangue in denunciation of war. Not a pleasant play, as originally written, and certainly in shocking taste; but an honest piece of work so far as it went. But Mr. Drury had pointed out that "his" public would never stand the original Lady Sylvia or the final degradation of the hero. There must be slight alterations— nothing inartistic, of course, but alterations, to make the thing more moving, more uplifting, more, in fact, true to human nature.

Because, Mr. Drury pointed out, if there was one thing you could rely on, it was the essential decency of human nature, and its immediate response to generous sentiments. His experience, he said, had proved it to him.

Scales had not given way without a struggle. He had fought

hard over every line. But there was the contract. And in the end, he had actually written the new scenes and lines himself, not because he wanted to, but because at any rate his own lines would be less intolerable than the united efforts of cast and producer to write them for themselves. So that he could not even say that he had washed his hands of the whole beastly thing. Like his own (original) hero, he had taken the line of least resistance. Mr. Drury had been exceedingly grateful to him and delighted to feel that author and management were working so well together in their common interest.

"I know how you feel," he would say, "about altering your artistic work. Any artist feels the same. But I've had twenty years' experience of the stage, and it counts, you know, it counts. You don't think I'm right—my dear boy, I should feel just the same in your place. I'm terribly grateful for all this splendid work you're putting in, and I know you won't regret it. Don't worry. All young authors come up against the same difficulty. It's just a question of experience."

Hopeless. Scales, in desperation, had enlisted the services of an agent, who pointed out that it was now too late to get the contract altered. "But," said the agent, "it's quite an honest contract, as these things go. Drury's management has always had a very good name. We shall keep an eye on these subsidiary rights for you—you can leave that to us. I know it's a nuisance having to alter things here and there, but it *is* your first play, and you're lucky to have got in with Drury. He's very shrewd about what will appeal to a West End audience. When once he's established you, you'll be in a much better position to dictate terms."

Yes, of course, thought Scales—to dictate to Drury, or to anybody else who might want that type of play. But in a worse position than ever to get anybody to look at his serious work. And the worst of it was that the agent, as well as the actor-manager, seemed to think that his concern for his own spiritual integrity didn't count, didn't matter—that he would be quite genuinely consoled by his royalties.

At the end of the first week, Garrick Drury practically said as much. His own experience had been justified by the receipts. "When all's said and done," he remarked, "the box-office is the real test. I don't say that in a commercial spirit. I'd always be ready to put on a play I believed in—as an artist—even if I lost money by it. But when the box-office is happy, it means the public is happy. The box-office is the pulse of the public. Get that and you know you've got the heart of the audience."

He couldn't see. Nobody could see. John Scales' own friends couldn't see; they merely thought he had sold himself. And as the play settled down to run remorselessly on, like a stream of treacle, John Scales realised that there would be no end to it. It was useless to hope that the public would revolt at the insincerity of the play. They probably saw through it all right, just as the critics had done. What stood in the way of the play's deserved collapse was the glorious figure of Garrick Drury. "This broken-backed play," said the *Sunday Echo*, "is only held together by the magnificent acting of Mr. Garrick Drury." "Saccharine as it is," said the *Looker-On*, "Bitter Laurel provides a personal triumph for Mr. Garrick Drury." "Nothing in the play is consistent," said the *Dial*, "except the assured skill of Mr. Garrick Drury, who——" "Mr. John Scales," said the *Daily Messenger*, "has constructed his situations with great skill to display Mr. Garrick Drury in all his attitudes, and that is a sure recipe for success We prophesy a long run for *Bitter Laurel*." A true prophecy, or so it seemed.

And there was no stopping i If only Mr. Drury would fall ill or die or lose his looks or h voice or his popularity, the beastly play might be buried and forgotten. There were circumstances under which the rights would revert to the author. But Mr. Drury lived and flourished and charmed the public, and the run went on, and after that there were the touring rights (controlled by Mr. Drury) and film rights (largely controlled by Mr. Drury) and probably radio rights and God only knew what else. And all Mr. Scales could do was to pocket the wages of sin and curse Mr. Drury, who had (so pleasantly) ruined his work, destroyed his reputation, alienated his friends, exposed him to the contempt of the critics and forced him to betray his own soul.

If there was one living man in London whom John Scales would have liked to see removed from the face of the earth, it was Garrick Drury, to whom (as he was daily obliged to admit to all and sundry) he owed so much. Yet Drury was a really charming fellow. There were times when that inexhaustible charm got so much on the author's nerves that he could readily have slain Mr. Drury for his charm alone.

Yet, when the moment came, on that night of the 15th-16th

161

April, the thing was not premeditated. Not in any real sense. It just happened. Or did it? That was a thing that even John Scales could not have said for certain. He may have felt a moral conviction, but that is not the same thing as a legal conviction. The doctor may have had his suspicions, but if so, they were not directed against John Scales. And whether they were right or wrong, nobody could say that it had made any difference; the real slayer may have been the driver of the car, or the intervening hand of Providence, sprinkling the tarmac with April showers. Or it may have been Garrick Drury, so courteously and charmingly accompanying John Scales in quest of a taxi, instead of getting straight into his own car and being whirled away in the opposite direction.

In any case, it was nearly one in the morning of Sunday when they got the film people off the premises, after a long and much-interrupted argument, during which Scales found himself, as usual, agreeing to a number of things he did not approve of but could see no way to prevent.

"My dear John," said Mr. Garrick Drury, pulling off his dressing-gown (he always conducted business interviews in a dressing-gown, if possible, feeling, with some truth, that its flowing outline suited him), "my dear John, I know exactly how you feel—Walter!—but it needs experience to deal with these people, and you can trust me not to allow anything inartistic— Oh, thank you, Walter. I'm extremely sorry to have kept you so late."

Walter Hopkins was Mr. Drury's personal dresser and faithful adherent. He had not the smallest objection to being kept up all night, or all the next morning for that matter. He was passionately devoted to Mr. Drury, who always rewarded his services with a kind word and the smile. He now helped Mr. Drury into his coat and overcoat and handed him his hat with a gratified murmur. The dressing-room was still exceedingly untidy, but he could not help that; towards the end of the conversation, the negotiations had become so very delicate that even the devoted Walter had had to be dismissed to lurk in an adjacent room.

"Never mind about all this," went on Mr. Drury, indicating a litter of grease-paint, towels, glasses, siphons, ash-trays, tea-cups (Mr. Drury's aunts had looked in), manuscripts (two optimistic authors had been given audience), mascots (five female admirers had brought Mickey Mice), flowers (handed in at the

162

stage-door) and assorted fan-mail, strewn over the furniture. "Just stick my things together and lock up the whisky. I'll see Mr. Scales to his taxi—you're sure I can't drop you anywhere, John? Oh! and bring the flowers to the car—and I'd better look through that play of young what's his name's—Ruggles, Buggles, you know who I mean—perfectly useless, of course, but I promised dear old Fanny—chuck the rest into the cupboard—and I'll pick you up in five minutes."

The night-watchman let them out; he was an infirm and aged man with a face like a rabbit, and Scales wondered what he would do if he met with a burglar or an outbreak of fire in the course of his rounds.

"Hullo!" said Garrick Drury, "it's started to rain. But there's a rank just down the Avenue. Now look here, John, old man, don't you worry about this, because—— Look out!"

It all happened in a flash. A small car, coming just a trifle too fast up the greasy street, braked to avoid a prowling cat, skidded, swung round at right angles and mounted the pavement. The two men leapt for safety—Scales rather clumsily, tripping and sprawling in the gutter. Drury, who was on the inside, made a quick backward spring, neat as an acrobat's, just not far enough. The bumper caught him behind the knee and flung him shoulder-first through the plate-glass window of a milliner's shop.

When Scales had scrambled to his feet, the car was half-way through the window, with its driver, a girl, knocked senseless over the wheel; a policeman and two taxi-drivers were running towards them from the middle of the street; and Drury, very white and his face bleeding, was extricating himself from the splintered glass, with his left arm clutched in his right hand.

"Oh, my God!" said Drury. He staggered up against the car, and between his fingers the bright blood spurted like a fountain.

Scales, shaken and bewildered by his fall, was for the moment unable to grasp what had happened; but the policeman had his wits about him.

"Never mind the lady," he said, urgently, to the taxi-men. "This gent's cut an artery. Bleed to death if we ain't quick." His large, competent fingers grasped the actor's arm, found the right spot and put firm pressure on the severed blood-vessel. The dreadful spurting ceased. "All right, sir? Lucky you 'ad the presence of mind to ketch 'old of yourself." He eased the actor down on the running board, without relaxing his grip.

"I got an 'andkercher," suggested one of the taxi-men.

"That's right," said the policeman. " 'Itch it round 'is arm above the place and pull it as tight as you can. That'll 'elp. Nasty cut it is, right to the bone, by the looks of it."

Scales looked at the shop-window and the pavement, and shuddered. It might have been a slaughter-house.

"Thanks very much," said Drury to the policeman and the taxi-man. He summoned up the ghost of a smile, and fainted.

"Better take him into the theatre," said Scales. "The stage-door's open. Only a step or two up the passage. It's Mr. Drury, the actor," he added, to explain this suggestion. "I'll run along and tell them."

The policeman nodded. Scales hurried up the passage and met Walter just emerging from the stage-door.

"Accident!" said Scales, breathless. "Mr. Drury—cut an artery—they're bringing him here.

Walter, with a cry, flung down the flowers he was carrying and darted out. Drury was being supported up the passage by the two drivers. The policeman walked beside him still keeping a strong thumb on his arm. They brought him in, stumbling over the heaps of narcissus and daffodil; the crushed blossom smelt like funeral flowers.

"There's a couch in his dressing-room," said Scales. His mind had suddenly become abnormally clear. "It's on the ground-floor. Round here to the right and across the stage."

"Oh, dear, oh, dear!" said Walter. "Oh, Mr. Drury! He won't die—he can't die! All that dreadful blood!"

"Now, keep your 'ead," admonished the policeman. "Can't you ring up a doctor and make yourself useful?"

Walter and the night-watchman made a concerted rush for the telephone, leaving Scales to guide the party across the deserted stage, black and ghostly in the light of one dim bulb high over the proscenium arch. Their way was marked by heavy red splashes on the dusty boards. As though the very sound of those boards beneath their tread had wakened the actor's instinct, Drury opened one eye.

"What's happened to those lights?" . . . Then, with returning consciousness, "Oh, it's the curtain line . . . Dying, Egypt, dying . . . final appearance, eh?"

"Rot, old man," said Scales, hastily, "You're not dying yet by a long chalk."

One of the taxi-drivers—an elderly man—stumbled and panted. "Sorry," said Drury, "to be such a weight . . . can't help you much . . . find it easier . . . take your grip further down . . ." The smile was twisted, but his wits and experience were back on the job. This was not the first or the hundredth time he had been "carried out" from the stage of the King's. His bearers took his gasping instructions and successfully negotiated the corner of the set. Scales, hovering in attendance, was unreasonably irritated. Of course, Drury was behaving beautifully. Courage, presence of mind, consideration for others—all the right theatrical gestures. Couldn't the fellow be natural, even at death's door?

Here, Scales was unjust. It was natural to Drury to be theatrical in a crisis, as it is to nine people out of ten. He was, as a matter of fact, providing the best possible justification for his own theories about human nature. They got him to the dressing-room, laid him on the couch, and were thanked.

"My wife," said Drury, ". . . in Sussex. Don't startle her . . . she's had 'flu . . . heart not strong."

"All right, all right," said Scales. He found a towel and drew some water into a bowl. Walter came running in.

"Dr. Debenham's out . . . away for the week-end. . . . Blake's telephoning another one . . . Suppose they're all away . . . whatever shall we do? . . . They oughtn't to *let* doctors go away like this."

"We'll try the police-surgeon," said the constable. "Here, you, come and 'old your thumb where I've got mine. Can't trust that there bandage. Squeeze 'ard, mind, and don't let go. And don't faint," he added sharply. He turned to the taxi-men. "You better go and see what's 'appened to the young lady. I blew me whistle, so you did oughter find the other constable there. You" (to Scales) "will 'ave to stay here—I'll be wanting your evidence about the accident."

"Yes, yes," said Scales, busy with the towel.

"My face," said Drury, putting up a restless hand. "Has it got the eye?"

"No, it's only a scalp-wound. Don't get excited."

"Sure? Better dead than disfigured. Don't want to end like Florrie. Poor old Florrie. Give her my love. . . . Cheer up, Walter. . . . Rotten curtain, isn't it? . . . Get yourself a drink. . . . You're certain the eye's all right? . . . You weren't hurt, were

165

you, old man? . . . Hell of a nuisance for you, too. . . . Stop the run. . . ."

Scales, in the act of pouring out whisky for himself and Walter (who looked nearly as ready to collapse as his employer) started, and nearly dropped the bottle. Stop the run—yes, it would stop the run. An hour ago, he had been praying for a miracle to stop the run. And the miracle had happened. And if Drury hadn't had the wits to stop the bleeding—if he had waited only one minute more—the run would have stopped, and the film would have stopped, and the whole cursed play would have stopped dead for good and all. He swallowed down the neat spirit with a jerk, and handed the second glass to Walter. It was as though he had made the thing happen by wishing for it. By wishing a little harder—— Nonsense! . . . But the doctor didn't come and, though Walter was holding on like grim death (*grim death!*) to the cut artery, the blood from the smaller vessels was soaking and seeping through the cloth and the bandages . . . there was still the chance, still the likelihood, still the *hope*. . . .

This would never do. Scales dashed out into the passage and across the stage to the night-watchman's box. The policeman was still telephoning. Drury's chauffeur, haggard and alarmed, stood, cap in hand, talking to the taxi-men. The girl, it appeared, had been taken to hospital with concussion. The divisional police-surgeon had gone to an urgent case. The nearest hospital had no surgeon free at the moment. The policeman was trying the police-surgeon belonging to the next division. Scales went back.

The next half-hour was a nightmare. The patient, hovering between consciousness and unconsciousness, was still worrying about his face, about his arm, about the play. And the red stain on the couch spread and spread. . . . .

Then with a bustle, a short, stout man came in, carrying a bag. He took a look at the patient, tested his pulse, asked a few questions, shook his head, muttering something about loss of blood and loss of time and weakness. The policeman, somewhere in the background, mentioned that the ambulance had arrived.

"Nonsense," said the doctor. "Can't possibly move him. Got to deal with it here and now." With a few brisk words of commendation, he dislodged Walter from his post. He worked quickly, cutting away the sodden sleeve, applying a proper tourniquet, administering some kind of stimulant, again assuring the patient that his eye was not damaged and that he was suffering from nothing but shock and loss of blood.

166

"You won't take my arm off?" said Drury, suddenly visited with a new alarm. "I'm an actor—I can't—I won't—you can't do it without telling me—you——"

"No, no, no," said the doctor. "Now we've stopped the bleeding. But you must lie still, or you might start it again."

"Shall I have the use of it?" The expressive eyes searched the doctor's face. "Sorry. But a stiff arm's as bad as no arm to me. Do your best . . . or I shall never play again. . . . Except in *Bitter Laurel*. . . . John, old man . . . funny, isn't it? Funny it's his arm. . . . Have to live on your play for the rest of my days . . the only, only play. . . ."

"Good God!" cried Scales, involuntarily.

"Now, I must have this room clear," said the doctor with authority. "Officer, get these people out and send me in those ambulance men.

"Come along," said the policeman. "And I'll take your statement now, sir."

"Not me!" protested Walter Hopkins, "I can't leave Mr. Drury. I can't. Let me stay. I'll help. I'll do anything——"

"The best way you can help," said the doctor, not unkindly but with determination, "is by giving me room to work. Now, please——"

Somehow they got Walter, struggling and hysterical, into the dressing-room across the passage. Here he sat, gathered together on the edge of a chair, starting at every sound from outside, while the constable interrogated and dismissed the two taxi-men. Then Scales found himself giving a statement, in the midst of which, the doctor put his head in to say:

"I want some of you to stand by. It may be necessary to make a blood-transfusion. We must get that arm stitched, but his pulse is very weak and I don't know how he'll stand it. I don't suppose any of you know which blood-group you belong to?"

"I'll do it!" cried Walter, eagerly "Please, sir, let it be me! I'd give all the blood in my body for Mr. Drury. I've been with him fifteen years, doctor——"

"Now, now," said the doctor.

"I'd sacrifice my life for Mr. Drury."

"Yes, I daresay," said the doctor, with a resigned look at the constable, "but there's no question of that. Where do people get these ideas? Out of the papers, I suppose. Nobody's being asked to sacrifice any lives. We only want a pint or so of blood—

trifling affair for a healthy man. It won't make the slightest difference to you—do you good, I shouldn't wonder. My dear sir, don't excite yourself so much. I know you're willing—very naturally—but if you haven't the right kind of blood you're no good to me."

"I'm very strong," said Walter, palpitating. "Never had a day's illness."

"It's nothing to do with your general health," said the doctor, a little impatiently. "It's a thing you're born with. I gather there is no relation of the patient's handy. . . . What? Wife, sister and son in Sussex—well that's rather a long way off. I'll test the two ambulance men first, but unfortunately the patient isn't a universal recipient, so we may not get the right grouping first go-off. I'd like one or two others handy, in case. Good thing I brought everything with me. Always do in an accident case. Never know what you may need, and time's everything."

He darted out, leaving behind him an atmosphere of mystery and haste. The policeman shook his head and pocketed his note-book.

"Dunno as blood-offerings is part of my dooty," he observed "I did oughter get back to me beat. But I'll 'ave to give that there car the once-over and see what my chum 'as to say about it. I'll look in again when I done that, and if they wants me they'll know where to find me. Now, then, what do *you* want?"

"Press," said a man at the door, succinctly. "Somebody phoned to say Mr. Drury was badly hurt. That true? Very sorry to hear it. Ah! Good evening, Mr. Scales. This is all very distressing. I wonder, can you tell me . . . ?"

Scales found himself helplessly caught up in the wheels of the Press—giving an account of the accident—saying all the right things about Drury—what Drury had done for him—what Drury had done for the play—quoting Drury's words—expatiating on Drury's courage, presence of mind and thought for others—manufacturing a halo round Drury—mentioning the strange (and to the newspaper man, gratifying) coincidence that the arm actually wounded was the arm wounded in the play—hoping that Eric Brand, the understudy, would be able to carry on till Mr. Drury was sufficiently recovered to play again—feeling his hatred for Drury rise up in him like a flood with every word he uttered—and finally insisting, with a passion and emphasis that he could not explain to himself, on his own immense personal gratitude and friendship towards Drury and his

168

desperate anxiety to see him restored to health. He felt as though, by saying this over and over again, he might stifle something—something—some frightful thing within him that was asserting itself against his will. The reporter said that Mr. Scales had his deepest sympathy. . . .

"Mr.—ha, hum——" said the doctor, popping his head in again.

"Excuse me," said Scales, quickly. He made for the door; but Walter was there before him, agitatedly offering his life-blood by the gallon. Scales thought he could see the pressman's ears prick up like a dog's. A blood-transfusion, of course, was always jam for a headline. But the doctor made short work of the reporter.

"No time for *you*," he said brusquely, pulling Scales and Walter out and slamming the door. "Yes—I want another test. Hope one of you's the right sort. If not," he added, with a sort of grim satisfaction, "we'll try bleeding the tripe-hound. Learn him not to make a fuss." He led the way back into Drury's dressing-room where the big screen which usually shrouded the wash-stand had been pulled round to conceal the couch. A space had been cleared on the table, and a number of articles laid out upon it: bottles, pipettes, needles, a porcelain slab oddly marked and stained, and a small drum of the sort used for protecting steri-lised instruments. Standing near the wash-basin, one of the ambulance men was boiling a saucepan on a gas-ring.

"Now then," said the doctor. He spoke in a low tone, perfectly clear, but calculated not to carry beyond the screen. "Don't make more noise than you can help. I'll have to do it here—no gas-ring in the other room, and I don't want to leave the patient. Never mind—it won't take a minute to make the tests. I can do you both together. Here, you—I want this slab cleaned —no, never mind, here's a clean plate; that'll do—it needn't be surgically sterile." He wiped the plate carefully with a towel and set it on the table between the two men. Scales recognised its pattern of pink roses; it had often held sandwiches while he and Drury, endlessly talking, had hammered out new dialogue for *Bitter Laurel* over a quick lunch. "You understand"—the doctor looked from one to the other and addressed himself to Walter, as though feeling that the unfortunate man might burst unless some notice was taken of him soon—"that your blood— everybody's blood—belongs to one or other of four different groups." He opened the drum and picked out a needle. "There's
169

no necessity to go into details; the point is that, for a transfusion to be successful, the donor's blood must combine in a particular way with the patient's. Now, this will only be a prick —you'll scarcely feel it." He took Walter by the ear and jabbed the needle into the lobe. "If the donor's blood belongs to an unsuitable group, it causes agglutination of the red cells, and the operation is worse than useless. He drew off a few drops of blood into a pipette. Walter watched and listened, seeming to understand very little, but soothed by the calm, professional voice. The doctor transferred two separate droplets of diluted blood to the plate, making a little ring about each with a grease pencil. "There is one type of person"—here he captured Scales and repeated the operation upon his ear with a fresh needle and pipette—"Group 4, we call them, who are universal donors; their blood suits anybody. Or, of course, if one of you belongs to the patient's own blood-group, that would do nicely. Unfortunately, he's a group 3, and that's rather rare. So far, we've been unlucky." He placed two drops of Scales's blood on the other side of the plate, drawing a pencil-mark from edge to edge to separate the two pairs of specimens, set the plate neatly between the two donors, so that each stood guard over his own property, and turned again to Walter:

"Let's see, what's your name?"

As though in answer, there was a movement behind the screen. Something fell with a crash, and the ambulance man put out a scared face, saying urgently, "Doctor!" At the same moment came Drury's voice, "Walter—tell Walter——!" trailing into silence. Walter and the doctor dived for the screen together, Scales catching Walter as he pushed past him. The second ambulance man put down what he was doing and ran to assist. There was a moment of bustle and expostulation, and the doctor said, "Come, now, give him a chance." Walter came back to his place at the table. His mouth looked as though he were going to cry.

"They won't let me see him. He asked for me."

"He mustn't exert himself, you know," said Scales, mechanically.

The patient was muttering to himself and the doctor seemed to be trying to quiet him. Scales and Walter Hopkins stood waiting helplessly, with the plate between them. Four little drops of blood—absurd, thought Scales, that they should be of so much importance, when you remembered that horrible welter

170

the street, on the couch. On the table stood a small wooden rack, containing ampoules. He read the labels, "Stock serum No. I," "Stock serum No. III"; the words conveyed nothing to him; he noticed, stupidly, that one of the little pink roses on the border of the plate had been smudged in the firing—that Walter's hands were trembling as he supported himself upon the table.

Then the doctor reappeared, whispering to the ambulance men, "Do try to keep him quiet." Walter looked anxiously at him. "All right, so far," said the doctor. "Now then, where were we? What did you say your name was?" He labelled the specimens on Walter's side of the plate with the initials "W.H."

"Mine's John Scales," said Scales. The doctor wrote down the initials of London's popular playwright as indifferently as though they had been those of a rate-collector and took from the rack the ampoule of Serum II. Breaking it, he added a little of the contents, first to a drop of the "J.S." blood and, next, to a drop of "W.H." blood, scribbling the figure II beside each specimen. To each of the remaining drops he added, in the same way, a little of Serum III. Blood and serum met and mingled; to Scales, all four of the little red blotches looked exactly alike. He was disappointed, he had vaguely expected something more dramatic.

"It'll take a minute or two," said the doctor, gently rocking the plate. "If the blood of either of you mixes with both sera without clumping the red corpuscles, then that donor is a universal donor, and will do. Or, if it clumps with Serum II and remains clear with Serum III, then the donor belongs to the patient's own blood-group and will do excellently for him. But if it clumps with both sera or with Serum III only, then it will do for the patient in quite another sense." He set the plate down and began to fish in his pocket.

One of the ambulance men looked round the screen again. "I can't find his pulse," he announced helplessly, "and he's looking very queer." The doctor clicked his tongue in a worried way against his teeth and vanished. There were movements, and a clinking of glass.

Scales gazed down at the plate. Was there any difference to be seen? Was one of the little blotches on Walter's side beginning to curdle and separate into grains as though someone had sprinkled it with cayenne pepper? He was not sure. On his own side of the plate, the drops looked exactly alike. Again he read the labels; again he noted the pink rose that had been smudged in the firing—the pink rose—funny about the pink rose—but what was funny about it? Certainly, one of Walter's drops was beginning to look different. A hard ring was forming about its edge, and the tiny, peppery grains were growing darker and more distinct.

"He'll do now," said the doctor, returning, "but we don't want to lose any time. Let's hope——"

He bent over the plate again. It was the drop labelled III that had the queer grainy look—was that the right way or the wrong way round? Scales could not remember. The doctor was examining the specimens closely, with the help of a pencil microscope. . . . Then he straightened his back with a small sigh of relief.

"Group 4," he announced; "we're all right now."

"Which of us?" thought Scales (though he was pretty sure of the answer). He was still obscurely puzzled by the pink rose.

"Yes," went on the doctor, "no sign of agglutination. I think we can risk that without a direct match-up against the patient's blood. It would take twenty minutes and we can't spare the time." He turned to Scales. "You're the man we want."

Walter gave an anguished cry.

"Not me?"

"Hush!" said the doctor, authoritatively. "No, I'm afraid we can't let it be you. Now, you"—he turned to Scales again— "are a universal donor; very useful person to have about. Heart quite healthy, I suppose? Feels all right. You look fit enough, and thank goodness, you're not fat. Get your coat off, will you and turn up your sleeve. Ah, yes. Nice stout-looking vein. Splendid. Now, you won't take any harm—you may feel a little faint perhaps, but you'll be as right as rain in an hour or so."

"Yes," agreed Scales. He was still looking at the plate. The smudged rose was on his right. Surely it had always been on his right. Or had it started on his left? When? Before the blood-drops had been put on? or after? How could it have altered its position? When the doctor was handling the plate? Or could Walter have caught the plate with his sleeve and swivelled it round when he made his mad rush for the screen? If so, was that before the specimens had been labelled? After, surely. No, before—*after* they were taken and *before* they were labelled. And that would mean. . . .

172

The doctor was opening the drum again ; taking out bandages, forceps, a glass flask. . . .

That would mean that his own blood and Walter's had changed places before the serum was added, and if so . . .

. . . Scissors, towels, a kind of syringe. . . .

If there was the slightest doubt, one ought to draw attention to it and have the specimens tested again. But perhaps either of their bloods would have done equally well ; in that case, the doctor would naturally give the preference to John Scales, rather than to poor Walter, shivering there like a leaf. Clump with II, clear with III ; clump with III clear with II—he couldn't remember which way it went. . . .

"No, I'm sorry," repeated the doctor. He escorted Walter firmly to the door and came back. "Poor chap—he can't make out why his blood won't do. Hopeless, of course. Just as well give the man prussic acid at once."

. . . The pink rose. . . .

"Doctor——" began Scales.

And then, suddenly, Drury's voice came from behind the screen, speaking the line that had been written to be spoken with a harsh and ugly cynicism, but giving it as he had given it now on the stage for nearly a hundred performances:

"All right, all right, don't worry—I'll rest on my laurels."

The hated, heartbreaking voice—the professional actor's voice —sweet as sugar plums—liquid and mellow like an intoxicated flute.

Damn him! thought Scales, feeling the rubber band tighten above his elbow, I hope he dies. Never to hear that damned-awful voice again. I'd give anything. I'd give. . . .

He watched his arm swell and mottle red and blue under the pressure of the band. The doctor gave him an injection of something. Scales said nothing. He was thinking:

Give anything. I would give my life. I would give my blood. I have *only* to give my blood—and say nothing. The plate *was* turned round. . . . No, I don't know that. It's the doctor's business to make sure. . . . I can't speak now. . . . He'll wonder why I didn't speak before. . . . Author sacrifices blood to save benefactor. . . . Roses to right of him, roses to left of him . . . roses, roses all the way. . . . I will rest on my laurels.

The needle now—plump into the vein. His own blood flowing, rising in the glass flask. . . . Somebody bringing a bowl of warm water with a faint steam rising off it. . . .

... His life for his friend ... right as rain in an hour or two ... blood-brothers ... the blood is the life ... as well give him prussic acid at once ... to poison a man with one's own blood ... new idea, for a murder. ... MURDER. ...

"Don't jerk about," said the doctor.

... and what a motive! ... murder to save one's artistic soul. ... Who'd believe that? ... and losing money by it ... your money or your life ... his life for his friend ... his friend for his life ... life or death, and not to know which one was giving ... not *really* know ... not know at all, *really* ... too late now ... absurd to say anything now ... nobody *saw* the plate turned round ... and who would ever imagine ... ?

"That'll do," said the doctor. He loosened the rubber band, dabbed a pad of wool over the puncture and pulled out the needle, all, it seemed to Scales, in one movement. He plopped the flask into a little stand over the bowl of water and dressed the arm with iodine. "How do you feel? A trifle faint? Go and lie down in the other room for a minute or two."

Scales opened his mouth to speak, and was suddenly assailed by a queer, sick qualm. He plunged for the door. As he went, he saw the doctor carry the flask behind the screen.

Damn that reporter! He was still hanging round. Meat and drink to the papers, this kind of thing. Heroic sacrifice by grateful author. Good story. Better story still if the heroic author were to catch him by the arm, pour into his ear the unbelievable truth—were to say, "I hated him, I hated him, I tell you—I've poisoned him—my blood's poison—serpent's blood, dragon's blood——"

And what would the doctor say? If this really had gone wrong, would he suspect? What *could he* suspect? He hadn't seen the plate move. Nobody had. He might suspect himself of negligence, but he wouldn't be likely to shout *that* from the housetops. And he *had* been negligent—pompous, fat, chattering fool. Why didn't he mark the specimens earlier? Why didn't he match-up the blood with Drury's? Why did he need to chatter so much and explain things? Tell people how easy it was to murder a benefactor?

Scales wished he knew what was happening. Walter was hovering outside in the passage. Walter was jealous—he had looked on enviously, grudgingly, as Scales came stumbling in from the operation. If only Walter knew what Scales had been doing, he might well look. ... It occurred to Scales that he had played a shabby trick on Walter—cheated him—Walter, who had wanted so much to sacrifice his right, his true, his life-giving blood. . . .

Twenty minutes . . . nearly half an hour. . . . How soon would they know whether it was all right or all wrong? "As well give him prussic acid," the doctor had said. That suggested something pretty drastic. Prussic acid was quick—you died as if struck.

Scales got up, pushed Walter and the pressman aside and crossed the passage. In Drury's room the screen had been pushed back. Scales, peeping through the door, could see Drury's face, white and glistening with sweat. The doctor bent over the patient, holding his wrist. He looked distressed—almost alarmed. Suddenly he turned, caught sight of Scales and came over to him. He seemed to take minutes to cross the room.

"I'm sorry," said the doctor. "I'm very much afraid—you did your best—we all did our best."

"No good?" Scales whispered back. His tongue and palate were like sawdust.

"One can never be certain with these things," said the doctor. "I'm very much afraid he's going." He paused and his eyes were faintly puzzled. "So much haemorrhage," he muttered as though explaining the trouble to himself. "Shock—cardiac strain—excitable"—and, in a worried voice—"he complained almost at once of pain in the back." He added, with more assurance: "It's always a bit of a gamble, you see, when the operation is left so late—and sometimes there is a particular idiosyncrasy. I should have preferred a direct test; but it's not satisfactory if the patient dies while you wait to make sure."

With a wry smile he turned back to the couch, and Scales followed him. If Drury could have acted death as he was acting it now! . . . Scales could not rid himself of the notion that he *was* acting—that the shine upon the skin was grease-paint, and the rough, painful breathing, the stereotyped stage gasp. If truth could be so stagy, then the stage must be disconcertingly like truth.

Something sobbed at his elbow. Walter had crept into the room, and this time the doctor made way for him.

"Oh, Mr. Drury!" said Walter.

Drury's blue lips moved. He opened his eyes: the dilated pupils made them look black and enormous.

"Where's Brand?"

175

The doctor turned interrogatively to the other two men. "His son?"

"His understudy," whispered Scales. Walter said, "He'll be here in a minute, Mr. Drury."

"They're waiting," said Drury. He drew a difficult breath and spoke in his old voice:

"Brand! Fetch Brand! The curtain must go up!"

Garrick Drury's death was very "good theatre."

Nobody, thought Scales, could ever know. He could never really know himself. Drury might have died, anyhow, of shock. Even if the blood had been right, he might have died. One couldn't be certain, now, that the blood hadn't been right; it might have been all imagination about the smudged pink rose. Or—one might be sure, deep in one's own mind. But nobody could prove it. Or—could the doctor? There would have to be an inquest, of course. Would they make a post-mortem? Could they prove that the blood was wrong? If so, the doctor had his ready explanation—"particular idiosyncrasy" and lack of time to make further tests. He *must* give that explanation, or accuse himself of negligence.

Because nobody could prove that the plate had been moved. Walter and the doctor had not seen it—if they had, they would have spoken. Nor could it be proved that he, Scales, had seen it —he was not even certain himself, except in the hidden chambers of the heart. And he, who lost so much by Drury's death —to suppose that he could have seen and not spoken was fantastic. There are things beyond the power even of a coroner to imagine or of a coroner's jury to believe.

SUSPICION

As the atmosphere of the railway carriage thickened with tobacco-smoke, Mr. Mummery became increasingly aware that his breakfast had not agreed with him.

There could have been nothing wrong with the breakfast itself. Brown bread, rich in vitamin-content, as advised by the *Morning Star*'s health expert; bacon fried to a delicious crispness; eggs just nicely set; coffee made as only Mrs. Sutton knew how to make it. Mrs. Sutton had been a real find, and that was something to be thankful for. For Ethel, since her nervous breakdown in the Summer, had really not been fit to wrestle with the untrained girls who had come and gone in tempestuous succession. It took very little to upset Ethel nowadays, poor child. Mr. Mummery, trying hard to ignore his growing internal discomfort, hoped he was not in for an illness. Apart from the trouble it would cause at the office, it would worry Ethel terribly, and Mr. Mummery would cheerfully have laid down his rather uninteresting little life to spare Ethel a moment's uneasiness.

He slipped a digestive tablet into his mouth—he had taken lately to carrying a few tablets about with him—and opened his paper. There did not seem to be very much news. A question had been asked in the House about Government typewriters. The Prince of Wales had smilingly opened an all-British exhibition of foot-wear. A further split had occurred in the Liberal party. The police were still looking for the woman who was supposed to have poisoned a family in Lincoln. Two girls had been trapped in a burning factory. A film-star had obtained her fourth decree nisi.

At Paragon Station, Mr. Mummery descended and took a

177

tram. The internal discomfort was taking the form of a definite nausea. Happily he contrived to reach his office before the worst occurred. He was seated at his desk, pale but in control of himself, when his partner came breezing in.

" 'Morning, Mummery," said Mr. Brookes in his loud tones, adding inevitably, "Cold enough for you?"

"Quite," replied Mr. Mummery. "Unpleasantly raw, in fact."

"Beastly, beastly," said Mr. Brookes. "Your bulbs all in?"

"Not quite all," confessed Mr. Mummery. "As a matter of fact I haven't been feeling——"

"Pity," interrupted his partner. "Great pity. Ought to get 'em in early. Mine were in last week. My little place will be a picture in the Spring. For a town garden, that is. You're lucky, living in the country. Find it better than Hull, I expect, eh? Though we get plenty of fresh air up in the Avenues. How's the missus?"

"Thank you, she's very much better."

"Glad to hear that, very glad. Hope we shall have her about again this winter as usual. Can't do without her in the Drama Society, you know. By Jove! I shan't forget her acting last year in *Romance*. She and young Welbeck positively brought the house down, didn't they? The Welbecks were asking after her only yesterday."

"Thank you, yes. I hope she will soon be able to take up her social activities again. But the doctor says she mustn't overdo it. No worry, he says—that's the important thing. She is to go easy and not rush about or undertake too much."

"Quite right, quite right. Worry's the devil and all. I cut out worrying years ago and look at me! Fit as a fiddle, for all I shan't see fifty again. *You're* not looking altogether the thing, by the way."

"A touch of dyspepsia," said Mr. Mummery. "Nothing much. Chill on the liver, that's what I put it down to."

"That's what it is," said Mr. Brookes, seizing his opportunity. "Is life worth living? It depends on the liver. Ha, ha! Well now, well now—we must do a spot of work, I suppose. Where's that lease of Ferraby's?"

Mr. Mummery, who did not feel at his conversational best that morning, rather welcomed this suggestion, and for half an hour was allowed to proceed in peace with the duties of an estate agent. Presently, however, Mr. Brookes burst into speech again.

"By the way," he said abruptly, "I suppose your wife doesn't know of a good cook, does she?"

"Well, no," replied Mr. Mummery. "They aren't so easy to find nowadays. In fact, we've only just got suited ourselves. But why? Surely your old Cookie isn't leaving you?"

"Good Lord, no!" Mr. Brookes laughed heartily. "It would take an earthquake to shake off old Cookie. No. It's for the Philipsons. Their girl's getting married. That's the worst of girls. I said to Philipson, 'You mind what you're doing,' I said. 'Get somebody you know something about, or you may find yourself landed with this poisoning woman—what's her name—Andrews. Don't want to be sending wreaths to your funeral yet awhile,' I said. He laughed, but it's no laughing matter and so I told him. What we pay the police for I simply don't know. Nearly a month now, and they can't seem to lay hands on the woman. All they say is, they think she's hanging about the neighbourhood and 'may seek situation as cook.' As cook! Now I ask you!"

"You don't think she committed suicide, then?" suggested Mr. Mummery.

"Suicide, my foot!" retorted Mr. Brookes, coarsely. "Don't you believe it, my boy. That coat found in the river was all eyewash. *They* don't commit suicide, that sort don't."

"What sort?"

"Those arsenic-maniacs. They're too damned careful of their own skins. Cunning as weasels, that's what they are. It's only to be hoped they'll manage to catch her before she tries her hand on anybody else. As I told Philipson——"

"You think Mrs. Andrews did it, then?"

"Did it? Of course she did it. It's plain as the nose on your face. Looked after her old father, and he died suddenly—left her a bit of money, too. Then she keeps house for an elderly gentleman, and *he* dies suddenly. Now there's this husband and wife—man dies and woman taken very ill, of arsenic poisoning. Cook runs away, and you ask, did she do it? I don't mind betting that when they dig up the father and the other old bird they'll find *them* bung-full of arsenic, too. Once that sort gets started, they don't stop. Grows on 'em, as you might say."

"I suppose it does," said Mr. Mummery. He picked up his paper again and studied the photograph of the missing woman. "She looks harmless enough," he remarked. "Rather a nice, motherly-looking kind of woman."

179

"She's got a bad mouth," pronounced Mr. Brookes. He had a theory that character showed in the mouth. "I wouldn't trust that woman an inch."

As the day went on, Mr. Mummery felt better. He was rather nervous about his lunch, choosing carefully a little boiled fish and custard pudding and being particular not to rush about immediately after the meal. To his great relief, the fish and custard remained where they were put, and he was not visited by that tiresome pain which had become almost habitual in the last fortnight. By the end of the day he became quite light-hearted. The bogey of illness and doctor's bills ceased to haunt him. He bought a bunch of bronze chrysanthemums to carry home to Ethel, and it was with a feeling of pleasant anticipation that he left the train and walked up the garden path of *Mon Abri*.

He was a little dashed by not finding his wife in the sitting-room. Still clutching the bunch of chrysanthemums he pattered down the passage and pushed open the kitchen door.

Nobody was there but the cook. She was sitting at the table with her back to him, and started up almost guiltily as he approached.

"Lor', sir," she said, "you give me quite a start. I didn't hear the front door go."

"Where is Mrs. Mummery? Not feeling bad again, is she?"

"Well, sir, she's got a bit of a headache, poor lamb. I made her lay down and took her up a nice cup 'o tea at half-past four. I think she's dozing nicely now."

"Dear, dear," said Mr. Mummery.

"It was turning out the dining-room done it, if you ask me," said Mrs. Sutton. "'Now, don't you overdo yourself, ma'am,' I says to her, but you know how she is, sir. She gets that restless, she can't abear to be doing nothing."

"I know," said Mr. Mummery. "It's not your fault, Mrs. Sutton. I'm sure you look after us both admirably. I'll just run up and have a peep at her. I won't disturb her if she's asleep. By the way, what are we having for dinner?"

"Well, I *had* made a nice steak-and-kidney pie," said Mrs. Sutton, in accents suggesting that she would readily turn it into a pumpkin or a coach-and-four if it was not approved of.

"Oh!" said Mr. Mummery. "Pastry? Well, I——"

"You'll find it beautiful and light," protested the cook, whisk-

180

ing open the oven-door for Mr. Mummery to see. "And it's made with butter, sir, you having said that you found lard indigestible."

"Thank you, thank you," said Mr. Mummery. "I'm sure it will be most excellent. I haven't been feeling altogether the thing just lately, and lard does not seem to suit me nowadays."

"Well, it don't suit some people, and that's a fact," agreed Mrs. Sutton. "I shouldn't wonder if you've got a bit of a chill on the liver. I'm sure this weather is enough to upset anybody."

She bustled to the table and cleared away the picture-paper which she had been reading.

"Perhaps the mistress would like her dinner sent up to her?" she suggested.

Mr. Mummery said he would go and see, and tiptoed his way upstairs. Ethel was lying snuggled under the eiderdown and looked very small and fragile in the big double-bed. She stirred as he came in and smiled up at him.

"Hullo, darling!" said Mr. Mummery.

"Hullo! You back? I must have been asleep. I got tired and headachy, and Mrs. Sutton packed me off upstairs."

"You've been doing too much, sweetheart," said her husband, taking her hand in his and sitting down on the edge of the bed.

"Yes—it was naughty of me. What lovely flowers, Harold. All for me?"

"All for you, Tiddley-winks," said Mr. Mummery, tenderly. "Don't I deserve something for that?"

Mrs. Mummery smiled, and Mr. Mummery took his reward several times over.

"That's quite enough, you sentimental old thing," said Mrs. Mummery. "Run away, now, I'm going to get up."

"Much better go to bed, my precious, and let Mrs. Sutton send your dinner up," said her husband. Ethel protested, but he was firm with her. If she didn't take care of herself, she wouldn't be allowed to go to the Drama Society meetings. And everybody was so anxious to have her back. The Welbecks had been asking after her and saying that they really couldn't get on without her.

"Did they?" said Ethel with some animation. "It's very sweet of them to want me. Well, perhaps I'll go to bed after all. And how has my old Hubby been all day?"

"Not too bad, not too bad."

181

"No more tummy-aches?"

"Well, just a *little* tummy-ache. But it's quite gone now. Nothing for Tiddley-winks to worry about."

Mr. Mummery experienced no more distressing symptoms the next day or the next. Following the advice of the newspaper expert, he took to drinking orange-juice, and was delighted with the results of the treatment. On Thursday, however, he was taken so ill in the night that Ethel was alarmed and insisted on sending for the doctor. The doctor felt his pulse and looked at his tongue and appeared to take the matter lightly. An inquiry into what he had been eating elicited the fact that dinner had consisted of pig's trotters, followed by a milk pudding, and that, before retiring, Mr. Mummery had consumed a large glass of orange-juice, according to his new régime.

"There's your trouble," said Dr. Griffiths cheerfully. "Orange-juice is an excellent thing, and so are trotters, but not in combination. Pigs and oranges together are extraordinarily bad for the liver. I don't know why they should be, but there's no doubt that they are. Now I'll send you round a little prescription and you stick to slops for a day or two and keep off pork. And don't you worry about him, Mrs. Mummery, he's as sound as a trout. *You're* the one we've got to look after. I don't want to see those black rings under the eyes, you know. Disturbed night, of course —yes. Taking your tonic regularly? That's right. Well, don't be alarmed about your hubby. We'll soon have him out and about again."

The prophecy was fulfilled, but not immediately. Mr. Mummery, though confining his diet to Benger's food, bread-and-milk and beef-tea skilfully prepared by Mrs. Sutton and brought to his bedside by Ethel, remained very seedy all through Friday, and was only able to stagger rather shakily downstairs on Saturday afternoon. He had evidently suffered a "thorough upset." However, he was able to attend to a few papers which Brookes had sent down from the office for his signature, and to deal with the household books. Ethel was not a business woman, and Mr. Mummery always ran over the accounts with her. Having settled up with the butcher, the baker, the dairy and the coal-merchant, Mr. Mummery looked up inquiringly.

"Anything more, darling?"

"Well, there's Mrs. Sutton. This is the end of her month, you know."

182

"So it is. Well. you're quite satisfied with her, aren't you, darling?'"

"Yes, rather—aren't you? She's a good cook, and a sweet, motherly old thing, too. Don't you think it was a real brain-wave of mine, engaging her like that, on the spot?"

"I do, indeed," said Mr. Mummery.

"It was a perfect providence, her turning up like that, just after that wretched Jane had gone off without even giving notice. was in absolute *despair*. It was a little bit of a gamble, of course, taking her without any references, but naturally, if she'd been looking after a widowed mother, you couldn't expect her to give references."

"N-no," said Mr. Mummery. At the time he had felt uneasy about the matter, though he had not liked to say much because, of course, they simply had to have somebody. And the experiment had justified itself so triumphantly in practice that one couldn't say much about it now. He had once rather tentatively suggested writing to the clergyman of Mrs. Sutton's parish, but, as Ethel had said, the clergyman wouldn't have been able to tell them anything about cooking, and cooking, after all, was the chief point.

Mr. Mummery counted out the month's money.

"And by the way, my dear," he said, "you might just mention to Mrs. Sutton that if she *must* read the morning paper before come down, I should be obliged if she would fold it neatly afterwards."

"What an old fuss-box you are, darling," said his wife.

Mr. Mummery sighed. He could not explain that it was some-how important that the morning paper should come to him fresh and prim, like a virgin. Women did not feel these things.

On Sunday, Mr. Mummery felt very much better—quite his old self, in fact. He enjoyed the *News of the World* over break-fast in bed, reading the murders rather carefully. Mr. Mummery got quite a lot of pleasure out of murders—they gave him an agreeable thrill of vicarious adventure, for, naturally, they were matters quite remote from daily life in the outskirts of Hull.

He noticed that Brookes had been perfectly right. Mrs. Andrews' father and former employer had been "dug up" and had, indeed, proved to be "bung-full" of arsenic.

He came downstairs for dinner—roast sirloin, with the pota-toes done under the meat and Yorkshire pudding of delicious lightness, and an apple tart to follow. After three days of invalid diet, it was delightful to savour the crisp fat and underdone lean. He ate moderately, but with a sensuous enjoyment. Ethel, on the other hand, seemed a little lacking in appetite, but then, she had never been a great meat-eater. She was fastidious and, besides, she was (quite unnecessarily) afraid of getting fat.

It was a fine afternoon, and at three o'clock, when he was quite certain that the roast beef was "settling" properly, it occurred to Mr. Mummery that it would be a good thing to put the rest of those bulbs in. He slipped on his old gardening coat and wandered out to the potting-shed. Here he picked up a bag of tulips and a trowel, and then, remembering that he was wearing his good trousers, decided that it would be wise to take a mat to kneel on. When had he had the mat last? He could not recollect, but he rather fancied he had put it away in the corner under the potting-shelf. Stooping down, he felt about in the dark among the flower-pots. Yes, there it was, but there was a tin of something in the way. He lifted the tin carefully out. Of course, yes—the remains of the weed-killer.

Mr. Mummery glanced at the pink label, printed in staring letters with the legend: "ARSENICAL WEED-KILLER. POISON," and observed, with a mild feeling of excitement, that it was the same brand of stuff that had been associated with Mrs. Andrews' latest victim. He was rather pleased about it. It gave him a sensation of being remotely but definitely in touch with important events. Then he noticed, with surprise and a little annoyance, that the stopper had been put in quite loosely.

"However'd I come to leave it like that?" he grunted. "Shouldn't wonder if all the goodness has gone off." He removed the stopper and squinted into the can, which appeared to be half-full. Then he rammed the thing home again, giving it a sharp thump with the handle of the trowel for better security. After that he washed his hands carefully at the scullery tap, for he did not believe in taking risks.

He was a trifle disconcerted, when he came in after planting the tulips, to find visitors in the sitting-room. He was always pleased to see Mrs. Welbeck and her son, but he would rather have had warning, so that he could have scrubbed the garden mould out of his nails more thoroughly. Not that Mrs. Welbeck appeared to notice. She was a talkative woman and paid little attention to anything but her own conversation. Much to Mr. Mummery's annoyance, she chose to prattle about the Lincoln Poisoning Case. A most unsuitable subject for the tea-table
184

thought, Mr. Mummery, at the best of times. His own "upset" was vivid enough in his memory to make him queasy over the discussion of medical symptoms, and besides, this kind of talk was not good enough for Ethel. After all, the poisoner was still supposed to be in the neighbourhood. It was enough to make even a strong-nerved woman uneasy. A glance at Ethel showed him that she was looking quite white and tremulous. He must stop Mrs. Welbeck somehow, or there would be a repetition of one of the old, dreadful, hysterical scenes.

He broke into the conversation with violent abruptness.

"Those Forsyth cuttings, Mrs. Welbeck," he said. "Now is just about the time to take them. If you care to come down the garden I will get them for you."

He saw a relieved glance pass between Ethel and young Welbeck. Evidently the boy understood the situation and was chafing at his mother's tactlessness. Mrs. Welbeck, brought up all standing, gasped slightly and then veered off with obliging readiness on the new tack. She accompanied her host down the garden and chattered cheerfully about horticulture while he selected and trimmed the cuttings. She complimented Mr. Mummery on the immaculacy of his garden paths. "I simply *cannot* keep the weeds down," she said.

Mr. Mummery mentioned the weed-killer and praised its efficacy.

"That stuff!" Mrs. Welbeck started at him. Then she shuddered. "I wouldn't have it in my place for a thousand pounds," she said, with emphasis.

Mr. Mummery smiled. "Oh, we keep it well away from the house," he said. "Even if I were a careless sort of person——"

He broke off. The recollection of the loosened stopper had come to him suddenly, and it was as though, deep down in his mind, some obscure assembling of ideas had taken place. He left it at that, and went into the kitchen to fetch a newspaper to wrap up the cuttings.

Their approach to the house had evidently been seen from the sitting-room window, for when they entered, young Welbeck was already on his feet and holding Ethel's hand in the act of saying goodbye. He manœuvred his mother out of the house with tactful promptness and Mr. Mummery returned to the kitchen to clear up the newspapers he had fished out of the drawer. To clear them up and to examine them more closely. Something had struck him about them, which he wanted to

185

verify. He turned them over very carefully, sheet by sheet. Yes —he had been right. Every portrait of Mrs. Andrews, every paragraph and line about the Lincoln poisoning case, had been carefully cut out.

Mr. Mummery sat down by the kitchen fire. He felt as though he needed warmth. There seemed to be a curious cold lump of something at the pit of his stomach—something that he was chary of investigating.

He tried to recall the appearance of Mrs. Andrews as shown in the newspaper photographs, but he had not a good visual memory. He remembered having remarked to Brookes that it was a "motherly" face. Then he tried counting up the time since the disappearance. Nearly a month, Brookes had said—and that was a week ago. Must be over a month now. A month! He had just paid Mrs. Sutton her month's money.

"Ethel!" was the thought that hammered at the door of his brain. At all costs, he must cope with this monstrous suspicion on his own. He must spare her any shock or anxiety. And he must be sure of his ground. To dismiss the only decent cook they had ever had out of sheer, unfounded panic, would be wanton cruelty to both women. If he did it at all, it would have to be done arbitrarily, preposterously—he could not suggest horrors to Ethel. However it was done, there would be trouble. Ethel would not understand and he dared not tell her.

But if by chance there was anything in this ghastly doubt— how could he expose Ethel to the appalling danger of having the woman in the house a moment longer? He thought of the family at Lincoln—the husband dead, the wife escaped by a miracle with her life. Was not any shock, any risk, better than that?

Mr. Mummery felt suddenly very lonely and tired. His illness had taken it out of him.

Those illnesses—they had begun, when? Three weeks ago he had had the first attack. Yes, but then he had always been rather subject to gastric troubles. Bilious attacks. Not so violent, perhaps, as these last, but undoubtedly bilious attacks.

He pulled himself together and went, rather heavily, into the sitting-room. Ethel was tucked up in a corner of the chesterfield.

"Tired, darling?"

"Yes, a little."

"That woman has worn you out with talking. She oughtn't to talk so much."

"No." Her head shifted wearily in the cushions. "All about that horrible case. I don't like hearing about such things."

"Of course not. Still, when a thing like that happens in the neighbourhood, people will gossip and talk. It would be a relief if they caught the woman. One doesn't like to think——"

"I don't want to think of anything so hateful. She must be a horrible creature."

"Horrible. Brookes was saying the other day——"

"I don't want to hear what he said. I don't want to hear about it at all. I want to be quiet. I want to be quiet!"

He recognised the note of rising hysteria.

"Tiddleywinks shall be quiet. Don't worry, darling. We won't talk about horrors."

No. It would not do to talk about them.

Ethel went to bed early. It was understood that on Sundays Mr. Mummery should sit up till Mrs. Sutton came in. Ethel was a little anxious about this, but he assured her that he felt quite strong enough. In body, indeed, he did; it was his mind that felt weak and confused. He had decided to make a casual remark about the mutilated newspapers—just to see what Mrs. Sutton would say.

He allowed himself the usual indulgence of a whisky-and-soda as he sat waiting. At a quarter to ten he heard the familiar click of the garden gate. Footsteps passed up the gravel—squeak, squeak, to the back-door. Then the sound of the latch, the shutting of the door, the rattle of the bolts being shot home. Then a pause. Mrs. Sutton would be taking off her hat. The moment was coming.

The step sounded in the passage. The door opened. Mrs. Sutton in her neat black dress stood on the threshold. He was aware of a reluctance to face her. Then he looked up. A plump-faced woman, her face obscured by thick horn-rimmed spectacles. Was there, perhaps, something hard about the mouth? Or was it just that she had lost most of her front teeth?

"Would you be requiring anything tonight, sir, before I go up?"

"No, thank you, Mrs. Sutton."

"I hope you are feeling better, sir." Her eager interest in his health seemed to him almost sinister, but the eyes behind the thick glasses, were inscrutable.

187

"Quite better, thank you, Mrs. Sutton."

"Mrs. Mummery is not indisposed, is she, sir? Should I take her up a glass of hot milk or anything?"

"No, thank you, no." He spoke hurriedly, and fancied that she looked disappointed.

"Very well, sir. Good night, sir."

"Good night. Oh! by the way, Mrs. Sutton——"

"Yes, sir?"

"Oh, nothing," said Mr. Mummery, "nothing."

Next morning Mr. Mummery opened his paper eagerly. He would have been glad to learn that an arrest had been made over the week-end. But there was no news for him. The chairman of a trust company had blown out his brains, and all the headlines were occupied with tales about lost millions and ruined shareholders. Both in his own paper and in those he purchased on the way to the office, the Lincoln Poisoning Tragedy had been relegated to an obscure paragraph on a back page, which informed him that the police were still baffled.

The next few days were the most uncomfortable that Mr. Mummery had ever spent. He developed a habit of coming down early in the morning and prowling about the kitchen. This made Ethel nervous, but Mrs. Sutton offered no remark. She watched him tolerantly, even, he thought, with something like amusement. After all, it was ridiculous. What was the use of supervising the breakfast, when he had to be out of the house every day between half-past nine and six?

At the office, Brookes rallied him on the frequency with which he rang up Ethel. Mr. Mummery paid no attention. It was reassuring to hear her voice and to know that she was safe and well.

Nothing happened, and by the following Thursday he began to think that he had been a fool. He came home late that night. Brookes had persuaded him to go with him to a little bachelor dinner for a friend who was about to get married. He left the others at eleven o'clock, however, refusing to make a night of it. The household was in bed when he got back but a note from Mrs. Sutton lay on the table, informing him that there was cocoa for him in the kitchen, ready for hotting-up. He hotted it up accordingly in the little saucepan where it stood. There was just one good cupful.

He sipped it thoughtfully, standing by the kitchen stove.

After the first sip, he put the cup down. Was it his fancy, or was there something queer about the taste? He sipped it again, rolling it upon his tongue. Is seemed to him to have a faint tang, metallic and unpleasant. In a sudden dread he ran out to the scullery and spat the mouthful into the sink.

After this, he stood quite still for a moment or two. Then, with a curious deliberation, as though his movements had been dictated to him, he fetched an empty medicine-bottle from the pantry-shelf, rinsed it under the tap and tipped the contents of the cup carefully into it. He slipped the bottle into his coat pocket and moved on tip-toe to the back door. The bolts were difficult to draw without noise, but he managed it at last. Still on tip-toe, he stole across the garden to the potting-shed. Stooping down, he struck a match. He knew exactly where he had left the tin of weed-killer, under the shelf behind the pots at the back. Cautiously he lifted it out. The match flared up and burnt his fingers, but before he could light another his sense of touch had told him what he wanted to know. The stopper was loose again.

Panic seized Mr. Mummery, standing there in the earthy-smelling shed, in his dress-suit and overcoat, holding the tin in one hand and the match-box in the other. He wanted very badly to run and tell somebody what he had discovered.

Instead, he replaced the tin exactly where he had found it and went back to the house. As he crossed the garden again, he noticed a light in Mrs. Sutton's bedroom window. This terrified him more than anything which had gone before. Was she watching him? Ethel's window was dark. If she had drunk anything deadly there would be lights everywhere, movements, calls for the doctor, just as when he himself had been attacked. Attacked—that was the right word, he thought.

Still with the same odd presence of mind and precision, he went in, washed out the utensils and made a second brew of cocoa, which he left standing in the saucepan. He crept quietly to his bedroom. Ethel's voice greeted him on the threshold.

"How late you are, Harold. Naughty old boy! Have a good time?"

"Not bad. You all right, darling?"

"Quite all right. Did Mrs. Sutton leave something hot for you? She said she would."

"Yes, but I wasn't thirsty."

Ethel laughed. "Oh! it was *that* sort of a party, was it?"

Mr. Mummery did not attempt any denials. He undressed and got into bed and clutched his wife to him as though defying death and hell to take her from him. Next morning he would act. He thanked God that he was not too late.

Mr. Dimthorpe, the chemist, was a great friend of Mr. Mummery's. They had often sat together in the untidy little shop on Spring Bank and exchange views on green-fly and club-root. Mr. Mummery told his story frankly to Mr. Dimthorpe and handed over the bottle of cocoa. Mr. Dimthorpe congratulated him on his prudence and intelligence.

"I will have it ready for you by this evening," he said, "and if it's what you think it is, then we shall have a clear case on which to take action."

Mr. Mummery thanked him, and was extremely vague and inattentive at business all day. But that hardly mattered, for Mr. Brookes, who had seen the party through to a riotous end in the small hours, was in no very observant mood. At half-past four, Mr. Mummery shut up his desk decisively and announced that he was off early, he had a call to make.

Mr. Dimthorpe was ready for him.

"No doubt about it," he said. "I used Marsh's test. It's a heavy dose, no wonder you tasted it. There must be four or five grains of pure arsenic in that bottle. Look, here's the mirror. You can see it for yourself."

Mr. Mummery gazed at the little glass tube with its ominous purple-black stain.

"Will you ring up the police from here?" asked the chemist.

"No," said Mr. Mummery. "No—I want to get home. God knows what's happening there. And I've only just time to catch my train."

"All right," said Mr. Dimthorpe. "Leave it to me. I'll ring them up for you."

The local train did not go fast enough for Mr. Mummery. Ethel—poisoned—dying—dead—Ethel—poisoned—dying— dead —the wheels drummed in his ears. He almost ran out of the station and along the road. A car was standing at his door. He saw it from the end of the street and broke into a gallop. It had happened already. The doctor was there. Fool, murderer that he was to have left things so late.

Then, while he was still a hundred and fifty yards off, he saw the front door open. A man came out followed by Ethel herself.

190

The visitor got into his car and was driven away. Ethel went in again. She was safe—safe!

He could hardly control himself to hang up his hat and coat and go in looking reasonably calm. His wife had returned to the armchair by the fire and greeted him in some surprise. There were tea-things on the table.

"Back early, aren't you?"

"Yes—business was slack. Somebody been to tea?"

"Yes, young Welbeck. About the arrangements for the Drama Society." She spoke briefly but with an undertone of excitement.

A qualm came over Mr. Mummery. Would a guest be any protection? His fact must have shown his feelings, for Ethel stared at him in amazement.

"What's the matter, Harold, you look so queer."

"Darling," said Mr. Mummery, "there's something I want to tell you about." He sat down and took her hand in his. "Something a little unpleasant, I'm afraid——"

"Oh, ma'am!"

The cook was in the doorway.

"I beg your pardon, sir—I didn't know you was in. Will you be taking tea or can I clear away? And oh, ma'am, there was a young man at the fishmonger's and he's just come from Grimsby and they've caught that dreadful woman—that Mrs. Andrews. Isn't it a good thing? It worritted me dreadful to think she was going about like that, but they've caught her. Taken a job as housekeeper she had to two elderly ladies and they found the wicked poison on her. Girl as spotted her will get a reward. I been keeping my eyes open for her, but it's at Grimsby she was all the time."

Mr. Mummery clutched at the arm of his chair. It had all been a mad mistake then. He wanted to shout or cry. He wanted to apologise to this foolish, pleasant, excited woman. All a mistake.

But there had been the cocoa. Mr. Dimthorpe. Marsh's test. Five grains of arsenic. Who, then——?

He glanced around at his wife, and in her eyes he saw something that he had never seen before. . . .

THE LEOPARD LADY

"IF the boy is in your way," said a voice in Tressider's ear, "ask at Rapallo's for Smith & Smith."

Tressider started and looked round. There was nobody near him—unless you counted the bookstall clerk, and the aged gentleman with crooked pince-nez half-way down his nose, who stood poring over a copy of *Blackwood*. Obviously, neither of these two could have uttered that sinister whisper. A yard or two away stood a porter, wearily explaining to a militant woman and a dejected little man that the 5.30 having now gone there was no other train before 9.15. All three were utter strangers to Tressider. He shook himself. It must have been his own subconscious wish that had externalised itself in this curious form. He must keep a hold on himself. Hidden wishes that took shape as audible promptings and whisperings were apt to lead to Colney Hatch—or Broadmoor.

But what in the world had suggested the names "Rapallo's" and "Smith & Smith"? Rapallo—that was a town in Italy or somewhere, he fancied. But the word had come to him as "Rapallo's" as though it were the name of a firm or person. And "Smith & Smith," too. Fantastic. Then he glanced up at the bookstall. Of course, yes—"W. H. Smith & Son"; that must have been the point from which the suggestion had started, and his repressed desires had somehow pushed their message past his censor in that preposterous sentence.

"If the boy is in your way, ask at Rapallo's for Smith & Smith."

He let his eye wander over the books and magazines spread out on the stall. Was there anything—yes, there was. A pile of little red books, of which the topmost bore the title: "How to ask for What you Want in ITALY." There was the other factor of the equation. "Italy" had been the match laid to the train, and the resulting spark had been, queerly but understandably enough, "Rapallo's."

Satisfied, he handed a shilling across the stall and asked for the *Strand Magazine*. He tucked his purchase under his arm and then, glancing at the station clock, decided that he had just time for a quick one before his train went. He turned into the buffet, pausing on the way to buy a packet of cigarettes at the kiosk, where the militant woman was already arming herself with milk-chocolate against her wait for the 9.15. He noticed, with a certain grim satisfaction, that the dejected man had made his escape, and was not altogether surprised to encounter him again in the buffet, hurriedly absorbing something yellow out of a glass.

He was some little time getting served, for there was quite a crowd about the bar. But even if he did miss his train, there was another in twenty minutes' time, and his odd experience had shaken him. The old gentleman with *Blackwood*'s had drifted up to the door by the time he left, and, indeed, nearly collided with Tressider in his short-sighted progress. Tressider absently apologised for what was not his fault, and made for the barrier. Here there was again a trifling delay while he searched for his ticket, and a porter who stood beside him with some hand-luggage eventually lost patience and pushed past him with a brief, "By your leave, sir." Eventually, however, he found himself in a first-class carriage with four minutes to spare.

He threw his hat up on to the rack and himself into a corner seat, and immediately, with an automatic anxiety to banish his own thoughts, opened his magazine. As he did so, a card fluttered from between the leaves on to his knee. With an exclamation of impatience directed against the advertisers who filled the pages of magazines with insets, he picked it up, intending to throw it under the seat. A line of black capitals caught his eyes:

SMITH & SMITH

and beneath, in smaller type:

Removals.

He turned the card over. It was about the size of an "At Home" card. The other side was completely blank. There was

193

G

no address; no explanation. An impulse seized him. He snatched up his hat and made for the door. The train was moving as he sprang out, and he staggered as his feet touched the platform. A porter sprang to his side with a warning shout.

"Shouldn't do that, sir," said the man, reprovingly.

"All right, all right," said Tressider, "I've left something behind."

"That's dangerous, that is," said the porter. "Against regulations."

"Oh, all *right,*" said Tressider, fumbling for a coin. As he handed it over, he recognised the porter as the man who had jostled him at the barrier and had stood behind him at the bookstall talking to the militant woman and the dejected man. He dismissed the man hastily, feeling unaccountably uneasy under his official eye. He ran past the barrier with a hasty word to the ticket collector who still stood there, and made his way back to the bookstall.

"*Strand Magazine,*" he demanded, curtly, and then, thinking he caught an astonished expression in the eye of the clerk, he muttered:

"Dropped the other."

The clerk said nothing, but handed over the magazine and accepted Tressider's shilling. Only when he was turning away did Tressider realise that he was still clutching the original copy of the *Strand* under his arm. Well, let the man think what he liked.

Unable to wait, he dived into the General Waiting Room and shook the new *Strand* open. Several insets flew out—one about learning new languages by gramophone, one about Insurance, one about Hire Purchase Payments. He gathered them up and tossed them aside again. Then he examined the magazine, page by page. There was no white card with the name "Smith & Smith."

He stood, trembling, in the dusty gas-light of the waiting room. Had he imagined the card? Was his brain playing tricks with him again? He could not remember what he had done with the card. He searched both magazines and all his pockets. It was not there. He must have left it in the train.

He *must* have left it in the train.

Sweat broke out upon his forehead. It was a terrible thing to go mad. If he had not seen that card—but he *had* seen it. He could see the shape and spacing of the black capitals distinctly.

After a moment or two, an idea came to him. A firm that advertised itself must have an address, perhaps a telephone number. But, of course, not necessarily in London. Those magazines went all over the world. What was the good of advertising without a name or address? Still, he would look. The words "Smith & Smith, Removals," in the London Telephone Directory would steady his nerves considerably.

He went out and sought the nearest telephone cabinet. The directory hung there on its stout chain. Only when he opened it did he realise how many hundred firms called "Smith & Smith" there might be in London. The small print made his eyes ache, but he persevered, and was at length rewarded by finding an entry: "Smith & Smith, Frntre Removrs & Haulage Cntrctrs," with an address in Greenwich.

That should have satisfied him, but it did not. He could not believe that a firm of Furniture Removers and Haulage Contractors at Greenwich would advertise, without address, in a magazine of world-wide circulation. Only firms whose name was a household word could do that kind of thing. And besides, in that second *Strand* there had been no advertisement.

Then how had that card got there? Had the bookstall clerk slipped it in? Or the militant woman who had stood beside him at the tobacco kiosk? Or the dejected man sipping whisky and soda in the buffet? Or the old gentleman who had passed him in the entrance? Or the porter who had waited behind him at the barrier? It came suddenly into his mind that all these five had been near him when he had heard the voice of his repressed wish whisper so persuasively, and so objectively:

"If the boy is in your way, ask at Rapallo's for Smith & Smith."

With a kind of greedy reluctance, he turned the pages of the telephone Directory backwards to R.

There it was. There could be no mistake about it this time.

"Rapallo's Sandwich & Cocktail Bar,"

with an address in Conduit Street.

A minute later, Tressider was hailing a taxi outside the station. His wife would be expecting him, but she must wait. He had often been detained in town before.

He gave the taxi the Conduit Street address.

It was a small place, but had nothing sinister about it. Clean, white-draped tables with individual lights and a big mahogany

bar, whose wide semi-circle took up nearly half the availabl
floor-space. The door closed behind Tressider with a comfort
able, chuckling click. He went up to the bar and, with an in
describable fluttering of the heart, said to the white-coate
attendant:

"I was told to ask here for Messrs. Smith & Smith."

"What name, sir?" asked the man, showing neither hesita
tion nor surprise.

"Jones," said Tressider, uninventively.

"Maurice, have we any message for a Mr. Jones from—whon
did you say, sir? Oh yes. From Messrs. Smith & Smith?"

The second barman turned round and enveloped Tressider i
a brief, searching glance.

"Oh, yes," he said. "Quite right, sir. Mr. Smith is expectin,
you. Will you step this way?"

He led Tressider to the back of the room, where a stoutish
middle-aged man in a dark tweed suit was seated at a tabl
eating an American sandwich.

The stout man looked up, revealing small chubby feature
beneath an enormous expanse of polished and dome-like skul
He smiled pleasantly.

"You are magnificently punctual," he said, in a clear, sol
voice, with a fluting quality which made it very delightful t
listen to. "I hardly expected you to get here quite so soon." An
then, as the barman turned away, he added:

"Pray sit down, Mr. Tressider."

"You look a little unnerved," said Mr. Smith. "Perhaps yo
had a rush from the station. Let me recommend one of Rapallo
special cocktails." He made a sign to the barman, who brough
over two glasses filled with a curious dark-coloured liqueu
"You will find it slightly bitter, but very effective. You need no
be alarmed, by the way. Choose whichever glass you like an
leave me the other. It is quite immaterial which."

Tressider, a little confounded by the smiling ease with whic
Mr. Smith read his thoughts, took one of the glasses at random
Mr. Smith immediately took the other and drank off one-ha
of the contents. Tressider sipped his. The liqueur was certainl
bitter but not altogether unpleasant.

"It will do you good," said Mr. Smith, prosaically. "The bo
I take it, is quite well?" he went on, almost in the same breatl

"Perfectly well," said Tressider, staring.

"Of course. Your wife takes such good care of him, doesn't she? A thoroughly good and conscientious woman, as most women are, bless their dear hearts. The child is six years old, I think?"

"Rising six."

"Just so. A long time to go yet before he attains his majority. Fifteen years—yes, a considerable time, in which very many things may happen. You yourself, for instance, will be hard on sixty—the best part of your life at an end, while his is just beginning. He is a young gentleman of great expectations, to quote the divine Dickens. And he is starting well, despite the sad handicap of losing both his parents at so early an age. A fine, healthy youngster, is he not? No measles? mumps? whooping-cough? that sort of thing?"

"Not so far," muttered Tressider.

"No. Your almost-parental care has shielded him from all the ills that youthful flesh is heir to. How wise your brother was, Mr. Tressider. Some people might have thought it foolish of him to leave Cyril in your sole guardianship, considering that there was only his little life between you and the Tressider estate. Foolish—and even inconsiderate. For, after all, it is a great responsibility, is it not? A child seems to hold its life by so frail a tenure. But your brother was a wise man, after all. Knowing your upright, virtuous wife and yourself so well, he did the best thing he could possibly have done for Cyril when he left him in your care. Eh?"

"Of course," said Tressider, thickly.

Mr. Smith finished his liqueur.

"You are not drinking," he protested.

"Look here," said Tressider, gulping down the remainder of his drink, "you seem to know a lot about me and my affairs."

"Oh, but that is common knowledge, surely. The doings of so rich and fortunate a little boy as Cyril Tressider are chronicled in every newspaper paragraph. Perhaps the newspapers do not know quite so much about Mr. Tressider, his uncle and guardian. They may not realise quite how deeply he was involved in the Megatherium catastrophe, nor how much he has lost in one way and another on the turf. Still, they know, naturally, that he is an upright English gentleman and that both he and his wife are devoted to the boy."

Tressider leaned his elbow on the table and, holding his head propped on his hand, tried to read Mr. Smith's countenance. He

197

found it difficult, for Mr. Smith and the room and everything about him seemed to advance and recede in the oddest manner. He thought he might be in for a dose of fever.

"Children . . . " Mr. Smith's voice fluted towards him from an enormous distance. "Accidents, naturally, will sometimes happen. No one can prevent it. Childish ailments may leave distressing after effects . . . babyish habits, however judiciously checked, may lead . . . Pardon me, I fear you are not feeling altogether the thing."

"I feel damned queer," said Tressider. "I—at the station today—hallucinations—I can't understand——"

Suddenly, from the pit in which it had lurked, chained and growling, Terror leapt at him. It shook his bones and cramped his stomach. It was like a palpable enemy, suffocating and tearing him. He gripped the table. He saw Mr. Smith's huge face loom down upon him, immense, immeasurable.

"Dear, dear!" The voice boomed in his ear like a great silver bell. "You are really not well. Allow me. Just a sip of this."

He drank, and the Terror, defeated, withdrew from him. A vast peace surged over his brain. He laughed. Everything was jolly, jolly, jolly. He wanted to sing.

Mr. Smith beckoned to the barman.

"Is the car ready?" he asked.

Tressider stood by Mr. Smith's side. The car had gone, and they were alone before the tall green gates that towered into the summer twilight. Mile upon mile they had driven through town and country; mile upon mile, with the river rolling beside them and the scent of trees and water blown in upon the July breeze. They had been many hours upon the journey and yet the soft dusk was hardly deeper than when they had set out. For them, as for Joshua, sun and stars had stood still in their courses. That this was so, Tressider knew, for he was not drunk or dreaming. His senses had never been more acute, his perceptions more vivid. Every leaf upon the tall poplars that shivered above the gates was vivid to him with a particular beauty of sound, shape and odour. The gates, which bore in great letters the name "SMITH & SMITH—REMOVALS," opened at Smith's touch. The long avenue of poplars stretched up to a squat grey house with a pillared portico.

Many times in the weeks that followed, Tressider asked him-

elf whether he had after all dreamed that strange adventure at
he House of the Poplars. From the first whisper by the station
ookstall to the journey by car down to his own home in Essex,
very episode had had a nightmare quality. Yet surely, no night-
are had ever been so consecutive nor so clearly memorable in
vaking moments. There was the room with its pale grey walls
nd shining floor—a luminous pool in the soft mingling of
lectric light and dying daylight from the high, unshuttered
vindows. There were the four men—Mr. Smith, of the restaur-
nt; Mr. Smyth, with his narrow yellow face disfigured by a
car like an acid burn; Mr. Smythe, square and sullen, with
hort, strong hands and hairy knuckles; and Dr. Schmidt, the
iggling man with the scanty red beard and steel-rimmed spec-
acles. And there was the girl with the slanting golden eyes like
 cat's, he thought. They called her "Miss Smith," but her name
hould have been Melusine.

Nor could he have dreamed the conversation, which was
usinesslike and brief.

"It has long been evident to us," said Mr. Smith, "that society
s in need of a suitable organisation for the Removal of un-
ecessary persons. Private and amateur attempts at Removal are
o frequently attended with subsequent inconvenience and even
langer to the Remover, who, in addition, usually has to carry out
is work with very makeshift materials. It is our pleasure and
rivilege to attend to all the disagreeable details of such Re-
ovals for our clients at a moderate—I may say, a merely
ominal—expense. Provided our terms are strictly adhered to,
ve can guarantee our clients against all unpleasant repercus-
ions, preserving, of course, inviolable secrecy as to the whole
ransaction."

Dr. Schmidt sniggered faintly.

"In the matter of young Cyril Tressider, for example," went
n Mr. Smith, "I can conceive nothing more unnecessary than
ne existence of this wearisome child. He is an orphan; his only
elations are Mr. and Mrs. Tressider who, however amiably
isposed they may feel towards the boy, are financially embar-
assed by his presence in the world. If he were to be quietly
emoved, who would be the loser? Not himself, for he would be
ared the sins and troubles of life on this ill-regulated planet;
ot his relations, for he has none but his uncle and aunt who
ould be better for his disappearance; not his tenants and
ependants, since his good uncle would be there to take his

199

place. I suggest, Mr. Tressider, that the small sum of one thousand pounds would be profitably spent in Removing this boy to that happy land 'far, far beyond the stars,' where he might play with the young-eyed cherubim (to quote our glorious poet), remote from the accidents of measles or stomach-ache to which, alas! all young children are so unhappily liable here below."

"A thousand?" said Tressider, and laughed, "I would give five, gladly, to be rid of the youngster."

Dr. Schmidt sniggered. "We should not like to be rapacious," he said. "No. One thousand pounds will amply repay the very trifling trouble."

"How about the risk?" said Tressider.

"We have abolished risk," replied Mr. Smith. "For us, and for our clients, the word does not exist. Tell me, the boy reside with you at your home in Essex? Yes. Is he a good little boy?"

"Decent enough kid, as far as that goes."

"No bad habits?"

"He's a bit of a liar, like lots of kids."

"How so, my friend?" asked Dr. Schmidt.

"He romances. Pretends he's had all kinds of adventures with giants and fairies and tigers and what not. You know the kind of thing. Doesn't seem able to tell the truth. It worries his aunt good deal."

"Ah!" Dr. Schmidt seemed to take over the interview at this point. "The good Mrs. Tressider, she does not encourage the romancing?"

"No. She does her best. Tells Cyril that he'll go to a bad place if he tells her stories. But it's wonderful how the little beggar persists. Sometimes we have to spank him. But he's damnably obstinate. There's a bad streak in the boy somewhere. Unsound. Not English, that sort of thing."

"Sad," said Dr. Schmidt, sniggering, so that the word became a long bleat. "Sa-a-d. It would be a pity if the poor little boy should miss the golden gates after all. That would distress me.

"It would be still more distressing, Schmidt, that a person with a failing of that kind should be placed in any position of importance as the owner of the Tressider estates. Honour and uprightness, coupled with a healthy lack of imagination, have made this country what it is."

"True," said Dr. Schmidt. "How beautifully you put it, my dear Smith. No doubt, Mr. Tressider, your little ward finds much cope for imaginative adventure when playing about in the deserted grounds of Crantonbury Place, situated so conveniently next door to your abode."

"You seem to know a lot," said Tressider.

"Our organisation," explained Dr. Schmidt, with a wave of the hand. "It is melancholy to see these fine old country mansions thus deserted, but one man's loss is the gain of the little boy next door. I should encourage little Cyril to play in the grounds of Crantonbury Hall. His little limbs will grow strong running about among the over-grown bushes and the straggling garden-beds where the strawberry grows underneath the nettle. I quote your Shakespeare, my dear Smith. It is a calamity that the fountains should be silent and the great fish-pond run dry. The nine men's morris is filled up with mud—Shakespeare again. Nevertheless, there are still many possibilities in an old garden."

He giggled and pulled at his thin beard.

If this fantastic conversation had never taken place, how was it that Tressider could remember every word so clearly. He remembered, too, signing a paper—the "Removal Order," Smith had called it—and a cheque for £1,000, payable to Smith & Smith, and post-dated October 1st.

"We like to allow a margin," said Mr. Smith. "We cannot at this moment predict to a day when the Removal will be carried out. But from now to October 1st should provide ample time. If you should change your mind before the Removal has taken place, you have only to leave word to that effect at Rapallo's. But after the Removal, it would be too late to make any alterations. Indeed, in such a case, there might be—er—unpleasantness of a kind which I should not care to specify. But, between gentlemen, such a situation could not, naturally, arise. Are you likely to be absent from home at any time in the near future?"

Tressider shook his head.

"No? Forgive me, but I think you would be well advised to spend—let us say the month of September—abroad. Or perhaps in Scotland. There is salmon, there is trout, there is grouse, there is partridge—all agreeable creatures to kill."

Dr. Schmidt sniggered again.

"Just as you like, of course," went on Mr. Smith. "But if you and perhaps your wife also——"

"My wife wouldn't leave Cyril."

201

"Yourself, then. A holiday from domesticity is sometimes an excellent thing."

"I will think about it," said Tressider.

He had thought often about it. He also thought frequentl' about the blank counterfoil in his cheque-book. That, at least was a fact. He was thinking about it in Scotland on Septembe 15th, as he tramped across the moors, gun on shoulder. It migh be a good thing to stop that cheque.

"Auntie Edith!"

"Yes, Cyril."

Mrs. Tressider was a thin woman with a strong, Puritan face a woman of narrow but fixed affections and limited outlook.

"Auntie, I've had a wonderful adventure."

Mrs. Tressider pressed her pale lips together.

"Now, Cyril. Think before hand. Don't exaggerate, dear. Yo' look very hot and excited."

"Yes, Auntie. I met a fairy——"

"Cyril!"

"No, *really*, Auntie, I did. She lives in Crantonbury Hall—in the old grotto. A real, live fairy. And she was all dressed in gold and lovely colours like a rainbow, red and green and blu' and yellow and *all* sorts of colours. And a gold crown on he' head and stars in her hair. And I wasn't a bit frightened, Auntie and she said——"

"Cyril, dear——"

"Yes, Auntie, *really*. I'm not 'zaggerating. She was ever s' beautiful. And she said I was a brave boy, just like Jack-and the-Beanstalk, and I was to marry her when I grew up, and liv' in Fairyland. Only I'm not big enough yet. And she had lion' and tigers and leopards all round her with gold collars an' diamonds on them. And she took me into her fairy palace——"

"Cyril!"

"And we ate fairy fruit off gold plates and she's going to teac' me the language of the birds and give me a pair of seven-leagu' boots all for myself, so that I can go *all* over the world and b' a hero."

"That's a very exciting story you've made up, darling, but o course it's only a story, isn't it?"

"No, 'tisn't only a story. It's quite true. You see if it isn't."

202

"Darling, even in fun you musn't say it's *true*. There couldn't be lions and tigers and leopards at Crantonbury Hall."

"Well . . . " the child paused. "Well, pr'aps I was 'zaggerating just a teeny, weeny bit. But there was two leopards."

"Oh, Cyril! Two leopards?"

"Yes, with golden collars and chains. And the fairy was ever so tall and beautiful, with lovely goldeny eyes just like the leopards'. She said she was the fairy of the leopards, and they were fairies too, and after we'd had the fairy feast the leopards grew wings and she got on their backs—on one of them's back, I mean—and flew *right* away over the roof."

Mrs. Tressider sighed.

"I don't think Nanny ought to tell you so many fairy tales. You know there aren't any fairies, really."

"That's all *you* know about it," said Cyril, rather rudely. "There is fairies, and I've seen one, and I'm to be the King of the Fairies when I'm bigger."

"You mustn't contradict me like that, Cyril. And it's *very* naughty to say what isn't true."

"But it *is* true, Auntie."

"You mustn't say that, darling. I've told you ever so many times that it's very nice to make up stories, but we mustn't ever forget that it's all make-believe."

"But I *did* see the fairy."

"If you say that any more, Auntie will be very cross with you——"

"But I did, I did. I *swear* I did."

"Cyril!" Mrs. Tressider was definitely shocked. "That is a very wicked word to use. You must go straight to bed without your supper, and Auntie doesn't want to see you again till you have apologised for being so rude and telling such naughty stories."

"But, Auntie——"

"That will do," said Mrs. Tressider, and rang the bell. Cyril was led away in tears.

"If you please, ma'am," said Nannie, catching Mrs. Tressider as she rose from the dinner-table, "Master Cyril don't seem very well, ma'am. He says he has a bad stomach-ache."

Cyril did seem feverish and queer when his aunt went up to him. He was flushed and feverish, and his eyes were unnaturally

203

bright and frightened. He complained of a dreadful pain und his pyjama-girdle.

"That's what happens to naughty little boys who tell stories said Mrs. Tressider, who had old-fashioned ideas about impro ing the occasion. "Now Nannie will have to give you som nasty medicine."

Nannie, advancing, armed with a horrid tumblerful of green grey liquorice powder, had her own moral to draw.

"I expect you've been eating them nasty old crab-apples o of the old garden," she remarked. "I'm sure I've told you tim and again, Master Cyril, to leave them things alone."

"I didn't eat nothing," said Cyril, " 'cept the fairy feast the palace with the leopard lady."

"We don't want to hear about the leopard-lady any more. said Mrs. Tressider. "Now, own up darling, that was all imagi ation and nonsense, wasn't it? He does look feverish," she adde in an aside to Nannie. "Perhaps we'd better send for Dr. Sim monds. With Mr. Tressider away, one feels rather anxious. Now Cyril, drink up your medicine and say you're sorry. . . . "

When Dr. Simmonds arrived an hour later (for he had bee out when summoned) he found his patient delirious and Mr Tressider thoroughly alarmed. Dr. Simmonds wasted no tim with liquorice powder, but used the stomach pump. His face wa grave.

"What has he been eating?" he asked, and shook his head a Nannie's suggestion of green applies. Mrs. Tressider, white an anxious, went into details about the child's story of the leopar lady.

"He looked feverish when he came in," she said, "but thought he was just excited with his make-believe games."

"Imaginative children are often unable to distinguish betwee fact and fancy," said the doctor. "I think he very probably di eat something that he shouldn't have done; it would be all par of the game he was playing with himself."

"I made him confess in the end that he was making it all up, said Mrs. Tressider.

"H'm," said Dr. Simmonds. "Well, I don't think you'd bette worry him about it any more. He's a highly-strung child an he'll need all his strength——"

"You don't mean he's in any danger, Doctor?"

"Oh, I hope not, I hope not. But children are rather kitt

little cattle and something has upset him badly. Is Mr. Tressider at home?"

"Ought I to send for him?"

"It might be as well. By the way, could you let me have a clean bottle? I should like to take away some of the contents of the stomach for examination. Just to be on the safe side, you know. I don't want to alarm you—it's just that, in a case of this kind, it is as well to know what one has to deal with."

Before morning, Cyril was collapsed, blue in the face and cold, and another doctor had been called in. Tressider, when he hurriedly arrived by the midnight train, was greeted by the news that there was very little hope.

"I am afraid, Mr. Tressider, that the boy has managed to pick up something poisonous. We are having an analysis made. The symptoms are suggestive of poisoning by solanine, or some alkali of that group. Nightshade—is there any garden nightshade at Crantonbury Hall?" Thus Dr. Pratt, a specialist and expensive.

Mr. Tressider did not know, but said he thought they might go and see next day. The search-party was accordingly sent out in the morning. They discovered no nightshade, but Dr. Pratt, prowling about the weed-grown kitchen garden made a discovery.

"Look!" he said. "These old potato-plants have got potato-apples on them. The potato belongs to the genus Solanum, and the apples, and sometimes even the tubers themselves, have occasionally given rise to poisonous symptoms. If the boy had happened to pluck and eat some of these berries——"

"He did, then," said Dr. Simmonds. "See here."

He lifted a plant on which a number of short stalks still remained to show where the potato-apples had been.

"I had no idea," said Tressider, "that the things were as poisonous as that."

"They are not as a rule," said Dr. Pratt. "But here and there one finds a plant which is particularly rich in the poisonous principle, solanine. There was a classical case, in 1885 or thereabouts——"

He prosed on. Mrs. Tressider could not bear it. She left them and went upstairs to sit by Cyril's bedside.

"I want to see the lovely leopard lady," said Cyril, faintly.

"Yes, yes—she's coming, darling," said Mrs. Tressider.

"With her leopards?"

"Yes, darling. And lions and tigers."

"Because I've got to be King of the Fairies when I grow up."

"Of course you have, darling."

On the third day, Cyril died.

The expert's analysis confirmed Dr. Pratt's diagnosis. Seeds and skin of the potato-apple had been identified in the contents of the stomach. Death was from solanine poisoning, a remarkable quantity of the alkali having been present in the potato-apples. An examination of other berries taken from the same plants showed that the potatoes in question were, undoubtedly, particularly rich in solanine. Verdict: Death by misadventure. Children, said the coroner, were very apt to chew and eat strange plants and berries, and the potato-apple undoubtedly had an attractive appearance—like a little green tomato—the jury had no doubt often seen it in their own gardens. It was, however, very seldom that the effects were so tragic as in the present sad case. No blame could possibly attach to Mr. and Mrs. Tressider, who had repeatedly warned the child not to eat anything he did not know the name of, and had usually found him an obedient child in this respect.

Tressider, to whom nobody had thought to mention the story of the leopard lady, showed a becoming grief at the death of his little ward. He purchased a handsome suit of black and ordered a new saloon car. In this he went about a good deal by himself in the days that followed the inquest, driving, on one occasion, as far as Greenwich.

He had looked up the address in the telephone-book and presently found himself rolling down a quiet riverside lane. Yes—there they were, on the right, two shabby green gates across which, in faded white lettering, ran the words:

SMITH & SMITH

REMOVALS

He got out of the car and stood, hesitating a little. The autumn had come early that year, and as he stood, a yellow poplar leaf, shaken from its hold by the wind, fluttered delicately to his feet.

He pushed at the gates, which opened slowly, with a rusty creaking. There was no avenue of poplars and no squat grey house with a pillared portico. An untidy yard met his gaze. At the back was a tumble-down warehouse, and on either side of the gate a sickly poplar whispered fretfully. A ruddy-faced man, engaged in harnessing a cart-horse to an open lorry, came forward to greet him.

"Could I speak to Mr. Smith," asked Tressider.

"It's Mr. Benton you'll be wanting," replied the man. "There ain't no Mr. Smith."

"Oh!" said Tressider. "Then which of the gentlemen is it that has a very high, bald forehead—a rather stoutish gentleman. I thought——"

"Nobody like that here," said the man. "You've made a mistake, mister. There's only Mr. Benton—he's tall, with grey 'air and specs, and Mr. Tinworth, the young gentleman, him that's a bit lame. Was you wanting a Removal by any chance?"

"No, no," said Tressider, rather hastily. "I thought I knew Mr. Smith, that's all. Has he retired lately?"

"Lord, no." The man laughed heartily. "There ain't been a Mr. Smith here, not in donkey's years. Come to think of it, they're all dead, I believe. Jim! What's happened to old Mr. Smith and his brother what used to run this show?"

A little elderly man came out of the warehouse, wiping his hands on his apron.

"Dead these ten years," he said. "What's up?"

"Gent here thought he knowed the parties."

"Well, they're dead," repeated Jim.

"Thank you," said Tressider.

He went back to the car. For the hundredth time he asked himself whether he should stop the cheque. The death of Cyril could only be a coincidence. It was now or never, for this was the 30th September.

He vacillated, and put the matter off till next day. At ten o'clock in the morning he rang up the bank.

"A cheque"—he gave the number—"for £1,000, payable to Smith & Smith. Has it been cashed?"

"Yes, Mr. Tressider. Nine-thirty this morning. Hope there's nothing wrong about it.'

"Nothing whatever, thanks. I just wanted to know."

Then he *had* drawn it. And somebody had cashed it.

Next day there was a letter. It was typewritten and bore no address of origin ; only the printed heading SMITH & SMITH and the date, 1 October.

"DEAR SIR,—

"With reference to your esteemed order of the 12th July for a Removal from your residence in Essex, we trust that this commission has been carried out to your satisfaction. We beg to acknowledge your obliging favour of One Thousand Pounds (£1,000), and return herewith the Order of Removal which you were good enough to hand to us. Assuring you of our best attention at all times,

"Faithfully yours,
"SMITH & SMITH."

The enclosure ran as follows:

"I, Arthur Tressider of (here followed his address in Essex) hereby confess that I murdered my ward and nephew, Cyril Tressider, in the following manner. Knowing that the child was in the habit of playing in the garden of Crantonbury Hall, adjoining my own residence, and vacant for the last twelve months, I searched this garden carefully and discovered there a number of old potato-plants, some of them bearing potato-apples. Into these potato-apples I injected with a small syringe a powerful solution of the poisonous alkali solanine, of which a certain quantity is always present in these plants. I prepared this solution from plants of solanum which I had already secretly gathered. I had no difficulty in doing this, having paid some attention as a young man to the study of chemistry. I felt sure that the child would be tempted to eat these berries, but had he failed to do so I had various other schemes of a similar nature in reserve, on which I should have fallen back if necessary. I committed this abominable crime in order to secure the Tressider estates, entailed upon me as next heir. I now make this confession, being troubled in my conscience.

"ARTHUR TRESSIDER"

"1 October, 193—"

The sweat stood on Tressider's forehead.

"How did they know I had studied chemistry?"

He seemed to hear the sniggering voice of Dr. Schmidt: "Our organisation——"

He burned the papers and went out without saying his customary farewell to his wife. It was not until some time later that he heard the story of the leopard lady, and he thought of Miss Smith, the girl with the yellow eyes like cat's eyes, who should have been called Melusine.

THE CYPRIAN CAT

r's extraordinarily decent of you to come along and see me
ike this, Harringay. Believe me, I do appreciate it. It isn't
very busy K.C. who'd do as much for such a hopeless sort of
lient. I only wish I could spin you a more workable kind of
tory, but honestly, I can only tell you exactly what I told
Peabody. Of course, I can see he doesn't believe a word of
t, and I don't blame him. He thinks I ought to be able to make
up a more plausible tale than that—and I suppose I could, but
where's the use? One's almost bound to fall down somewhere
f one tries to swear to a lie. What I'm going to tell you
s the absolute truth. I fired one shot and one shot only, and
hat was at the cat. It's funny that one should be hanged for
hooting at a cat.

Merridew and I were always the best of friends; school
and college and all that sort of thing. We didn't see very
much of each other after the war, because we were living
at opposite ends of the country; but we met in Town from
ime to time and wrote occasionally and each of us knew that
he other was there in the background, so to speak. Two years
ago, he wrote and told me he was getting married. He was
ust turned forty and the girl was fifteen years younger, and
ae was tremendously in love. It gave me a bit of a jolt—
you know how it is when your friends marry. You feel they
will never be quite the same again; and I'd got used to the
dea that Merridew and I were cut out to be old bachelors.
But of course I congratulated him and sent him a wedding
present, and I did sincerely hope he'd be happy. He was
obviously over head and ears; almost dangerously so, I thought,
considering all things. Though except for the difference of age
t seemed suitable enough. He told me he had met her at—of
all places—a rectory garden-party down in Norfolk, and that

she had actually never been out of her native village. I mean, literally—not so much as a trip to the nearest town. I'm not trying to convey that she wasn't pukka, or anything like that. Her father was some queer sort of recluse—a mediævalist, or something—desperately poor. He died shortly after their marriage.

I didn't see anything of them for the first year or so. Merridew is a civil engineer, you know, and he took his wife away after the honeymoon to Liverpool, where he was doing something in connection with the harbour. It must have been a big change for her from the wilds of Norfolk. I was in Birmingham, with my nose kept pretty close to the grindstone, so we only exchanged occasional letters. His were what I can only call deliriously happy, especially at first. Later on, he seemed a little worried about his wife's health. She was restless; town life didn't suit her; he'd be glad when he could finish up his Liverpool job and get her away into the country. There wasn't any doubt about their happiness, you understand—she'd got him body and soul as they say, and as far as I could make out it was mutual. I want to make that perfectly clear.

Well, to cut a long story short, Merridew wrote to me at the beginning of last month and said he was just off to a new job—a waterworks extension scheme down in Somerset; and he asked if I could possibly cut loose and join them there for a few weeks. He wanted to have a yarn with me, and Felice was longing to make my acquaintance. They had got rooms at the village inn. It was rather a remote spot, but there was fishing and scenery and so forth, and I should be able to keep Felice company while he was working up at the dam. I was about fed up with Birmingham, what with the heat and one thing and another, and it looked pretty good to me, and I was due for a holiday anyhow, so I fixed up to go. I had a bit of business to do in Town, which I calculated would take me about a week, so I said I'd go down to Little Hexham on June 20th.

As it happened, my business in London finished itself off unexpectedly soon, and on the sixteenth I found myself absolutely free and stuck in an hotel with road-drills working just under the windows and a tar-spraying machine to make things livelier. You remember what a hot month it was— flaming June and no mistake about it. I didn't see any point in waiting, so I sent off a wire to Merridew, packed my bag and

ook the train for Somerset the same evening. I couldn't get
compartment to myself, but I found a first-class smoker
ith only three seats occupied, and stowed myself thankfully
to the fourth corner. There was a military-looking old boy,
n elderly female with a lot of bags and baskets, and a girl.
thought I should have a nice, peaceful journey.

So I should have, if it hadn't been for the unfortunate way
m built. It was quite all right at first—as a matter of fact,
think I was half asleep, and I only woke up properly at
even o'clock, when the waiter came to say that dinner was
n. The other people weren't taking it, and when I came back
om the restaurant car I found that the old boy had gone,
nd there were only the two women left. I settled down in
y corner again, and gradually, as we went along, I found a
orrible feeling creeping over me that there was a cat in the
ompartment somewhere. I'm one of those wretched people who
an't stand cats. I don't mean just that I prefer dogs—I mean
hat the presence of a cat in the same room with me makes
e feel like nothing on earth. I can't describe it, but I believe
uite a lot of people are affected that way. Something to do
vith electricity, or so they tell me. I've read that very often the
islike is mutual, but it isn't so with me. The brutes seem to
nd me abominably fascinating—make a bee-line for my legs
very time. It's a funny sort of complaint, and it doesn't make
e at all popular with dear old ladies.

Anway, I began to feel more and more awful and I realised
hat the old girl at the other end of the seat must have a
at in one of her innumerable baskets. I thought of asking her
o put it out in the corridor, or calling the guard and having
t removed, but I knew how silly it would sound and made
p my mind to try and stick it. I couldn't say the animal
vas misbehaving itself or anything, and she looked a pleasant
ld lady; it wasn't her fault that I was a freak. I tried to
istract my mind by looking at the girl.

She was worth looking at, too—very slim, and dark with
ne of those dead-white skins that make you think of magnolia
lossom. She had the most astonishing eyes, too—I've never
een eyes quite like them; a very pale brown, almost amber,
et wide apart and a little slanting, and they seemed to have
kind of luminosity of their own, if you get what I mean.
don't know if this sounds—I don't want you to think I was
owled over, or anything. As a matter of fact she held no

sort of attraction for me, though I could imagine a different type of man going potty about her. She was just unusual, that was all. But however much I tried to think of other thing I couldn't get rid of the uncomfortable feeling, and eventuall I gave it up and went out into the corridor. I just mentio this because it will help you to understand the rest of th story. If you can only realize how perfectly awful I feel whe there's a cat about—even when it's shut up in a basket—you' understand better how I came to buy the revolver.

Well, we got to Hexham Junction, which was the neares station to Little Hexham, and there was old Merridew waitin on the platform. The girl was getting out too—but not th old lady with the cat, thank goodness—and I was just handin her traps out after her when he came galloping up and haile us.

"Hullo!" he said, "why that's splendid! Have you introduce yourselves?" So I tumbled to it then that the girl was Mr Merridew, who'd been up to Town on a shopping expeditior and I explained to her about my change of plans and she sai how jolly it was that I could come—the usual things. I notice what an attractive low voice she had and how graceful he movements were, and I understood—though, mind you, I didn share—Merridew's infatuation.

We got into his car—Mrs. Merridew sat in the back and got up beside Merridew, and was very glad to feel the ai and to get rid of the oppressive electric feeling I'd had i the train. He told me the place suited them wonderfully and had given Felice an absolutely new lease of life, so t speak. He said he was very fit, too, but I thought myself tha he looked rather fagged and nervy.

You'd have liked that inn, Harringay. The real, old-fashione stuff, as quaint as you make 'em, and everything genuine—non of your Tottenham Court Road antiques. We'd all had ou grub, and Mrs. Merridew said she was tired; so she went u to bed early and Merridew and I had a drink and went fo a stroll round the village. It's a tiny hamlet quite at the othe end of nowhere; lights out at ten, little thatched houses wit pinched-up attic windows like furry ears—the place purred i its sleep. Merridew's working gang didn't sleep there of cours —they'd run up huts for them at the dams, a mile beyond th village.

The landlord was just locking up the bar when we cam

n—a block of a man with an absolutely expressionless face. His wife was a thin, sandy-haired woman who looked as though he was too down-trodden to open her mouth. But I found out afterwards that was a mistake, for one evening when he'd taken one or two over the eight and showed signs of wanting to make a night of it, his wife sent him off upstairs with a gesture and a look that took the heart out of him. That first night she was sitting in the porch, and hardly glanced at us as we passed her. I always thought her an uncomfortable kind of woman, but she certainly kept her house most exquisitely neat and clean.

They'd given me a noble bedroom, close under the eaves with long, low casement window overlooking the garden. The sheets smelt of lavender, and I was between them and asleep almost before you could count ten. I was tired, you see. But later in the night I woke up. I was too hot, so took off some of the blankets and then strolled across to the window to get a breath of air. The garden was bathed in moonshine and on the lawn I could see something twisting and turning oddly. I stared a bit before I made it out to be two cats. They didn't worry me at that distance, and I watched them for a bit before I turned in again. They were rolling over one another and jumping away again and chasing their own shadows on the grass, intent on their own mysterious business—taking themselves seriously, the way cats always do. It looked like a kind of ritual dance. Then something seemed to startle them, and they scampered away.

I went back to bed, but I couldn't get to sleep again. My nerves seemed to be all on edge. I lay watching the window and listening to a kind of soft rustling noise that seemed to be going on in the big wistaria that ran along my side of the house. And then something landed with a soft thud on the sill —a great Cyprian cat.

What did you say? Well, one of those striped grey and black cats. Tabby, that's right. In my part of the country they call them Cyprus cats, or Cyprian cats. I'd never seen such a monster. It stood with its head cocked sideways, staring into the room and rubbing its ears very softly against the upright bar of the casement.

Of course, I couldn't do with that. I shooed the brute away, and it made off without a sound. Heat or no heat, I shut and fastened the window. Far out in the shrubbery, I thought I

213

heard a faint miauling; then silence. After that, I went straight off to sleep again and lay like a log until the girl came in to call me.

The next day, Merridew ran us up in his car to see the place where they were making the dam, and that was the first time I realized that Felice's nerviness had not been altogether cured. He showed us where they had diverted part of the river into a swift little stream that was to be used for working the dynamo of an electrical plant. There were a couple of planks laid across the stream, and he wanted to take us over to show us the engine. It wasn't extraordinarily wide or dangerous, but Mrs. Merridew peremptorily refused to cross it, and got quite hysterical when he tried to insist. Eventually he and I went over and inspected the machinery by ourselves. When we got back she had recovered her temper and apologized for being so silly. Merridew abased himself, of course, and I began to feel a little *de trop*. She told me afterwards that she had once fallen into a river as a child and been nearly drowned, and it had left her with a what d'ye call it—a complex about running water. And but for this one trifling episode, I never heard a single sharp word pass between them all the time I was there; nor, for a whole week, did I notice anything else to suggest a flaw in Mrs. Merridew's radiant health. Indeed, as the days wore on to midsummer and the heat grew more intense, her whole body seemed to glow with vitality. It was as though she was lit up from within.

Merridew was out all day and working very hard. I thought he was overdoing it and asked him if he was sleeping badly. He told me that, on the contrary, he fell asleep every night the moment his head touched the pillow, and—what was most unusual with him—had no dreams of any kind. I myself felt well enough, but the hot weather made me languid and disinclined for exertion. Mrs. Merridew took me out for long drives in the car. I would sit for hours, lulled into a half-slumber by the rush of warm air and the purring of the engine, and gazing at my driver, upright at the wheel, her eyes fixed unwaveringly upon the spinning road. We explored the whole of the country to the south and east of Little Hexham, and once or twice went as far north as Bath. Once I suggested that we should turn eastward over the bridge and run down into what looked like rather beautiful wooded country, but Mrs. Merridew didn't care for the idea; she said it was a bad road and that the scenery on that side was disappointing.

214

Altogether, I spent a pleasant week at Little Hexham, and
f it had not been for the cats I should have been perfectly
omfortable. Every night the garden seemed to be haunted by
hem—the Cyprian cat that I had seen the first night of my
tay, and a little ginger one and a horrible stinking black Tom
vere especially tiresome, and one night there was a terrified
vhite kitten that mewed for an hour on end under my window.
flung boots and books at my visitors till I was heartily weary,
ut they seemed determined to make the inn garden their
endezvous. The nuisance grew worse from night to night ; on
ne occasion I counted fifteen of them, sitting on their hinder-
nds in a circle, while the Cyprian cat danced her shadow-dance
mong them, working in and out like a weaver's shuttle. I
ad to keep my window shut, for the Cyprian cat evidently
nade a habit of climbing up by the wistaria. The door, too ; for
once when I had gone down to fetch something from the sitting-
oom, I found her on my bed, kneading the coverlet with her
aws—pr'rp, pr'rp, pr'rp—with her eyes closed in a sensuous
cstasy. I beat her off, and she spat at me as she fled into
he dark passage.

I asked the landlady about her, but she replied rather curtly
hat they kept no cat at the inn, and it is true that I never saw
any of the beasts in the daytime ; but one evening about dusk
I caught the landlord in one of the outhouses. He had the
inger cat on his shoulder, and was feeding her with something
hat looked like strips of liver. I remonstrated with him for
ncouraging the cats about the place and asked whether I could
ave a different room, explaining that the nightly caterwauling
isturbed me. He half opened his slits of eyes and murmured
hat he would ask his wife about it ; but nothing was done,
nd in fact I believe there was no other bedroom in the house.

And all this time the weather got hotter and heavier, working
ip for thunder, with the sky like brass and the earth like iron,
nd the air quivering over it so that it hurt your eyes to look
t it.

All right, Harringay—I am trying to keep to the point. And
'm not concealing anything from you. I say that my relations
vith Mrs. Merridew were perfectly ordinary. Of course, I saw
a good deal of her, because as I explained Merridew was out
ll day. We went up to the dam with him in the morning and
rought the car back, and naturally we had to amuse one
nother as best we could till the evening. She seemed quite

pleased to be in my company, and I couldn't dislike her. I can't tell you what we talked about—nothing in particular. She was not a talkative woman. She would sit or lie for hours in the sunshine, hardly speaking—only stretching out her body to the light and heat. Sometimes she would spend a whole afternoon playing with a twig or a pebble, while I sat by and smoked. Restful! No. No—I shouldn't call her a restful personality, exactly. Not to me, at any rate. In the evening she would liven up and talk a little more, but she generally went up to bed early, and left Merridew and me to yarn together in the garden.

Oh! about the revolver. Yes. I bought that in Bath, when I had been at Little Hexham exactly a week. We drove over in the morning, and while Mrs. Merridew got some things for her husband, I prowled round the second-hand shops. I had intended to get an air-gun or a pea-shooter or something of that kind, when I saw this. You've seen it, of course. It's very tiny—what people in books describe as "little more than a toy," but quite deadly enough. The old boy who sold it to me didn't seem to know much about firearms. He'd taken it in pawn some time back, he told me, and there were ten rounds of ammunition with it. He made no bones about a licence or anything—glad enough to make a sale, no doubt, without putting difficulties in a customer's way. I told him I knew how to handle it, and mentioned by way of a joke that I meant to take a pot-shot or two at the cats. That seemed to wake him up a bit. He was a dried-up little fellow, with a scrawny grey beard and a stringy neck. He asked me where I was staying. I told him at Little Hexham.

"You better be careful, sir," he said. "They think a heap of their cats down there, and it's reckoned unlucky to kill them." And then he added something I couldn't quite catch about a silver bullet. He was a doddering old fellow, and he seemed to have some sort of scruple about letting me take the parcel away, but I assured him that I was perfectly capable of looking after it and myself. I left him standing at the door of his shop, pulling at his beard and staring after me.

That night the thunder came. The sky had turned to lead before evening, but the dull heat was more oppresive than the sunshine. Both the Merridews seemed to be in a state of nerves—he sulky and swearing at the weather and the flies, and she wrought up to a queer kind of vivid excitement. Thunder affects
216

ome people that way. I wasn't much better, and to make things worse I got the feeling that the house was full of cats. I couldn't see them but I knew they were there, lurking behind the cupboards and flitting noiselessly about the corridors. I could scarcely sit in the parlour and I was thankful to escape to my room. Cats or no cats I had to open the window, and I sat there with my pyjama jacket unbuttoned, trying to get a breath of air. But the place was like the inside of a copper furnace. And pitch-dark. I could scarcely see from my window where the bushes ended and the lawn began. But I could hear and feel the cats. There were little scrapings in the wistaria and scufflings among the leaves, and about eleven o'clock one of them started the concert with a loud and hideous wail. Then another and another joined in—I'll swear there were fifty of them. And presently I got that foul sensation of nausea, and the flesh crawled on my bones, and I knew that one of them was slinking close to me in the darkness. I looked round quickly, and there she stood, the great Cyprian; right against my shoulder, her eyes glowing like green lamps. I yelled and struck out at her, and she snarled as she leaped out and down. I heard her thump the gravel, and the yowling burst out all over the garden with renewed vehemence. And then all in a moment there was utter silence, and in the far distance there came a flickering blue flash and then another. In the first of them I saw the far garden wall, topped along all its length with cats, like a nursery frieze. When the second flash came the wall was empty.

At two o'clock the rain came. For three hours before that I had sat there, watching the lightning as it spat across the sky and exulting in the crash of the thunder. The storm seemed to carry off all the electrical disturbance in my body; I could have shouted with excitement and relief. Then the first heavy drops fell; then a steady downpour; then a deluge. It struck the iron-backed garden with a noise like steel rods falling. The smell of the ground came up intoxicatingly, and the wind rose and flung the rain in against my face. At the other end of the passage I heard a window thrown to and fastened, but I leaned out into the tumult and let the water drench my head and shoulders. The thunder still rumbled intermittently, but with less noise and farther off, and in an occasional flash I saw the white grille of falling water drawn between me and the garden.

It was after one of these thunder-peals that I became aware

217

of a knocking at my door. I opened it, and there was Merridew
He had a candle in his hand, and his face was terrified.

"Felice!" he said, abruptly. "She's ill. I can't wake her. Fo
God's sake, come and give me a hand."

I hurried down the passage after him. There were two bec
in his room—a great four-poster, hung with crimson damas
and a small camp bedstead drawn up near to the window. Th
small bed was empty, the bedclothes tossed aside; evidently h
had just risen from it. In the four poster lay Mrs. Merridev
naked, with only a sheet upon her. She was stretched flat upo
her back, her long black hair in two plaits over her shoulder
Her face was waxen and shrunk, like the face of a corpse, an
her pulse, when I felt it, was so faint that at first I cou
scarcely feel it. Her breathing was very slow and shallow an
her flesh cold. I shook her, but there was no response at all.
lifted her eyelids, and noticed how the eyeballs were turned u
under the upper lid, so that only the whites were visible. Th
touch of my finger-tip upon the sensitive ball evoked no reactio
I immediately wondered whether she took drugs.

Merridew seemed to think it necessary to make some explana
tion. He was babbling about the heat—she couldn't bear s
much as a silk nightgown—she had suggested that he shoul
occupy the other bed—he had slept heavily—right through th
thunder. The rain blowing in on his face had aroused him. H
had got up and shut the window. Then he had called to Felice t
know if she was all right—he thought the storm might hav
frightened her. There was no answer. He had struck a light. He
condition had alarmed him—and so on.

I told him to pull himself together and to try whether, b
chafing his wife's hands and feet, we could restore the circula
tion. I had it firmly in my mind that she was under the influenc
of some opiate. We set to work, rubbing and pinching and slap
ping her with wet towels and shouting her name in her ear
It was like handling a dead woman, except for the very sligh
but perfectly regular rise and fall of her bosom, on which—wit
a kind of surprise that there should be any flaw on its magnoli
whiteness—I noticed a large brown mole, just over the hear
To my perturbed fancy it suggested a wound and a menace
We had been hard at it for some time, with the sweat pourin
off us, when we became aware of something going on outsid
the window—a stealthy bumping and scraping against the pane
I snatched up the candle and looked out.

218

On the sill, the Cyprian cat sat and clawed at the casement. Her drenched fur clung limply to her body, her eyes glared into mine, her mouth was opened in protest. She scrabbled furiously at the latch, her hind claws slipping and scratching on the woodwork. I hammered on the pane and bawled at her, and she struck back at the glass as though possessed. As I cursed her and turned away she set up a long, despairing wail.

Merridew called to me to bring back the candle and leave the brute alone. I returned to the bed, but the dismal crying went on and on incessantly. I suggested to Merridew that he should wake the landlord and get hot-water bottles and some brandy from the bar and see if a messenger could not be sent for a doctor. He departed on this errand, while I went on with my massage. It seemed to me that the pulse was growing still fainter. Then I suddenly recollected that I had a small brandy-flask in my bag. I ran out to fetch it, and as I did so the cat suddenly stopped its howling.

As I entered my own room the air blowing through the open window struck gratefully upon me. I found my bag in the dark and was rummaging for the flask among my shirts and socks when I heard a loud, triumphant mew, and turned round in time to see the Cyprian cat crouched for a moment on the sill, before it sprang in past me and out at the door. I found the flask and hastened back with it, just as Merridew and the landlord came running up the stairs.

We all went into the room together. As we did so, Mrs. Merridew stirred, sat up, and asked us what in the world was the matter.

I have seldom felt quite such a fool.

Next day the weather was cooler; the storm had cleared the air. What Merridew had said to his wife I do not know. None of us made any public allusion to the night's disturbance, and to all appearances Mrs. Merridew was in the best of health and spirits. Merridew took a day off from the waterworks, and we all went for a long drive and picnic together. We were on the best of terms with one another. Ask Merridew—he will tell you the same thing. He would not—he could not, surely—say, otherwise. I can't believe, Harringay, I simply cannot believe that he could imagine or suspect me—I say, there was nothing to suspect. Nothing.

Yes—this is the important date—the 24th of June. I can't

tell you any more details; there is nothing to tell. We came back and had dinner just as usual. All three of us were together all day, till bedtime. On my honour I had no private interview of any kind that day, either with him or with her. I was the first to go to bed, and I heard the others come upstairs about half an hour later. They were talking cheerfully.

It was a moonlight night. For once, no caterwauling came to trouble me. I didn't even bother to shut the window or the door. I put the revolver on the chair beside me before I lay down. Yes, it was loaded. I had no special object in putting it there, except that I meant to have a go at the cats if they started their games again.

I was desperately tired, and thought I should drop off to sleep at once, but I didn't. I must have been overtired, I suppose. I lay and looked at the moonlight. And then, about midnight, I heard what I had been half expecting: a stealthy scrabbling in the wistaria and a faint miauling sound.

I sat up in bed and reached for the revolver. I heard the "plop" as the big cat sprang up on to the window-ledge; I saw her black and silver flanks, and the outline of her round head, pricked ears and upright tail. I aimed and fired, and the beast let out one frightful cry and sprang down into the room.

I jumped out of bed. The crack of the shot had sounded terrific in the silent house, and somewhere I heard a distant voice call out. I pursued the cat into the passage, revolver in hand—with some idea of finishing it off, I suppose. And then, at the door of Merridew's room, I saw Mrs. Merridew. She stood with one hand on each doorpost, swaying to and fro. Then she fell down at my feet. Her bare breast was all stained with blood. And as I stood staring at her, clutching the revolver, Merridew came out and found us—like that.

Well, Harringay, that's my story, exactly as I told it to Peabody. I'm afraid it won't sound very well in Court, but what can I say? The trail of blood led from my room to hers; the cat must have run that way; I *know* it was the cat I shot. I can't offer any explanation. I don't know who shot Mrs. Merridew, or why. I can't help it if the people at the inn say they never saw the Cyprian cat; Merridew saw it that other night, and I know he wouldn't lie about it. Search the house, Harringay—that's the only thing to do. Pull the place to pieces, till you find the body of the Cyprian cat. It will have my bullet in it.

NEL BESTSELLERS

Crime

T013 332	CLOUDS OF WITNESS	*Dorothy L. Sayers*	40p
W002 871	THE UNPLEASANTNESS AT THE BELLONA CLUB	*Dorothy L. Sayers*	30p
W003 011	GAUDY NIGHT	*Dorothy L. Sayers*	40p
T010 457	THE NINE TAILORS	*Dorothy L. Sayers*	35p
T012 484	FIVE RED HERRINGS	*Dorothy L. Sayers*	40p
T012 492	UNNATURAL DEATH	*Dorothy L. Sayers*	40p

Fiction

W002 775	HATTER'S CASTLE	*A. J. Cronin*	60p
W002 777	THE STARS LOOK DOWN	*A. J. Cronin*	60p
T010 414	THE CITADEL	*A. J. Cronin*	60p
T010 422	THE KEYS OF THE KINGDOM	*A. J. Cronin*	50p
T001 288	THE TROUBLE WITH LAZY ETHEL	*Ernest K. Gann*	30p
T003 922	IN THE COMPANY OF EAGLES	*Ernest K. Gann*	30p
T012 271	THE WARSAW DOCUMENT	*Adam Hall*	40p
T011 305	THE STRIKER PORTFOLIO	*Adam Hall*	30p
T007 243	SYLVIA SCARLETT	*Compton Mackenzie*	30p
T007 669	SYLVIA AND ARTHUR	*Compton Mackenzie*	30p
T007 677	SYLVIA AND MICHAEL	*Compton Mackenzie*	35p
W002 772	TO THE CORAL STRAND	*John Masters*	40p
W002 788	TRIAL AT MONOMOY	*John Masters*	40p
T009 084	SIR, YOU BASTARD	*G. F. Newman*	30p
T009 769	THE HARRAD EXPERIMENT	*Robert H. Rimmer*	40p
T010 252	THE REBELLION OF YALE MARRATT	*Robert H. Rimmer*	40p
T010 716	THE ZOLOTOV AFFAIR	*Robert H. Rimmer*	40p
T012 522	THURSDAY MY LOVE	*Robert H. Rimmer*	40p
T013 820	THE DREAM MERCHANTS	*Harold Robbins*	75p
W002 783	79 PARK AVENUE	*Harold Robbins*	60p
T012 255	THE CARPETBAGGERS	*Harold Robbins*	80p
T011 801	WHERE LOVE HAS GONE	*Harold Robbins*	80p
T013 707	THE ADVENTURERS	*Harold Robbins*	75p
T006 743	THE INHERITORS	*Harold Robbins*	60p
T009 467	STILETTO	*Harold Robbins*	50p
T010 406	NEVER LEAVE ME	*Harold Robbins*	30p
T011 771	NEVER LOVE A STRANGER	*Harold Robbins*	70p
T011 798	A STONE FOR DANNY FISHER	*Harold Robbins*	60p
T011 461	THE BETSY	*Harold Robbins*	75p
T010 201	RICH MAN, POOR MAN	*Irwin Shaw*	80p
T005 194	THE PILLARS OF MIDNIGHT	*Elleston Trevor*	30p
W002 186	THE PLOT	*Irving Wallace*	75p
W002 761	THE SEVEN MINUTES	*Irving Wallace*	75p
T009 718	THE THREE SIRENS	*Irving Wallace*	75p
T010 341	THE PRIZE	*Irving Wallace*	80p

Historical

T009 750	THE WARWICK HEIRESS	*Margaret Abbey*	30p
T011 607	THE SON OF YORK	*Margaret Abbey*	30p
T011 585	THE ROSE IN SPRING	*Eleanor Fairburn*	30p
T009 734	RICHMOND AND ELIZABETH	*Brenda Honeyman*	30p
T011 593	HARRY THE KING	*Brenda Honeyman*	35p
T009 742	THE ROSE BOTH RED AND WHITE	*Betty King*	30p
W002 479	AN ODOUR OF SANCTITY	*Frank Yerby*	50p
W002 824	THE FOXES OF HARROW	*Frank Yerby*	50p
W002 916	BENTON'S ROW	*Frank Yerby*	40p
W003 010	THE VIXENS	*Frank Yerby*	40p
T006 921	JARRETT'S JADE	*Frank Yerby*	40p
T010 988	BRIDE OF LIBERTY	*Frank Yerby*	30p

Science Fiction

W003 002	SWORDS OF MARS	*Edgar Rice Burroughs*	30p
W003 003	CARSON OF VENUS	*Edgar Rice Burroughs*	30p
W002 449	THE MOON IS A HARSH MISTRESS	*Robert Heinlein*	40p
W002 697	THE WORLDS OF ROBERT HEINLEIN	*Robert Heinlein*	25p
W002 839	SPACE FAMILY STONE	*Robert Heinlein*	30p
W002 844	STRANGER IN A STRANGE LAND	*Robert Heinlein*	60p
T006 778	ASSIGNMENT IN ETERNITY	*Robert Heinlein*	25p
T007 294	HAVE SPACESUIT – WILL TRAVEL	*Robert Heinlein*	30p
T009 696	GLORY ROAD	*Robert Heinlein*	40p
T011 844	DUNE	*Frank Herbert*	75p
W002 814	THE WORLDS OF FRANK HERBERT	*Frank Herbert*	30p
W002 911	SANTAROGA BARRIER	*Frank Herbert*	30p
W003 001	DRAGON IN THE SEA	*Frank Herbert*	30p
T012 298	DUNE MESSIAH	*Frank Herbert*	40p

War

W002 686	DEATH OF A REGIMENT	*John Foley*	30p
W002 921	WOLF PACK	*William Hardy*	30p
W002 484	THE FLEET THAT HAD TO DIE	*Richard Hough*	25p
W002 805	HUNTING OF FORCE Z	*Richard Hough*	30p
W002 632	THE BASTARD BRIGADE	*Peter Leslie*	25p
T006 999	KILLER CORPS	*Peter Leslie*	25p
T011 445	TRAWLERS GO TO WAR	*Lund and Lundlam*	40p
W005 051	GÖRING	*Manvell & Fraenkel*	52½p
W005 065	HIMMLER	*Manvell & Fraenkel*	52½p
W002 423	STRIKE FROM THE SKY	*Alexander McKee*	30p
W002 831	NIGHT	*Francis Pollini*	40p
T010 074	THE GREEN BERET	*Hilary St. George Saunders*	40p
T010 066	THE RED BERET	*Hilary St. George Saunders*	40p
W005 018	THE ZIMMERMAN TELEGRAM	*Barbara W. Tuchman*	25p

Western

T010 619	EDGE – THE LONER	*George Gilman*	25p
T010 600	EDGE – TEN THOUSAND DOLLARS AMERICAN	*George Gilman*	25p
T010 929	EDGE – APACHE DEATH	*George Gilman*	25p

General

T011 763	SEX MANNERS FOR MEN	*Robert Chartham*	30p
W002 531	SEX MANNERS FOR ADVANCED LOVERS	*Robert Chartham*	30p
W002 835	SEX AND THE OVER FORTIES	*Robert Chartham*	30p
T010 732	THE SENSUOUS COUPLE	*Dr. C.*	25p
P002 367	AN ABZ OF LOVE	*Inge and Sten Hegeler*	60p
P011 402	A HAPPIER SEX LIFE	*Dr. Sha Kokken*	70p
W002 584	SEX MANNERS FOR SINGLE GIRLS	*Georges Valensin*	25p
W002 592	THE FRENCH ART OF SEX MANNERS	*Georges Valensin*	25p
W002 726	THE POWER TO LOVE	*E. W. Hirsch M.D.*	47½p

Mad

S003 491	LIKE MAD	30p
S003 494	MAD IN ORBIT	30p
S003 520	THE BEDSIDE MAD	30p
S003 521	THE VOODOO MAD	30p
S003 657	MAD FOR BETTER OR VERSE	30p
S003 716	THE SELF MADE MAD	30p

- - - - - - - - - - - - - - - - - -

NEL, P.O. BOX 11, FALMOUTH, CORNWALL

Please send cheque or postal order. Allow 6p per book to cover postage and packing.

Name..

Address ....

....

Title ....

(AUGUST)